Deception

is the

Old Black

A Viv Fraser Mystery

V. Clifford

Inverardoch Press

Also by V.Clifford

The Viv Fraser Mysteries:

Beyond Cutting

Finding Tess

Digging up the Dead

Non Fiction

Freud's Converts

Chapter One

It was the first hot day of August and Festival revellers filled the streets. Viv Fraser blew out a long breath before slamming the Rav's door – an illegal parking space in King's Stables Road was better than none. Irritated, she wove her way through crowds milling around the cobbled heart of Edinburgh's Old Town.

She mumbled curses to herself at the sight of white awnings stretching as far as the eye could see. How much council tax did she pay for unknown traders to set up stalls on *her* parking spaces for a month? Distracted, she cut straight through a group of tourists huddled round a map then raised her hands by way of an apology. She didn't comprehend their language but it ceased for a moment before resuming as if only a breeze had disturbed them. She stepped off the pavement to avoid a cluster of men staggering out of the Black Bull. Two of them, arms round each other's shoulders, fell to their knees red faced, laughing and completely uninhibited. Nervous of the kind of laughter that preceded vomit or collapse, Viv skipped ahead but had to dodge another drunken man stumbling backward into the road. The drunk was narrowly missed by a cyclist who swerved and gesticulated by ripping out his ear-buds and holding them up as if they were good enough reason for his cycling the wrong way up a one-way street. No bell either, Viv noticed. Since medieval times drovers had brought their animals here to fatten for sale before blowing their gains on whisky. It felt as if things hadn't changed.

The pavement outside each pub and café was crammed with tables and chairs. Creative publicans had installed plastic shrubs to mark their boundaries – occupation being nine tenths of the law. Viv glanced in through the door of Bella's bistro and waved to her friend who squeezed on tiptoe between seated customers. With her hands full Bella could only raise her eyebrows and grin in response. Viv knew that the Festival caused bedlam but was vital to keep businesses going through fallow months. Right now the street was an international melting pot, but come September the battle to fill tables would commence.

Viv edged into Mo's mini-market to pick up supplies. She'd left that morning on an empty stomach because the cupboards were bare. Most days she could rely on clients to offer sustenance, even home baking, but today not a muffin or scone had been in sight. She lifted a pack of espresso and a bottle of gold top milk: the bread shelf was empty. She grabbed a box of oatcakes then decided she'd bake bread and added a bag of flour. She was a trier.

As she stood in the queue to pay, a tall man stretched his head round to look at her and said, 'Do I know you?'

His accent was typical of Edinburgh, a city colonised by those who'd gone to one of its many public schools.

Viv, startled by his proximity, stepped away. 'I don't think so.'

'Yes, yes I do. You used to cut my hair.'

Viv stared at him. A flicker of recognition came to her but she was certain she'd never cut his hair. If she'd fingered round someone's neck and ears, been close enough to count the open pores on their nose, she never forgot. Cutting hair was intimate. 'I used to work in the West End. Maybe that's it?'

He looked doubtful. Disappointed. 'Oh. Well, maybe. I've seen you in Bella's.'

'Now that is a possibility. You must be local.'

'How so?'

'Only locals call it Bella's. That's not the name above the door.'

'Right enough.' He reached his hand out and said. 'Angus. Gus to my friends.'

She swapped the grocery basket to her other arm and shook his large calloused hand. 'Viv. I live in the West Bow. You?'

'Two doors up. Top floor. The one with the tiny roof garden. You've maybe seen it from the other side of the main road.'

'Oh, my God. Really? Wow. I'm so jealous. Have you been there long?'

'A few years.'

It was her turn to look doubtful. If he'd lived there that long surely she'd have noticed him before now.

As if reading her thoughts he said, 'I've been away a lot.'

Mo coughed from behind the counter; it was Viv's turn to pay. 'You make a good pair,' he nodded. 'Look, he's addicted to chocolate digestives as well.'

Viv checked to see what Gus was carrying. 'Alas, no good, I'm an exclusively milk chocolate woman.'

Gus interrupted. 'I'm easy. I can eat either.'

Viv laughed. No one was that easy but his piercing blue eyes intrigued her. 'What is it you do up there in your garret?'

'I'm a writer.'

She laughed again. 'You and everyone else I meet these days. What sort of things do you write?' What kind of writing caused such rough hands?

'Biographies.'

'Plural? So you've written more than one?'

He flushed. 'Getting on for six.'

Viv was impressed. 'Anyone I might know?'

'I ghost. A few politicians. No one that would interest you, I don't suppose.'

'Well that's a leap from not knowing my name to knowing my politics.'

'Oh I didn't mean it as a . . .'

She waved her hand. 'It's fine. I'm teasing.' She felt colour rising up her neck. What the heck was going on? She packed her groceries into her rucksack and squeezed past him to get to the door. 'Nice to meet you.'

He paid for his biscuits and followed right behind her. 'Don't suppose you'd fancy a coffee sometime?'

Her flush deepened. She wasn't usually the bashful type but she was bordering on it now. 'Sure. That would be great.' She walked off.

He called after her. 'When? You should come up and see my roof terrace.'

She stopped, turned and laughed. 'I thought you were going to say puppies. But the terrace is just as much of a carrot. I'd love to.' She swung her rucksack off her shoulder and rummaged around in the side pocket. 'Here.' She handed him a card with her email address on it.

He grinned, exposing a set of slightly crooked white teeth, offset by his tan. It couldn't be Scottish. And those cool blue eyes? He probably soaked them in a solution overnight.

'How about now?'

She hesitated, grotty after a day of cutting hair. But he was nodding, eager with anticipation. She relented. 'Okay, just a quick visit.'

Chapter Two

They reached his building and he led the way to the top floor of the close. Paint flaked from the walls, rubbish bags and boxes full of Heineken empties occupied threadbare doormats and each door had many names taped to it. She felt grateful for the sedate neighbours that she had in her own stair.

'Sorry about the mess,' he said. 'A transient student population doesn't make for a loyal stair committee.'

She laughed. 'I struck lucky. In our building there are only a couple of flats that change hands, and almost always to post grads or visiting fellows. Although we've had our moments.'

His home couldn't have been more different from hers. With blond wooden floors and flush doors, steel and leather furniture with white curtains, it was all too minimalist for her. They did, however, share a love of books. She ran her fingers along shelf after shelf crammed with titles from history of art to engineering, cooking to container gardening. She could have spent the rest of the day scanning them. She said. 'Eclectic . . .'

'Thanks. I sometimes think it's an illness. I can never say no to a book. Come on, it's up here.'

She followed him into a small sitting room. 'But it's not an illness you'd want to cure?'

'No.'

He pressed the heel of his hand against the wall and an invisible panel clicked open. They stepped into a steep, narrow staircase that wound up towards the roof through an open glass hatch. They emerged onto a wooden platform.

She blinked, adjusting to the bright sunlight. 'Oh, my God. This is fabulous. Unbelievable. And not so tiny.'

The terrace shared much of the view that she had from her windows in the West Bow, the magnificent towers of George Heriot's School and the Old Royal Infirmary both significant architectural landmarks. Her own building was further up the hill and had the full panorama of the Pentlands, but this flat had the bonus view of the castle perched on its volcanic rock, transcending the chaos of the street. To the north, the tenements on Johnston Terrace defied Newtonian logic and looked as if they might slide down into the gardens at any moment. 'Do you have a garden as well?'

'Yes.' He pointed to some neat grassy terraces. 'It's not much to look at, but it's somewhere else to sit away from the crowds at this time of year.'

'I'm so envious. There is nowhere to sit out in the Bow. I genuinely have stared up at this place and fantasised about having one on my roof.'

A small gazebo, painted a National Trust shade of green, sat at the back corner of the decking. A few large pots with energetic plants spilling over their tops surrounded its entrance. He pushed the door inwards. 'Here, take a seat and I'll go and put some coffee on.'

She stepped inside and the noise of bustle from the Grassmarket below abated. Two white basket-weave chairs and a matching table with coffee stains and crumbs took up a third of the floor space. A newspaper rack crammed with old copies of *The Guardian* sat to the side of one of the chairs. She wouldn't have tagged him as a *Guardian* reader – *FT* if anything. Nice to be wrong. She plonked herself down on one of the chairs. With windows on all sides it was like an aquarium. Viv wasn't big on acquisitions but this definitely brought out her green-eyed monster.

After a few minutes of planning one of these for her own patch of roof, a tray appeared through the hatch and she went out to help him. But he had the process down to a fine art and was already lifting it back up from the decking. 'No worries, I do this every day.'

'I can't believe how fabulous this is. Who built it?'

'I did.'

'No way! Really! Oh my God.' She flushed, cringing at the sound of a Hollywood bimbo coming out of her mouth. What was she up to?

He grinned. Her enthusiasm infectious.

She stood inside the gazebo and made a turn of 360 degrees. 'It's perfect. I thought my place was good because of the views but you have the whole . . .' She didn't know what to say. So she sat down and looked at him. 'How the hell did you do it? I mean how did you get all the material up those stairs?'

'Same way you'd eat an elephant. One bite at a time.'

Viv laughed. She'd rarely heard anyone else use the phrase. She loved it – it was a good way to slow people down. Now that they were inside she sensed that the space was more suited to one person. She imagined him sitting with his laptop on his knees, long legs stretched out, or feet perched up on the extra chair. What a great place to work. The smell of coffee floated round the confined space. He'd brought a plate of digestives, both milk and dark chocolate.

He handed her a demi-tasse. 'Milk and sugar?'

'No thanks.' She examined the tiny cup. 'Posh wee cup.' She sipped the strong velvety brew and made noises of appreciation. 'So what are you working on at the moment? Or does a ghost have to keep it entirely to himself?'

He nodded. 'Afraid so. First Ministers hate their public to think they can't write their own stuff.'

She almost choked on her coffee. 'I see.'

He handed her a paper napkin. 'Everything all right?'

She nodded as she dabbed her mouth. 'I'm fine, thanks. But how does it work? I'm guessing you tape an interview where they tell you everything that they want people to know, but nothing of importance?'

'That's about the size of it. Anything that I write that they don't like is taken out, so it's not worth straying. They even line up interviews with "friends" and family for me. So everyone's primed. Although occasionally, just occasionally, someone blurts out a nugget that's worth knowing but can't go into the book.' He smiled.

Intrigued, she continued. 'So you have stacks of notes on famous people that could destroy their reputations?'

'I have to sign a clause.'

She thought as much. 'But what if they're stolen?'

He stared at her, his eyebrows knitting. 'Now where might this be going?'

Viv, realising that she'd shifted into interrogation mode, shook her head. 'Oh, ignore me. I'm a nosey sod.'

'So what *is* it that you do?'

'I *am* a hairdresser . . . But I've absolutely never cut that hair.' She pointed at his head.

He looked puzzled, as if the hairdressing question had been a ruse that had backfired. 'Okay, okay. So where do you work?'

'I'm independent. But I do other things as well.' This was her least favourite conversation and frustration had crept into her tone.

'Such as?'

'Well, I've written the odd column for a newspaper.'

He stopped short with his cup almost to his lips and nodded. 'Well, that's unusual.'

She couldn't be bothered justifying her existence. Time to take her leave. She nodded and swigged the remains of her coffee. 'Thanks for that. I've got loads to do.' She gestured at the cup. 'Delicious.'

'Good. You'll come again.' It was a question disguised as a statement.

'I might. But only since you had milk chocolate digestives.'

'But you didn't have one.'

'No, I didn't. But it was nice of you to make the effort.'

As he stood up he said. 'Do you know Sal Chapman?'

'Yes . . . I did . . . I mean I do. I bought the flat from her.'

He thrust his hands deep into his pockets and hunched his shoulders. 'She came to see this place when I was building it.'

It had been a while since she'd thought about Sal's previous life. Now her mind skipped into overdrive, trying to make sense of what his relationship with Sal could be. How well had he known her? How long had they been friends? What should she now make of the 'coincidence' of him stopping her?

Wary, she walked back over to the hatch.

'Go down backwards. It's safer.'

She swung round and descended in seconds. Her rucksack wasn't where she'd left it. She glanced round as he stepped into the room.

'Oh, I put your bag into the fridge since there was milk in it.'

How domestic. Had he gone through it? Was she paranoid? Yes, she was. She rolled her shoulders.

'It was good to meet you.' He said it tentatively, as if he sensed he'd lost her.

'Yes. Likewise.' Then she heard a strange voice, sounding bizarrely like her own, saying, 'We must do it again sometime.'

'Great, I'd like that.'

His hallway was cramped and she didn't want to get trapped in it with him. She made for the door, opened it and in one smooth move was on the landing swinging her rucksack over her shoulder.

Chapter Three

Viv lived just above the curve of the West Bow, at the lower end of Victoria Street. As soon as the heavy outside door clicked behind her, quiet descended and she sighed, relishing sanctuary in the midst of chaos. She took the stairs at her usual pace, two at a time, reaching the top floor slightly out of breath, and unlocked her door. Her landline was ringing. Few people used it and since she'd seen her sister earlier, she'd lay money on it being her mum. She missed the call but her mother's number registered in the display. Within seconds the light on the answering machine began blinking. She pressed Play.

Her mum's voice said, 'I've just spoken to Amanda.'

Viv braced herself for what was coming next, but was surprised when her mum sighed and said, 'Oh, never mind. I'm going to a tea dance so you'll not get me in.'

The clatter of her mum unravelling the cord on her phone before resting it on its cradle took up another minute of tape. Viv smiled. Her mum was no shrinking violet, but she was averse to technology, and especially suspicious of the telephone.

She stripped off to have a shower. The downside of being a hairdresser were tiny bits of newly cut hair that got stuck everywhere. She'd once spent forever trying to remove a shard embedded in her nipple. Adjusting the water temperature she stood, allowing a cool stream to rinse her working day down the drain. She towelled her hair then pulled on joggers and an over-sized tee shirt. Not yet adept at making bread, she measured ingredients into a bowl and kneaded them as if she was in a gestalt session. She covered the bowl with a linen tea towel and sighed with satisfaction, but as she rinsed her hands she wondered what Angus' ulterior motive could be.

Once armed with a proper sized cup of industrial strength coffee she booted up her laptop. As she waited for it to come to life she glanced round her sitting room, reflecting on what it said about her. It might be described as anti-minimalist, since although tiny, it was decorated in a way that would have been a comfort to the Victorian Holmes and Watson. A large Chesterfield covered by a deep red velvet throw took up almost one wall. Embossed French wallpaper, terracotta on terracotta, provided a lush background for numerous paintings and prints in gilt or black frames. A huge oak desk sat to the right of a window that faced south onto the spectacular view that she shared with Angus.

She Googled 'Angus Buchanan' since that was the name on his buzzer. He was a Fettesian, which accounted for his clipped accent, a journalist for *The Independent* and he'd travelled a lot, which accounted for the tan. No sign of a partner, either in the flat or online, but that didn't mean he didn't have one.

She groaned as her inbox pinged and pinged, filling with message after message. As her finger hovered over the delete key the door buzzer sounded. She was tempted to ignore it – she'd already taken in deliveries for a couple of neighbours this week – but whoever it was persisted and she stomped up the hall and pressed the button on the entry system. 'Yes?'

A familiar voice shouted, 'You letting me in or what?'

She released the catch, allowing Mac in, and nipped through to the kitchen to put the kettle back on. He arrived at her door a few seconds later breathless, but leant against the doorjamb pretending not to be.

'Here, I haven't seen you in a while.' She held out the cup of coffee.

'Ah, you're a mind reader.'

She pointed to a high cupboard. 'Sugar's in there.'

Marcus Marconi, known to his close friends as Mac for reasons that we know and others just guessed at, rubbed a hand over his flat belly. 'No extra calories for me.'

Viv snorted and shook her head. 'What would possess you to police your food?'

'Well, since you mention it, I'm going on an outward-bound weekend.'

Viv grinned. 'You're taking the piss.'

He shook his head. 'It'll be fantastic. Team building.'

'Now I know you're kidding. You. Outward-bound. What have you been on?'

'That's why I'm here.'

The mock serene look on his face made Viv guarded. 'No. No way. Absolutely no way.' She backed up the hall into the sitting room.

'I haven't even asked you yet.'

She studied his face. 'You don't need to. I can tell by that look.'

'What look?'

'That look.' She pointed at his face. 'The look that's saying, how the hell am I going to persuade her that it'll be fantastic when I'm lying my pants off.'

'At least let me tell you about it.'

She held up her hands. 'No. No. And triple no. There is nothing you could say or do to persuade me.'

'What if it was an order?'

'I'd tell you to go f . . . '

'Okay, I get it.' He held up his free hand. 'Great coffee by the way.'

'Don't even go there with the smooth operator routine.'

'How do you stand living here at this time of year? It's like the United Nation's end of year party out there.'

'I'm warning you. I won't be bought with smarmy comments.'

He held up his cup. 'Any more where this came from?'

'Sure. I'll get it. How you doing anyway? Heard from Ruddy recently?' She threw this over her shoulder as she went back to the kitchen for his refill.

'You know you shouldn't call him that. But now you mention him . . .'

'Shit,' she whispered to herself. She should have kept her mouth shut.

'He asked me to recruit you for this weekend.'

She handed him his cup, trying to work out whether he was serious. If he were, that was a game changer. Suddenly the room was stifling and she tugged open the window to let in some air, but the noise of a piper warming up made her push it shut again. She loved the pipes but they sounded like an animal in pain until they were in full flow.

'So what are you saying?'

'Beats me why he's so keen on you coming along but I'm only following orders.'

She tossed a cushion at him. 'Liar! You hate following orders.' This wasn't exactly true but it allowed her to vent.

He dodged the cushion, managing to keep the coffee inside his mug. Mac was the head of a police unit called the National Task Force (NTF), which seemed to have an opaque remit that included responding to terrorist threats, whatever that happened to mean. Viv was their go-to-girl when they needed help with unorthodox cyber stuff. She wasn't really part of the official team. But having informal status suited both her and them. Being ordered around wasn't her kind of thing. It was unusual for Mac to pull rank with her. She was intrigued.

She felt herself relaxing so she stiffened her shoulders in an attempt to bolster her psyche against its own curiosity. 'Sorry Mac, as much as I'd like to help you out, no can do.'

He went to speak but she held up her hands. 'Don't. Please.' As soon as 'please' was out she wished she hadn't said it. It was a sign of weakness but it was too late.

Mac placed his cup on a coaster on a large metal chest that doubled as a side table. He squared the edge of the coaster with the edge of the chest. 'Okay. Your call.'

Why would he say that? Viv got the feeling this wasn't going to be his last attempt at persuasion but she replied, 'Yes, it is my call.'

'Great coffee. No one else I know can make coffee that . . .'

She cut him off with a shake of her head. 'Okay, okay, are we done here?' She nodded towards the door.

He shrugged and headed back down the hall. 'If you change your mind . . . it's in the interest of National Security.'

She raised her eyebrows. 'Do me a favour . . .'

Once she'd closed the door behind him she stood with her back against it. What was he up to? Viv had done outward-bound stuff at school and with the OTC at university. She'd found it hard going although nowhere like as tough as the course that Ruddy had forced her to complete before he'd let her loose on any job for the service. She could think of nothing worse than spending a weekend with a group of office staff forced to push their physical limits. The real challenges were psychological. Everything was in the mind.

A memory surfaced of that last outward-bound weekend. She'd returned to find that Dawn, her then partner, had gone off with a younger model – a much younger model. Viv had collapsed, too exhausted to do anything, until Dawn's hysterical phone calls in the middle of the night, crying with shame and regret, had worn her down – and she'd taken her back. It hadn't been Dawn's first betrayal, but it had been her last.

Surprised and cheered by how little this recollection now disturbed her, she pushed herself off the door and headed through to resume deleting emails. She was meeting Ellie, a friend who had been working in the Netherlands for the last three years. They had a lot to catch up on.

Chapter Four

What was Mac up to? Making a fuss about a weekend away wasn't his style. She considered what his next move might be. If Ruddy had requested she go with him, Mac would find a way.

The evening was still warm but that could change in a heartbeat, so she chose layers, a tee shirt beneath a shirt with a pullover and a jacket round her shoulders.

Neither Ellie nor Viv had had much luck in the relationship department. Ellie only dated married men, a sure sign of her commitment phobia, but also a reason for her never to judge Viv. As soon as a man edged towards leaving his wife or hinted for her to move in, Ellie donned her super Nikes and took off.

Viv's relationships hadn't been much to recommend her, but so far she had avoided the married. Since Dawn's death she had had the odd fling, but nothing serious enough to frighten her – until Sal. Tonight the plan was to have a good gossip with Ellie over a pizza and a few Peronis.

She punched back her dough and said, 'Prove it!' Then scrubbed her hands again, before slipping into the kit she'd laid out on the bed. They were starting off in Carwash on the Mound, which was an easy walk from the flat. She nipped her cheeks, messed up her hair and headed out, pulling the street door firmly behind her, then rechecking that it was secure – Friday nights carried the high risk of a passing drunk availing him or herself of a place to rest or worse. She crossed the road and walked up Victoria Street. At the steps leading to Victoria Terrace a young woman struggling to bump a baby in a pushchair blocked the way. Viv took hold of the bottom of the pushchair and in seconds they'd carried it to the top. The woman looked exhausted but grateful and opened her mouth to say thanks. Viv waved a hand at her. 'No worries.' She peeked at the baby. 'Cutie.' Then carried on to the Upper Bow.

The Old Town was a maze of higgledy-piggledy closes and vennels. Locals could scurry between high tenements and arches and cut twenty minutes off a journey. Thus it was for Viv. She'd no sooner stepped onto the High Street, also known as the Royal Mile, than a few more steps would take her through Lady Stairs Close onto the Mound, right to the door of the pub. It was a short safe journey in daylight, not so much after dark.

Viv squeezed through a throng of drinkers outside the pub, their pints held aloft, when someone called her name, 'Vivian.' Instinctively she turned and spotted a hand beckoning to her from inside a dark blue saloon parked at the kerb. She cursed and wandered over.

'No one calls me Vivian except my mother. And even then I'd have to have done something badly wrong.'

Ruddy smiled from the passenger seat. 'I hear you're too busy to join the circus.'

She leant against the car roof and grinned. 'You heard wrong then.'

Ruddy's eyebrows appeared to move independently of the rest of his face. His complexion, the kind associated with a bottle of scotch before breakfast, was entirely natural. In the genes with a dash of Scotland's extreme weather.

'It's not that I'm too busy. It's that I don't need another, "She'll be Wearing Pink Pyjamas" moment any time soon.'

He frowned. 'Ah! So that's it . . . Marconi needs you there. It's the NTF. We have a mole.' His tone was determined as he checked the immaculate fingernails on his solid freckled hands. He raised his eyebrows again and pursed his lips. This time not so much in a question as, refusal was not an option.

Viv looked skyward and blew out a breath. 'Why me?'

'You already know that.'

'So what sort of digging do you want?'

'Whatever it takes.'

She bit the inside of her cheek. 'When is it?'

'Leaving tomorrow at 9.30am from Fettes.'

'No can do. I've got a wedding . . .'

'You can sort that. We're relying on you, Viv. I know you won't disappoint.' The glint never left his eye.

The car window rose as the saloon pulled away from the pavement. Viv stood and watched as Ruddy's driver steered seamlessly into the flow of traffic heading down towards Princes Street. Ruddy's power over her was of her own making: she wanted to please him. He reminded her of her father. He wasn't physically like him but rather everything her father stood for. She turned and saw Ellie standing at the pub door, looking well, not as skinny as she often was.

'Hi you. I see you're still into that undercover malarkey.'

Viv didn't rise.

Ellie nudged her arm. 'C'mon, what was all that about?'

'Oh, nothing.'

They hugged, but Ellie pressed her. 'Didn't look like nothing to me.'

Viv grinned, 'I see you're still on the demon fags.'

Ellie lifted her hand and stuck a mock cigarette under Viv's nose. 'No longer the real thing. Looks good though, eh? What d'you think?'

It was convincing. 'Brilliant. I'd never have been able to tell. Well at least not until you kept smoking the same fag with the same amount of ash teetering perilously close to dropping onto your new trousers.'

They hugged again. 'Great to see you, Viv, but come on who was that?'

Ellie, a lawyer in The Hague, at the Court of Human Rights, was as sharp as a tack. She'd never let Viv off the hook.

Viv linked her arm through Ellie's and said, 'C'mon, let's get a drink and I'll fill you in.'

The bar was heaving but Viv managed to catch the eye of a barman who gave her the thumbs up.

Ellie pointed to a couple folding up their street guide. 'Guess where I'm heading.' And off she went, pressing past bodies to get to the table. The couple were in no rush and Viv watched as Ellie hovered conspicuously. Discretion was not her forte. It didn't need to be.

Eventually the barman nodded. 'Right, what'll it be?'

By the time Viv made it to the table she'd lost at least a third from both pints. 'Half measures at this rate.' They clinked glasses and gulped their cool beers.

Viv was first to come up for air. 'So I'm guessing you'll never let it rest until I tell you, so here's what you want to know. The man in the car with the red hair and the ruddy complexion is the all-but-invisible-boss of someone that I've done the occasional job for.'

'I'm guessing you're not talking about cutting hair?'

Viv shook her head. 'Not exactly, but I did meet up with Mac . . . actually you probably remember him, Marcus Marconi. Used to live in the Grove. Four older sisters.'

Ellie screwed up her eyes. 'The Catholics?'

Viv shook her head. 'Crikey Ells, is that the only thing you remember about them?'

'I never really knew them.'

'Well never mind. Mac, that's what he was called in primary school. I met up with him on a hairdressing job. We'd also clashed at uni so it was good to catch up.'

Ellie nudged her arm. 'So what's he like then, this Mac?'

'It's nothing like that.' Viv raised her eyes. 'You've got a one-track mind. You know I've done a bit of cyber stuff?' She hesitated, waiting for a wisecrack from Ellie.

'So that's what you call it now, is it? In my world we still call it illegal intrusion, or simply hacking. Which is what you also used to call it if my memory serves me correctly.'

'Oh piss off. You know what it means. Anyway, Mac dropped by earlier and asked me to go on an outward-bound course – allegedly to bond with other members of the department. Actually I don't mean "other" because I'm not officially a member of the department.'

'What department is it?'

Viv looked around. 'It doesn't matter. I'm not in any department. I just help out now and again.'

It was Ellie's turn to roll her eyes. 'Give me some credit, Viv. I haven't been on the game in The Hague.'

Viv nodded but hesitated again. Signing the Official Secrets Act wasn't something she had done lightly. But it occurred to her that Ellie might also have signed it. She decided that the NTF itself was no secret. 'Fair enough. It's called the NTF, National Task Force.'

Ellie seemed to know what Viv was talking about and nodded. 'Yes I remember something about the time it took for them to choose a name for it.' She sniggered. 'Bureaucrats – you gotta love them. The Hague's hoatching with them. That's why I'm back.' She gestured with her hand for Viv to continue.

Viv took another gulp of her pint. 'I've got to make a decision asap. I told Mac that I wasn't up for it, but he's been out-ranked. Otherwise I wouldn't have had that wee visit.' She pointed out to the street. 'Oh, never mind that. What's brought you back?'

Ellie wasn't ready to be distracted by her own story. 'If I know you there's no way you'll pass up a bit of action. What else would you be doing this weekend?'

Viv wrapped her hands round her glass and brought it up to cool her forehead.

Ellie continued. 'Exactly. Nowt. I can already see how bored you are. Look at you. Slumped or what? Not to mention the look on your face. Get yourself into the zone, girl. You'll only mope for the weekend if you don't go.'

'I'm doing hair for a wedding!' Her tone sounded more defensive than she intended.

Ellie changed tack and launched into what she'd been up to, giving Viv a blow by blow account of the latest married man who, as Viv had already guessed, was threatening to leave his wife. Viv and Ellie had known each other since their early teens and lived within spitting distance of each other but gone to different schools and universities. Viv often thought that that was probably what had kept them together. Ellie, a couple of years younger than Viv, did law at Glasgow then a post grad on international law at Durham, while Viv went to Edinburgh to read anthropology, before a post grad in psychotherapy, which led nicely onto her doctorate on Sigmund Freud. Viv, a late developer, had spent her weekends in a salon washing and sweeping hair, while Ellie had been an impressive athlete who'd played for the east of Scotland hockey team, although was unable to beat Viv in a sprint.

They finished their pints and wandered down the Mound, stopping occasionally to listen to a street performance. Eventually, after trawling along George Street, being knocked back by every eatery, they secured the last table in Pizza Express on Queensferry Street. They chatted about their families, spending too much time on their sisters, and Viv managed to wheedle the real story of Ellie's latest man friend, who had got too close for Ellie's comfort and been given the heave. They laughed and laughed at the inevitability of their circumstances, so familiar with each other that they barely needed to finish their sentences. Weird to think that in the passage of three years neither had done anything that was a surprise to the other. Perhaps that was the definition of friendship.

Ellie kept stifling yawns and soon Viv shouted above the racket, 'Look why don't we call it a night? You're knackered, we can catch up properly when the Festival's over.'

Ellie gestured for the bill. 'This is on me.'

Viv started to argue but Ellie held up her hand, 'No point. You did it last time.'

'Fair enough. It's good to have you back, Ells.'

They strolled up Queensferry Street and waited among queues of tourists on Shandwick Place, then bear-hugged as Ellie's bus approached. Viv wandered home via King's Stables Road, her mind full of questions about the outward-bound weekend. Why her? What was really at stake? Whatever it was had to be significant. Mac wouldn't pull the 'National Security' number without good reason. Or would he?

As she turned into the West Bow she spotted the saloon from earlier. She sauntered over to it and the window lowered. Ruddy smiled at her. 'Slight change of plan. Get in.'

She checked inside the car. Only Ruddy and his driver. She opened the back door and slipped in. 'So what's this about?'

'You'll see.' He handed her a folder. Inside there were photographs of boats. Some splendid cruisers, some sailing boats. 'Taking me on a cruise?'

His eyebrows twitched.

The car pulled away from the kerb and drove towards the West Port. She flicked through the folder. At the end there were two gruesome pictures of a severed forearm, both showing the same tattoo but from different angles.

She screwed up her face. 'Extreme way to lose your tats.' She stared at him. 'Still not sure what any of this has to do with me.'

They had reached Corstorphine Road, the main route to the west of Edinburgh. 'Where are we off to?'

Ruddy smiled. 'Patience, Vivian.'

The driver glanced in the rear view mirror and smiled. They turned onto the old Turnhouse road and stopped at the gates of an airfield. With a few words from the driver to a uniformed man in a small sentry box the barrier rose and they drove through. They parked on a strip of tarmac secured by a fence, twenty feet high topped with a round of rip wire. Ruddy got out and made his way to her side but she'd already jumped out. The blades of a nearby chopper began to turn.

She swung round and stared at Ruddy then pointed. 'Is that for us?'

He nodded. She tried but failed to stifle a grin. Excitement brimmed into every area of her body. 'I haven't been on one of these since OTC.'

He nodded.

She shook her head. 'Silly me. You already know that.' Her words tailed off as the blades gathered momentum and the chug chug chug became too much to compete with. Once on board they were both given a headset and goggles.

Ruddy confidently put on his headset and raised his voice above the engines. 'Welcome to Special Services.'

Her belly was knitting socks. This was more Hollywood than Edinburgh. Once she was strapped in with her own headset on the chopper took off. She felt as if she'd won the lottery for free rides at the fun fair. If this was what

Special Services meant, she was in. Trying to keep her wits about her she glanced down at the fields and the ribbon of the M8. It was not yet dark enough for drivers to have their headlights on, but the twinkle of sidelights made an impressive snake far into the distance. They were definitely travelling west. At some point the chopper scudded round on a more northerly trajectory. Light pollution receded and they raced through valleys where mountains rose above them on either side and lochs glistened below. Eventually they made it to the coast. The sun dipped close to the horizon. Her jumper wasn't adequate for this 2,000 feet high adventure. She hauled on her jacket.

Ruddy must have noticed her shiver and rooted around behind his seat and pulled out a blanket. Nice touch. She wrapped it over her knees and tucked her hands inside. They circled over a small bay where there were three boats, all lit up; the largest of them a white and silver gin palace. The other two most likely fishing boats.

The pilot spoke into his microphone. 'You can use the infra-red now. Put your goggles on.'

She was intrigued at how clear the stars were before it was completely dark. She put the goggles on and immediately the world beneath her changed. She could actually see the skeletons in shades of green of everyone on board the vessels.

She couldn't help herself grinning. Amazed that she was circling around in a chopper and that she was using military tech as if she were one of the boys. 'Wow! These things are excellent. Couldn't they be used in medical diagnosis?'

Ruddy ignored her question. 'The cruiser. What do you see on the cruiser?'

There were four people above deck and two, maybe three, lying below deck. 'I can see people lying below deck.'

Ruddy nodded. His head swivelled and he pointed to one of the fishing boats.

Same thing. Four above and perhaps three below. The magnification was terrific.

Viv laughed. 'If these were any stronger I could see their Adam's apples moving.'

Ruddy said, 'You think fishermen bring crew aboard to take a sleep?' He coughed and pointed again.

She followed the line of his finger. There was a faint trail of heat beneath the water. Not skeletons but definitely a line, or transmission, something showing up with pockets of green, making a connection between the gin palace and the fishing boat. These goggles were amazing and she briefly wondered if Special Services would miss a set.

'We know that there's a ring using this area of coastline. We're just not sure what they're bringing in.'

She was fascinated. 'People. D'you think it's people?'

He shrugged. 'We're hoping you'll find us a few more clues.'

She hauled the goggles off. Her eyes took a minute to adjust. 'Me?'

He nodded. 'Killing two birds with one stone.'

'They must know that you're on to them. This chopper isn't exactly discreet.'

'They're pretty cocky. Don't seem to think they're at risk.' He pointed to a couple of buildings on the shore. 'That's your destination tomorrow.'

She pulled the goggles back on and made out five people sitting round a table. In the gloaming the landscape was vague but she spotted a herd of deer and grinned again at the weird movement of their entire frames. Perfectly designed. She turned her head to face the boats again. One of the fishing boats was moving out to open sea.

She nudged Ruddy and nodded.

He shouted. 'They'll have to be efficient sailors to get to the other side of the Old Hag. She's taken down far bigger boats than that.' He tapped the pilot on the shoulder and made an upward spiral gesture. The chopper immediately rose and banked, turning back in the direction they'd come. She reopened and scanned the folder with the photographs in it. The tattoos were very specific, botanically accurate. Must have been done by a steady hand. By the time they were parallel with the M8 again headlights were on full. The sky was as clear as it had been in the west, but she couldn't make out nearly so many stars here. The same driver was waiting for them when they touched down.

Ruddy said as they got back into the car, 'We think that the west coast stuff is probably drugs, vodka, maybe even mock designer labels, but that's not all they're up to. It's as if that stuff is a decoy.'

She swallowed and buckled up. 'You thinking trafficking?'

He shrugged. 'Who knows? But we suspect ties to an extremist cell.'

'That doesn't make sense. Are they extreme nationalists? . . . Why would they bring in foreigners? Surely they want to get rid of them?'

He shook his head. 'Or . . .? Wakey, wakey, Viv. Take a guess at what they'd do with them. This is all unconfirmed but we're hoping something might turn up at the centre.'

'What exactly am I supposed to do on this dreaded outward-bound weekend?'

He grinned. 'Do what you're best at.'

She thought of what she'd done for him in the recent past. Her most fruitful results came from cyber snooping. She was about to say that the west coast of Scotland was hardly a cyber hot spot when she remembered how well equipped even nomads in the furthest reaches of the Gobi desert were. 'Okay. I'll do what I can.'

He gave a nod. 'I thought you would. Like father, like daughter.'

Surprised by this she said, 'Did you know him?'

'Yes.'

She stuttered. 'We . . . well what did you know about him?'

'Nothing that you probably couldn't guess. He was committed to justice and . . .' He gave the slightest shake of his head.

'And?'

'Best we stick to the present.'

'What is that supposed to mean?'

She could see that he wasn't going to be drawn.

They dropped her on the West Bow and she stood on the pavement staring at the saloon gliding slowly up towards George IV Bridge. What was she getting herself into? How had Ruddy known her dad? Her dad had been an ordinary detective, or so she believed.

She put her key into the outer door of her building and turned to wave, but the car was already gone. She even wondered for a moment if she'd dreamt the expedition. In the flat she was greeted by the smell of fresh dough. She stuck it into the oven and while waiting for it to bake packed a few things into a rucksack. The hair she was doing in the morning was a favour for a client and not the client themselves, so she didn't feel too bad when she changed the time of her arrival. Besides, brides-to-be never slept the night before the big day. The loaf hadn't risen and felt like an oversized brick. Baking clearly wasn't her strong point, but she still went to bed with the smell of fresh bread lulling her into a sense that all was well.

Chapter Five

Viv was an exceptional time-keeper and arrived with two minutes to spare at the home of the bride's mother. As she rang the bell she heard a screech coming from upstairs. She took a deep breath and released it slowly. This could be fun. The mother of the bride swung the door open and with a dramatic flourish bade Viv enter, while the screeches continued from above.

The mother said, 'This way. We thought it would be useful for you to have a mirror and lots of space. We've put you in here.' She opened the door to a large bedroom with wall-to-wall mirrored wardrobes. The wedding gown was hanging on a high window catch blocking out the light. Next to it hung a row of small puffy bridesmaid's dresses in lilac. Fortunately Viv had only agreed to sort out the bride's hair. The bridesmaids were being taken care of by their parents.

After about five minutes, with Viv becoming increasingly tetchy, the bride waltzed in. Her swollen eyes and veined cheeks would take a miracle to calm before the ceremony. Not Viv's problem. They'd had a trial run for the hair the week before and Viv set to. Mother brought in a bottle of champagne and poured a glass for her daughter. She offered Viv one but she refused; she would need to be alert for the rest of the day. Mother and daughter couldn't have cared less. They gulped it down as if it was water. If she needed this much alcohol to get married perhaps there were questions to be asked. Viv noticed that the bride was wearing a bra and ankle socks.

'I wonder if it might be an idea to take off your bra and socks.'

The girl looked sideways at her.

'Your dress is strapless. All you'll see are bra marks. Ditto the socks. I'd lose them and not have deep tracks for the photographs.'

The bride swung round and shrieked at her mother, 'You should have told me. If these marks spoil my photographs . . .'

Her mother, obviously used to being spoken to in this way, just about turned with her glass in her hand and left the room without a reply. Viv continued without missing a beat and, once she was finished, silently packed up her kit and retreated to the front door, where Mother smiled and said, 'I'll send you a cheque.'

Viv nodded, relieved to escape the asylum. When she reached the Rav a woman had double parked, blocking her in. Viv drummed on the steering wheel as she waited for three young children to be strapped in and given whatever toys they needed to keep them quiet. By the time she got going time was tight.

An architectural carbuncle built for function, Police HQ at Fettes hadn't improved with time. As if crime didn't happen at weekends, its large car park was almost empty and Viv pulled into a space opposite the minibus. She hauled her rucksack from the boot of the Rav and swung it over her shoulder. It was 9.25am, and there were people already on the bus. She saw Mac and one other man, storing luggage in a hold at the side.

Viv coughed.

Mac didn't look up but said, 'Nice you could make it, Dr Fraser.'

Either he was seriously pissed off or he was an excellent actor. He stood and held out his hand. Viv slipped her rucksack off her shoulder and handed it to him. She tried to make eye contact but he turned away and shoved her sack into the hold. She guessed this was part of the deal and stepped inside the bus. There were fourteen seats but only four aboard so far, a great ratio of people to seats. Lynx deodorant made a big impression as she passed the three blokes sitting nearest the front, although the cheese and onion crisps one of them was scoffing added to the cocktail.

Her heart sank when she recognised Gordon, a cyber analyst she had worked with before, who immediately said, 'Ah, if it isn't our very own

Bletchley girl.' His tone more facetious than she remembered it.

At the mention of this name the others looked up from their various technologies and in turn introduced themselves. 'Hi, I'm Archie.' His mouth still full of crisps.

And with a wave, 'I'm David, Davie.'

And a nod from, 'Robert, Robbie,' who was now busy checking the tachograph at the side of the driver's seat.

The only female aboard mumbled something incomprehensible before returning to scrolling through her phone.

Viv slipped onto the long seat at the back and stretched her legs into the aisle. She placed her jacket on one side and her ipod on the other, her territorial imperative showing no signs of diminishing. From this position she could keep her eye on the horizon and check out her companions – not a decent haircut amongst them. No one had used their full name, and consequently they sounded like a bunch of cocktail waiters. She was the only person who'd been graced with a last name and it wasn't her own. She glared at Gordon, wondering what he was up to and why he had introduced her in that way. She wasn't yet sure what any of their jobs were – even Mac's, if she thought about it hard enough. But they all worked together in some capacity for the NTF cyber unit.

Mac came aboard and handed out folders. 'Right. Read these and sign at the bottom of the last page.'

Viv glanced at the first page, decided she wasn't signing anything and closed the folder, then slipped it beneath her butt.

Mac saw her and frowned a warning.

It was too early in the morning to start toeing the line but she sighed and retrieved the folder. Since when did the police start giving out welcome packs? She rubbed a hand across her face and through her hair. The woman glanced at her and smiled. Viv shook her head and raised her eyes skyward in a what-the-fuck gesture.

Robbie fired up the engine but Gordon said, 'Wait!' and rushed off the bus and back into the building. Five minutes later he sauntered back and took his seat without apology.

Robbie glanced at Mac, who nodded. They were off with only seven on board. Time for reading was over for Viv. She leaned her head against the window, but caught a reflection of Archie gnawing on his fingernails. She shuddered and closed her eyes, wondering what he was so worried about. For the first twenty minutes she visualised the route along the Queensferry Road, out towards the Forth Bridges then the turn off towards Bo'ness. Once they reached the M9 she settled down properly with a fleece behind her head. There was an hour of motorway ahead and other than the Kelpies and Stirling castle, which she'd had an eyeful of recently, there was too much flat green land to look at. Once they were onto the Callander road and into the Trossachs the scenery would be more dramatic.

She dozed until their first stop at the Green Welly Cafe, about two hours from the outskirts of Edinburgh. The bus began to empty. The female bumped into Archie and shot him a schoolgirl death stare as if it had been his fault.

He said, 'Sorry, Frances.' Then skipped in front of her to join the others as they headed inside the building. Mac was chatting to the driver outside the bus and as much as she wanted to ask Mac a few questions she didn't feel it was right to interrupt them. Besides, she was getting the hang of his silent treatment. Mac took off into the building, but Robbie just stretched and cracked his knuckles at the door of the bus. No opportunity for her to snoop around the others' stuff.

One by one they returned to the bus, except Gordon. Eventually, just as Mac was about to go to look for him, he wandered out reading a newspaper. Not in any hurry.

Mac said, 'Move it, Gordon.' But all Gordon did was slowly fold his paper.

On the next leg of the journey Viv remained alert. To work in the NTF they'd all have been to Tulliallan for training, but she wondered how they would fare this weekend. Gordon was carrying a little too much weight and Archie moved as if he was in pain. Being a cyber geek still meant you were a police officer, although looking at a screen all day did nothing for physical fitness.

Davie, sitting next to Gordon, started singing, 'Nellie the Elephant

Packed her Trunk'. There was an outburst of laughter as they realised he was tipping the wink at John Le Carré, who had called MI5 'the circus' before they adopted it as their own. They all joined in for a couple of choruses before the song fizzled out and they bowed heads again to the church of technology.

The first opportunity Viv saw to chat she engaged Archie, then Davie joined them. She learnt that both were 'listeners' in the cyber side of policing. Archie said he'd studied law, not gone into the family firm of solicitors but bummed around the Far East before doing a post graduate course on software development, for which he found he had a flair. Davie on the other hand had been a computer geek ever since he'd set fire to his dad's shed while making some sort of electronic device when he was eleven. Safe to say that although he was a geek he reckoned he was a creative geek. They told her that Gordon had actually been a cop, on the beat, but had done in-house training in computing and worked his way through the ranks. Gordon himself occasionally chipped in to the conversation but only to add a sarcastic comment. Frances kept her head down reading her book.

The road to the isles now meandered through a stunning landscape where Munroes stretched their compulsory 3,000 feet above lochs that glistened like mirrors. Still dark water reflected gnarled, lichen-covered trees stunted and battered by the prevailing wind. Ancient people had made their homes on crannogs in the middle of these lochs. Secret causeways beneath the waterline were the only way to reach them, and were known only to a privileged few. There was all manner of speculation about why people had chosen to build homes in such inhospitable places. Damp sites with plagues of midgies – insects that descended to fight a battle more fierce than any human could provoke. Archaeologists had found evidence of domestic habitation, which put paid to the notion that they were ritual sites. Clay cooking pots, even a round of cheese had been preserved by the peaty waters of the loch, and the telltale charcoal of fires meant habitation over a significant time. If this lot on the bus thought they were in for a tough weekend they should at least be grateful that Goretex had been invented. Winter days with howling winds and driving rain weighed down by woollen plaid couldn't have been much fun for the early settlers in this part of the Highlands.

Frances, who was in the seat in front and opposite glanced up from her book and turned to Viv. What was it with overly blue eyes? She reprimanded herself for being cynical. Then nodded and said, 'Good book?'

'Not bad.' She exposed the cover of a thriller. 'Passing the time really. So what do you think this weekend will be like?'

'Have you been on an outward-bound course before?' Viv asked.

Frances shook her head. 'No. I've done some of the stuff we'll be expected to do, I mean we've all been to Tulliallan right? Seems a bit of an indulgence if you ask me.'

Viv snorted. The weekend would be many things but indulgent wasn't how she'd imagined it. 'How much time did you spend at Tulliallan?'

'The usual. Initiation training then the odd top up. Not counting our health check, they fairly put us through our paces this year. You? What is it that you do?'

'I did some stuff at uni.' Suitably vague.

'Yes, but what are you doing here this weekend?'

Viv looked right and left, then in a low voice said, 'There's some funny business at this centre. I'm just an extra pair of eyes.' The bus screeched to a halt then reversed. Robbie had missed the turn-off.

Eventually the minibus bumped onto a track and began a slow descent over rough ground. The view out to sea took in Islay and Jura, but a bleak landscape stretched for miles on either side of the track. Acre upon acre of heather and bracken, with the occasional rock breaking the surface, looked benign. Everywhere seemed benign when the sun shone.

The bus rocked and jerked for about a mile before it slowed and changed to a lower gear for an even steeper descent, until it shuddered to a halt outside a large wooden building with a moss covered roof. Viv glanced back to where they'd come from but couldn't see anything except heather. They were hidden in a dip. A crescent of white sand nestled beneath steep cliffs in the distance. Off to the left lay an open sided shed with outdoor equipment stored in racks. Moss was obviously the in thing, since the shed roof also blended into the landscape like the accommodation block.

Canoes and kayaks in bright colours were stacked in racks one above the other, and the back wall was hung with yellow safety vests. Viv guessed they would be using those.

Everyone piled off the bus and stretched. The first yawn went round like a Mexican wave, missing Viv and the female with the thriller. Either they were too distracted, or both sociopaths. Viv's rucksack was last on so first off. She walked toward the building but turned briefly to check what Mac was up to. She stared transfixed when she caught Archie running his hand down Gordon's back. It was over in a second but she didn't imagine it. Mac was on his knees with his head stuck in the hold so she continued.

A person with the most incredible head of reddish-blond dreadlocks, wearing khaki shorts, a navy polo shirt and a ring in her nose stood just outside the door holding a clipboard with a list pinned to it. She allocated Viv a room named Jura, and directed her to it. The tiny room had two single beds and an en suite shower with wc. Not the Ritz but not roughing it either. Hurrah to no communal washing. She stared out of the window. The view out to sea was spectacular. The surface of a horseshoe shaped bay with rocks circling its edges shimmered beneath the high sun. She recognised nothing from her trip the night before. Everything had looked entirely alien from the air and behind those goggles. No sign of any boats. Good time of day to swim.

She imagined they'd be split into groups to do domestic duties like making dinner. She lay on one of the beds checking it for comfort – perfectly good. The ceiling had a hairline crack right across the middle as if defining the boundary between the beds. It suited her to have her space clarified. What was she expected to do this weekend? One task for Ruddy with such a vague remit that what were her chances of succeeding? Slim, she thought. Bosses could shift their goal-posts, so unless she was absolutely clear what they were after she was bound to fail. And for Mac the NTF had perceived a mole, someone they believed posed a threat to 'National Security', and they'd tasked her with rooting them out. She felt her belly clench at the notion of failing in such easy tasks. Surely she was skilled enough to prise details out of the others. People always gave more away than they thought, especially if they were trying to conceal something. If she couldn't discover anything suspect over the weekend she'd have to find a way to check out their consoles at Fettes – with or without Mac's permission. She needed them to talk about themselves, and fortunately most people loved to do that, given the right circumstances. But first she'd have to snoop around. There had to be an office of sorts somewhere. With this thought she sighed and relaxed.

She was adjusting her pillow when the door opened and Frances came in. Viv grinned. 'Not too shabby. Don't even have to pad down the hall for a pee.' She nodded to the door of the shower room.

Frances blew out a breath and tossed her pack onto the bed opposite. 'Could be worse, I suppose.'

'What did you expect? Butler service?'

The woman raised her eyes and shook her head. 'No, but I can think of better things to be doing this weekend.'

'Couldn't we all? But our country calls.' Viv was being facetious but could see that thriller woman wasn't sure how to take her. 'Chill, I'm kidding!'

The woman flopped onto the edge of her bed and began to pull things from her pack. Viv wasn't one for unpacking and decided to leave her to it and have a nose around instead.

Once she'd got the layout of the building, noting that the office had no lock on it, she headed out the front door.

Mac shouted, 'Oi, Viv! Where do you think you're off to?' His voice more stern than he needed to be.

'Just thought I'd have a wander. Maybe a swim.'

'You'll get your swim soon enough. For now keep your eyes and ears peeled for Frances.'

An old-fashioned bell rang, the kind used in primary schools to call children in from playtime. Viv immediately revisited the memory of disappointment at returning to lessons. The woman with the bell, the same woman who had allocated their rooms, stood in the doorway looking as if she was relishing the task. Intrigued, she stared at the woman's piercings, and consigned them to the realm of self-harm, ditto her dreadlocks. The idea of not washing her hair every day, having a good scrub of her scalp, freaked her out. She'd once had someone come to her who wanted rid of dreadlocks. No easy task cutting hair that had been matted for years. And the stench that rose when hot water hit the hair and scalp was as noxious as damp farmyard animals. Scalps are living breathing skins and don't like confinement any more than other bits of the body. Some people did manage to sponge their heads regularly but it was no substitute for a good lathered up scrub.

Mac nodded and said, 'Game on.' He looked at Viv for confirmation.

She glared at him.

They went indoors to a large, long room with a wall of windows facing the sea, and a refectory table with benches on either side. A wood burner at the far end of the room would have been more welcoming if it had been lit, but instead it sat like a black mark against a stonewall. The outside of the building was clad in wood but it appeared as if an older stone property had been there first and the centre had grown up around it. A low door at the far end of the room, near the fire, led to the kitchen. A large wooden dresser, home to mugs and glasses, took up a chunk of wall. Right next to the dresser sat a large electric urn and a selection of herbal teas in boxes. The smell of the place reminded her of Henderson's vegetarian restaurant on Hanover Street, with sea dampness added to the mix.

Mac coughed and took charge. 'You'll all have read the info in the folders that I gave you on the bus. Those make clear the objectives of the weekend.'

There was a loud grumble of dissent.

'It's not as difficult as you think. But it's good for us to do some team building, to be forced out of comfort zones.' He pointed as he spoke. 'The first task for you all is to swim over to that small peninsula. It's cut off at high tide so you'll become isolated.'

They all groaned.

He continued. 'It's not far. You'll spend the night foraging for food and water. And Viv here is writing a piece for Police Scotland magazine, so you might want to keep in her good books.'

Noisy objections from the group rose and Viv eyeballed Mac. He didn't flinch. No smirk. Complete deadpan. This was all news to her but there was no getting out of it and she knew it. They all knew it.

'Shit,' she whispered to herself. 'Boy, will he pay for this.'

Mac continued. 'Before you organise yourself for the trip I'd like you to pair up with a buddy.' Now he did stare at Viv. 'You may as well choose your roommate. The point is . . .' Groans from the group continued until Mac put up his hands. 'Calm down! You know there's no way out of any of this so buckle up for the ride and enjoy pushing yourself to your limits.'

Viv shook her head. She couldn't believe it was Mac speaking. He sounded as if he'd swallowed a motivational manual. She looked around for Frances, who hadn't appeared yet. She glanced at Mac and raised her eyebrows.

He also looked around and approached the woman with the dreadlocks. 'Can I use that bell you had earlier?'

She went into another room and returned with the bell. He took the bell and rang it again. Still Frances didn't appear. If she was upstairs, Viv wondered how safe her things were. Might her roommate be going through her kit? Viv had nothing to hide that wasn't on her person, although in her rucksack she had a little survival box with waterproof matches in it. It would be a pity if those went missing now that they were going swimming.

Mac said, 'Viv, could you check the room? Let's see what she's up to.'

When Viv opened the door of the room she grinned. Frances was lying on the bed with her eyes closed and ear-buds in, oblivious to the bell outside or Viv's entry. She touched her leg. Frances kicked out, missing Viv's knee by a hair's breadth.

'What the f . . .' She hauled the ear-buds out.

Viv headed back out the door gesturing with her thumb. 'Downstairs. Roll call.'

Mac eyeballed Frances, but said to the whole group, 'I shouldn't need to remind you that you're here on a team building exercise. No man is an island and all that.'

Frances whispered to Viv, 'What's happening?'

Viv pointed to the bay. 'That's what's happening. We're swimming over there and spending the night.'

'No way.' Shock written all over her face.

Viv snorted. 'Yes way.'

'Any questions?' Mac said.

Gordon said, 'Back here for a fry-up in the morning, then?'

Mac said, 'No such luck. You'll route march over the island, find canoes that were left earlier, you're lucky the weather's fine, but don't dally because there's a storm forecast for tomorrow.'

Gordon said, 'Since when have you known a forecast to be right?'

'I'm just letting you know what's possible.'

Viv was about to wander back upstairs to collect her things, but made a detour to the kitchen to see if she could find large bin bags. She'd like to get to the other side with some spare dry clothes. Gordon obviously had the same idea and had found them already.

'Every man for himself, eh, Viv?'

It was too early in the weekend to get het up about gender-biased language, so she just accepted the roll of bags and pulled a few off.

As she turned to leave he said, 'What's this about then? Why are you really here?'

She feigned ignorance and shrugged.

'You think I'm buying that?' He held up crossed fingers. 'You and Marconi are like two peas in a pod.'

She wasn't sure where he was coming from since Mac was his team leader, his boss in other words. Viv wasn't even staff. Asking him what he meant would only lead to further questions, so she laughed and said, 'Nobody's ever called me a pea before but I'll take that as a compliment.'

He followed her out of the kitchen then hesitated before turning towards the men's corridor, leaving her to go upstairs and retrieve her stuff.

The Goretex rucksack she'd brought was a serious bit of kit, but for a night in the open she'd need something warm. She hauled out spare trousers, socks and underwear and left them on the bed. This made little difference to the weight. Everything was essential, especially the sealed box of survival things that included the waterproof matches. She'd found them in an outdoor shop in Callander, the only useful thing to come out of her last visit. She had a ball of string, a midge net, probably more important than any of the other stuff. No point in taking tissues but she'd keep the tiny first aid kit as a just-in-case. It was only for one night after all.

Chapter Six

On her way to the shore Viv caught the others huddled in a conversation that hushed as she drew close. She continued towards a rocky edge on the shore and stripped down to her swimsuit. Gordon and Archie began kicking about in the shallows further to her right. With her rucksack on her shoulders and her boots tied in a bag she tiptoed across the rocks and peered into the water. There was no way to tell how deep it was. Even in August the seas around Scotland were unforgiving. She slipped off the edge. When her toes touched the surface she caught her breath and a painful chill ran up her limbs reaching her breasts before her feet touched the bottom. No going back. She struck out.

The sea was calm and from the shore she reckoned it would take fifteen minutes, but that was only a guess. Now that she was in the water it seemed much further. This was the first test of mind over matter. If she were in the pool at Warrender baths she'd swim hard for thirty minutes without stopping and think nothing of it. The business of not being able to touch the bottom or make it to the side was the challenging bit. Best not to over-think and keep moving.

She'd had a look at a Harvey map before setting off and hoped that the beach on the other side was pebbled, but she had no way of knowing if there was a rocky shelf to negotiate before she got that far. She kept up a steady rhythm and besides one large jellyfish, which she spotted in time to swim around, the sea was clean and invigorating. It would have been a whole lot easier without the rucksack but the option of wearing every item was not a wise one.

She thought she heard someone call out, but decided it was a trick of her mind. Then a head bobbed up in front of her but immediately disappeared. She was gently bumped from below the water. She gasped, her imagination working over time. There were basking sharks on the west coast and although they wouldn't attack they were huge creatures, up to fifty feet long. She swallowed again and put more power into her strokes. The creature bobbed up again then swam beneath her and surfaced with its head only a couple of feet in front. It made eye contact. She was face to face with a seal. It seemed to want to play, and as much as Viv was relieved and delighted to see the animal close up, she wasn't in a position to oblige. The rucksack was cumbersome; she couldn't hang about. It continued to swim beneath her, round her, ducking and diving and nudging her with its nose. It was unbelievable, a once in a lifetime experience. The seal, possibly disappointed in her, disappeared as quickly as it had arrived.

Her sights fell on the far shore. Even on a hot day in Scotland the sea temperature was never going to be much above fourteen degrees. Cold bore deep into her bones.

She picked up her pace. Numb thighs were a bad sign. Before long she sensed the water getting warmer, which either meant it was shallower or she had the beginnings of hypothermia. She pushed on until it was easier to walk than to swim, then dragged herself without dignity onto a silver pebbled beach. Puffing and shivering she shook the water off as best she could then foraged in a bin bag from her pack for a fleece. All the while looking out to sea.

With the fleece on she rubbed her arms and hopped around vigorously before putting the rest of her kit on. Essential to keep moving. Although it was the last thing she felt like doing, she forced herself to run up over the pebbles onto a stretch of machair, where she star jumped and ran on the spot. She took off at a sprint for as far as she could, a couple of hundred metres, before turning and repeating it. What were the chances of swimming with a seal? If the rest of the weekend turned into a disaster, she'd always have that memory to treasure. There was no sign of her little friend on the horizon and she began to wonder if she had imagined it.

She was about to give up her exercise when she saw Gordon and Archie lying collapsed just beyond the waterline. Breathless, she jogged over to check that they were okay. They had made their lives more difficult by swimming with tee shirts on: human skin was designed to repel water – fabric was not. Archie rolled onto his side and vomited. Served him right for snacking on rubbish on the minibus. Gordon made it onto his knees and tried to calm his breathing.

'Look, guys, I know it's the last thing that you feel like doing, but it's worth keeping moving. Once the chitters set in . . .'

Gordon glared at her and through gasps said, 'Since when did you become our designated super-hero?'

Viv shrugged and walked back to where she'd left her rucksack. She slung it over her shoulder and made her way inland. The only sound above her own breathing was a pair of curlews having a domestic in the distance. So far only three of the seven who'd been on the bus had made it. Not a great turnout. Perhaps the others resisted setting off. Viv, a deferred gratification woman, always kept the best 'til last.

The land away from the shore was as it had been on either side of the track back at the centre. Heather, bracken with boulders peeking through, was paradise for ticks. She checked that her trousers were well tucked into her socks then continued to stride out, looking for somewhere to light a fire. After a short time someone shouted her name. She turned and saw Gordon waving at her from the beach. She hesitated, sighed, and ran back towards him. He was gesticulating wildly towards the sea. Her gaze followed his and she saw Frances' head dip below the surface.

Instinctively she dropped her pack and ran, tearing off her kit as she went. When she reached the water's edge, and while struggling to remove her boots, she glared at Gordon. 'Why aren't you going in? Don't just stand there, you arsehole.'

Frances' arms were raised above her head, flailing about thirty metres from the shore. Then her head sank again. Viv's limbs were still recovering from her own swim, but there was nothing else for it. In her hardest front crawl she swam out to where Frances had been. She dived and swam around; it wasn't too deep but was murky since the sand had been disturbed. She surfaced, gasped for air and dived again. This time she saw her and tried to grab her by the arms but Frances kicked out in panic. Winded, Viv began to sink down and down into the murky water. When her feet bumped onto the sea floor she pushed off propelling herself back to the surface. She gasped and spluttered. No sign of Frances. Viv's strength was waning but she took another huge breath then dived again. This time she swam beneath Frances and shoved her towards the surface. Frances gasped, and punched and kicked, then suddenly went limp. Viv, seriously close to her limit, finally managed to grip Frances' chin and, holding her head above the water as best she could, swam towards the shore. With each laborious stroke she questioned her sanity for attempting this when she was already spent. Twice she went under, but some primal survival instinct asserted itself and she managed to reach the shallows. The final act of hauling Frances' dead weight away from the water's edge forced her to collapse. Gordon and Archie pulled Frances further up the beach while Viv lay fighting for her breath. Once it steadied she got to her knees and crawled to Frances' side and checked her pulse. Nothing. Gordon and Archie stood in silence, shivering like lemmings. Clearly neither had been in the Boy Scouts.

Eventually Gordon said without any conviction, 'Is there anything I can do?'

Viv, too distracted to reply, set about CPR. She'd never done CPR on a real body. Compressing the chest to the rhythm of the Bee Gee's *Staying Alive* was all very well but what had happened to mouth to mouth? Was she right in thinking it was no longer recommended? During her second go at pumping Frances' chest the woman's eyes flickered and she spluttered, spewing out seawater and coughing herself into action.

Viv collapsed onto the pebbles and stared in disbelief at the sky. A breeze tickled the goose-bumps on her arms so she rolled onto her knees, stood up, and dragged herself back to where she'd discarded her kit. For the second time in ten minutes she wiped salty water from her limbs then pulled on her clothes, remembering to tuck her trousers back into her socks. She retrieved another bin liner from her sack and went to where Frances was lying in a foetal position. Viv wrapped the bag round her and huddled down beside her to keep her warm.

Viv, seething at the lack of initiative from Archie and Gordon, said, 'Right guys, you asked if there was anything you could do, well now's your chance. Either build a fire or take over here. She needs as much body warmth round her as we can give her. After that little episode we've got to stop hypothermia setting in.'

Both men looked at each other, then Archie hunkered down and lay awkwardly along Frances' back.

Gordon got down and backed himself as best he could onto her front. A tricky operation with her knees curled up. 'Cosy or what?' he said, embarrassment evident in his tone.

The fact was that they would all benefit from more warmth. 'I'll go find somewhere to light a fire. Once I've got that going I'll come back and get you. Mean time keep huddled,' she ordered.

She heard Gordon make a sarcastic comment but let it go. She couldn't think what the hell had got into him. What had prevented him from trying to save Frances? And what was with all the sarcasm? There was no need for him to take against her. They had worked together on a couple of things and although they were not buddies there weren't enemies either.

Terrain that looked benign from the bunkhouse had dips and troughs every few feet. Such hard going. Viv scanned the horizon, hoping to find a big boulder for shelter. There were plenty of them, but finding one with a large indent on the side away from the prevailing wind was tricky. Eventually she discovered one and dumped her sack before making her way back to the beach to gather driftwood. There wasn't much around so she supplemented what she had with stalks of heather and moss. It took about twenty minutes to get the fire going and another ten until she was confident that it wouldn't go out as soon as she left it unattended.

She jogged back to the beach and nodded to Gordon and Archie. They both rolled away from Frances and sat waiting as if for their next order. Viv hadn't planned on leading but someone had to take the initiative.

'Get going then. Help her over to the fire then gather as much rubbish, wood, rope, anything that'll burn, from along the coast line.'

Frances stood up and snapped, 'Thank you. I'll manage.' She was wobbly on her feet but Viv shrugged. No one could force her to have help. The two men took off in opposite directions along the pebbles.

What would Mac think? Why hadn't either of them gone back in to rescue Frances? She'd find out soon enough, but meantime they'd have to find food. She was beginning to feel lightheaded but studied the horizon and saw another head swimming steadily across the bay. Perhaps competence was on its way.

The sun was still high. A breeze wasn't making much impact on the temperature, which suited them while they were damp from their swim. One of the fabulous things about Scotland were the endless summer nights. And as long as the sun shone they were safe from the mayhem of midgies. Her midge net could be used for fishing rather than protection.

Further round the bay, over a rocky outcrop, she found a series of pools with seaweed gathering at the edges. Viv nibbled a sliver and screwed up her nose. She stood and scanned the horizon. There was little chance of catching fish so she bent back down to the seaweed. Should she gather for herself or for the collective? 'Should' was super-ego shit, but she collected more than enough. There had been no mention of being self-sufficient and one reference to 'no man is an island', so she was covered.

From a high point she identified Jura by its Paps. The area was famous for its ragged inhospitable coastline and impossible currents. The Gulf of Corryvreckan between Islay and Scarba, was home to Scotland's strongest whirlpool, and played havoc with the tides. What was it that Ruddy had called it? Viv took in a long breath of fresh sea air and felt her townie genes begin to twitch. What the hell was she doing here, foraging around a shoreline picking up kelp that tasted of old wet socks? She countered this by convincing herself that since it was only for one night she could go without until the morning. Gordon's comment to Mac about a fry-up came to mind. Nevertheless the pile of seaweed would do someone if they were desperate. She noticed limpets sticking to the edge of a rock and knelt to prise one off. Even with her knife it was too much like hard work for so little gain. If the others wanted them she would point the way. While she was down on her hunkers she wondered exactly what Ruddy was hoping she'd find. But if he knew that she wouldn't be here. If Frances was up to no good she was now indebted to Viv. You wouldn't hurt someone who'd saved your life, or would you?

When Viv arrived back at the fireside she was surprised to see Mac. Frances was still gripping onto the black bin bag, legs and arms crossed, uncomfortable with Mac's proximity, or was it his questions? Tension occupied the metre between them.

Mac glanced up. 'Ah, the heroine approaches. Frances has just been telling me that she got cramp.'

This was news to Viv, but that was as good an explanation for Frances going under as any. Viv held up the straggly seaweed. 'Hungry anyone?'

Frances turned away and put her hand over her mouth as if she might gag.

Mac grinned. 'I might have known you'd be the Bear Grylls on the team. Thanks but not for me.' He shot Viv a look that she couldn't quite make out.

She furrowed her brows in a question. But he shook his head and turned to Frances. 'You think you'll be okay to do the overnight?'

Viv nudged at the fire and was about to answer, but realised he was talking to Frances.

Frances shrugged. 'I suppose so. Although I don't know what the fuck we need to be here for in the first place.'

'Don't you?' He stood up, casting a shadow over Frances and the fire. 'Canoes are being delivered in the morning. You're expected to make your own way back to the centre tomorrow.'

Viv said. 'In time for afternoon tea . . .? Where do we pick up the canoes?'

He raised his eyebrows. 'You'll find them.'

This sounded ominous. But since they weren't here for a jolly, any equipment that might help them would have to be fought for. Sleeping under the stars in August was no real hardship, so there must be another catch lined up. In the meantime she built the fire up, hoping the others would arrive back laden with stuff to burn. Mac surely wouldn't stay, but she didn't ask.

He wandered off.

Viv said to Frances, 'You really going to be okay? That was quite a display you put on there.'

Frances' eyes filled. 'I'll be okay. The whole thing is only for two days. Surely we can all make it through two fucking days.'

This was rich, coming from someone who almost didn't make it through the first challenge. Cramp was unbearable on dry land. Viv had seen Olympic swimmers, blokes in the Corps, brought to tears by it. At sea the consequences were a lot more terrifying. Maybe Frances had some kind of death wish.

'Well, if you need food I spotted limpets on the rocks over there. Or I'm sure that seaweed is delicious.' She grinned and nodded to the pile, which she'd tossed onto the boulder.

Chapter Seven

The chatter of voices rolled over the heather, growing closer and closer. Archie, Gordon and Davie approached with arms full of driftwood.

Viv jumped up. 'Wow. Great job, guys. All we need to do now is to get our voices into shape for a campfire singsong.'

Davie sang a perfect round of 'Kookaburra' and they all laughed. Even Frances smiled.

Archie plonked himself close to the fire and opened his rucksack. 'Dinner!' He held up small tins of fish, a selection that would have done Sainsbury proud.

'I thought the idea was we'd fish for our dinner or at least forage,' Davie said. 'But I suppose you've been foraging at the supermarket?' He nudged Archie. 'I'll have the mackerel if it's going begging.'

Archie handed round the tins. Who would refuse the gift of dinner?

Viv settled on a rock opposite him. 'No wonder you were knackered when you landed on the beach. What the hell else have you got in that sack?'

He grinned and pulled out small tins of Guinness and a few miniature bottles of Macallan.

'For God's sake.' Viv shook her head but was no less grateful for the fact that she didn't need to use her midge net to catch her supper. 'You've forgotten the silver.'

He sank his hand back into the sack and everyone roared. But he only pulled out his Swiss army knife. Viv had brought a Gerber: total alpha female, with pliers, wire cutters and screwdrivers. What she thought she'd be doing with these in the wilderness she'd no idea. Perhaps she'd over-estimated. However, if she did need to break into a high security facility any time this weekend she was prepared.

Archie said, 'This do?'

They all laughed again when each one in turn produced a similar knife. Viv kept the Gerber under wraps, reassured that the others had planned ahead.

Viv skipped the Guinness but was grateful for a small tin of smoked mussels. The others made juvenile comments about how much easier they were to eat from a tin than from their shells slathered in butter and garlic. The sun slowly dropped towards the horizon. Viv pointed to clouds in the distance – a mackerel sky.

Every group has its unique life, so if they were going with the forming-norming-storming-performing-ending routine, she guessed they were 'norming'. Gordon and Archie had a go at the seaweed but spat it out. Viv smiled. At least they gave it a go. It defo wasn't her thing. Slimy she didn't do.

Davie said, 'Okay, who's got any ghost stories?'

They looked from one to another. Davie had one or two up his sleeve, otherwise he wouldn't have asked. Sure enough. 'Right. Once upon a time . . .'

He spoke slowly in a lowered tone that drew everyone in. It wasn't dark but behind the boulder the sun had disappeared from sight and they'd all gathered closely round the fire to hear Davie's tale. At one point Viv saw Frances nod off, but she woke up when her head dropped. She must be exhausted. Davie knew how to tell a story, no matter how shallow the plot. He had them hanging on his every word. The punch line was like a damp squib, but the journey had been worth it and they applauded, asking for more.

It could be a long night. Viv banked up the fire and said, 'I'm going to put my head down, try and get some kip.'

Gordon said, 'Tired out after so much super hero action? I thought you'd be keeping an eye on us for lover boy.'

Viv saw the others looking bemused. Best policy was to ignore him, but she was slightly surprised that no one came to her defence, not even Frances. Ungrateful sod. Viv took another bin bag from her rucksack and wrapped it round her shoulders. She laid her head on one of her boots, but yanked it away deciding that a clod of moss was more comfy. She pulled her boots back on and curled up with her hand resting on the moss. Although Davie started another story, one by one the group followed Viv's lead, organising themselves for sleep, or at least rest. For the adrenals to recover from a day's activity, the body needed to be horizontal. Even if you don't sleep your system gains equilibrium. That was probably as much as they could hope for tonight. Although the sun had gone completely the sky was light and she stared up at a vast starry canopy. It could be a cold night, but if the payoff was good settled weather tomorrow, it would be worth it. Counting stars was much the same as counting sheep.

She must have dozed, because she woke with someone whispering right next to her head. The menacing tone took a few seconds to sink in, but she caught, 'Don't move or make a sound.'

She felt warm breath on her ear as Frances promised to stick whatever sharp object she was holding against Viv's carotid artery. Viv opened her mouth to speak, but was rewarded with a sharp prick on her neck. Frances beckoned her to get up and she complied. Frances held her arm in a vice-like grip, showing no sign of her earlier fatigue. The two women stumbled over rocky heather surrounding the fire, neither speaking until they were some distance from the others.

Frances spoke. 'You didn't think I was stupid enough to believe you wanted me alive. You were pulling me under. You tried to stop me from breathing. But I fought back. I came back.' She shook Viv's arm violently to add credibility to her words.

It took a couple of seconds for Viv to realise that Frances was describing accurately what had happened but her interpretation of why she had done it was seriously off. Frances thought that Viv had tried to kill her. 'No you've got it wrong . . .'

Frances tightened her grip. 'Shut it. There's no way you're going to get rid of me. You're the one who's having an accident.'

Viv's mind was birling. How the hell was she to reason with this kind of craziness? She remained quiet.

'That's not going to work either. Don't think I wasn't paying attention in the psych classes. I've known other bitches like you. Cool, distant, always seeking attention. I've seen how Marconi looks at you. Don't take me for a fool.'

Viv went to speak. 'But . . .'

'I said shut it! Now you just follow me and we'll be at the cliffs in no time.'

Cliffs. Shit. Viv hadn't reckoned on the cliffs. The rock around the bay was basalt. Cliffs would be unforgiving. She halted and yanked her arm out of Frances' hold. But Frances had other ideas and somehow gripped onto Viv's pocket.

Then the oddest thing happened. One minute Frances was as forceful as a Musketeer, the next she collapsed to the ground taking Viv with her. It was like a comedy sketch. Viv landed on top of Frances' now limp body. She was out cold and in the process had released her grip on Viv's pocket. Viv rolled away and got to her feet. Frances lay limp, but still breathing. Viv shook her and slapped Frances' face. It didn't make any impression. She loosened the zip of Frances' jacket and saw an insulin pen hanging round her neck. 'Shit!' She'd never administered insulin to anyone and wasn't sure whether now was the right time. She held back, reciting the motto, 'When in doubt do nowt'. Instead she rooted around in her own pockets to see if she had any old chewing gum or Tic-tacs. The only thing she came up with was half an oatcake. Worth a try. She shoved a piece into Frances' mouth and held it shut. Not very sympathetic, but first aid wasn't, it was practical.

There wasn't much more she could do with Frances, other than try and get her back to the camp. But first she had to find the weapon that had pricked her neck. Luckily she soon spotted a small silver toothpick glinting inches from Frances' hand. Viv pocketed it, then holding her beneath the arms tried dragging her, but she kept stumbling. It still wasn't entirely dark but shadows on the land were difficult to read in the half-light. Viv hoisted her up and pulled her arm around her shoulder. She was no lightweight but it was easier than hauling her backwards. Ten metres from the fire she stopped, astonished that despite all her huffing and puffing none of the others had stirred. Finally she laid Frances back onto her sleeping bag, checked her pulse and her eyes. Her pulse seemed normal and her eyes had stopped rolling. The oatcake was dissolving.

Chapter Eight

Viv rubbed her face and raked her hands through her hair. What was going on? Only a few hours ago she'd saved Frances' life. Why would she turn that into a conspiracy theory? Viv wasn't trying to kill her. Did she think that someone was, or was she just in need of medication? Whatever the answer she shouldn't be on this course. Why hadn't she told Mac about this? All medication had to be declared in this job. Something like diabetes could be managed but they'd have to know about it. Viv banked up the dwindling embers and lay back in her spot with her hands behind her head. Too many unanswered questions swirling in her head. No chance of sleeping now.

In the distance the call of a pair of oystercatchers pierced the silence. She drew in a long slow breath. There was no doubt about her proximity to the sea; the air was heavy with smells that just wouldn't occur in town. Archie turned onto his back and began to snore, a comic snore. She tried to visualise which funny man it reminded her of and opted for Stan Laurel. She rose onto her elbows to watch his long intake of breath and his whistling out breath – maybe more Deputy Dawg than Laurel but so funny.

Then she must have dozed again, because she surfaced to the smell of coffee brewing.

Archie grinned at her as she roused. 'Got all your gourmet needs here.'

She smiled and rubbed her hair. Archie was looking rough. His dark shadow didn't do much for him, unlike Gordon who looked a lot less officious with patches of growth on his chin. Although the coffee smelled good, Viv couldn't function without first brushing her teeth. It wasn't until she stood up and stretched that she noticed Frances had gone.

'Anyone seen Frances?'

Archie nodded to the other side of the boulder. 'She went that-a-way.'

Viv took off in the direction he'd pointed and didn't have to go far before she spotted her squatting in a dip. Viv turned her back and got on with her own tooth regime. Frances nodded as she passed Viv, as if nothing had happened in the night. She was pale and rubbing her upper arms.

Viv shook her head. 'What? You not even going to remark on your little performance last night?'

Frances stopped and shot Viv a confused look. 'I don't . . .' She clenched and unclenched her fists. 'Did I do something in the night?'

Viv snorted. 'What? You don't remember?'

Frances looked genuinely alarmed. 'Okay. So I'm guessing from that look that I did something, but since I've no clue what, you'll have to enlighten me.'

Viv stared at her. 'Are you for real? You have no memory of waking me in the night?'

'Nope. None at all.' She scuffed her boot on a boulder. 'But it wouldn't be the first time I'd done something weird in my sleep.'

Viv thought about this. But didn't believe that Frances could have been so active without being aware of it. 'Sleep walking?'

'I know it sounds mad, but yes.'

Viv shook her head in disbelief and brought out the toothpick from her pocket. 'Recognise this?'

Frances' eyes widened. 'Shit! What did I do?'

Viv slipped the pick back into her jacket. 'You can have it back when we get home.' She headed back to the fire.

'If there's any of that coffee left I'd love some.'

Archie handed her a steaming paper cup. 'I've already put dried milk and sugar in it.'

Viv screwed up her face. 'Yuck.'

'You'll thank me for it when we're canoeing round that headland.'

Gordon yawned, stretched, then cracked his neck from side to side.

'Everyone sleep like babies?'

Davie stirred. 'Babies? Who said babies?'

Archie tossed a packet at him. 'Here, use these.'

Davie held up a pack of baby wipes. 'The smell of these makes me gag.'

Archie replied. 'Yeah, well, the smell of you makes us gag. Get using.'

Gordon, Archie and Frances sniggered. Viv stood with her hands wrapped round the cup of coffee. Who were these guys? None of them seemed likely to cause the NTF any difficulties beyond wearing too much deodorant. Besides, what hardened criminal carries baby wipes?

Once they'd packed up their gear Viv pulled the fire apart. 'Don't think we'll be back. Can't wait to find the canoes and get across that bay for a hot shower.' She started off over the heather towards the other side of the peninsula. If Mac meant them to paddle around it he'd have left the canoes in the most inaccessible position, otherwise what challenge would they have had? During the night Frances had talked about cliffs. Had that been her imagination or were there actually cliffs on this part of the peninsula? She took a quick look at her map but decided all she had to do was follow the shoreline and she'd eventually find them. If only she'd paid more attention in geography classes.

Walking was hard going. At times she had to lift her knees almost to waist height to clear the heather. Once she made it to the machair, she stopped. Relieved, she dropped her backpack, laid her hands on her hips and caught her breath. She stared out to sea. It was cool but a low mist was clearing revealing a pale blue sky. If it continued like this it could get hot. The others began to catch up, each one more out of breath than the last. But it was best to keep moving. She had to admit that despite her allergy to wide open spaces it was unbelievably beautiful. Islay and Jura dominated the view and she felt an odd pull over the sea. The coastline became rockier and the land began to rise so that the path was higher and further from the sea.

Archie appeared at her side. 'Not want to slow down and enjoy the view?'

'Sure. But I'm worried that if we don't get round the headland before too long the sun will be up and we'll all get frazzled.'

He nodded. 'I hadn't thought of that. I suppose you're right.'

Gordon, dripping with sweat, lumbered up, 'How much further d'you think we'll have to walk before we find the canoes?' He glared at Viv.

She shrugged. 'Hang on, I'll just consult my crystal ball and let you know.'

He continued, 'It's not as if you're not in on all of this.'

Viv turned to face him. 'Look, I don't know where you're getting your conspiracy theories, but they are so far off the mark as to be laughable. I'm as much in the dark about this as the rest of you, so ease up on the speculation.'

He snorted. 'Give me some credit. You're in Marconi's pocket.'

Viv stopped and turned to him with her hands still on her hips. 'What is it with you?' She shook her head and reminded herself not to rise. 'Let's get our maps out and find the least hospitable spot on this coastline and see if we can't get hold of these canoes.'

She knelt on the ground and spread out her map. Gordon stood above her shadowing the map. Viv waited. Sighed and waited. 'For fuck sake Gordon, grow up. Either get down here and . . .'

'Now, now, Viv. Don't you go losing it.' Archie and Davie had made up on them. Archie kneeled beside Viv and swept his huge hand over the map, pinning down the corners. 'Move it, Gordon, we can't see a sodding thing. You're shadowing the map.'

Gordon stepped away.

Viv poked her finger at a spot on the map. There. A cave at the bottom of a cliff. 'I bet that's where they are. It's still quite a walk so we better get a move on.'

Archie said to Gordon, 'Better forget your fantasy of having a fry-up for brunch. We'll be lucky if we get to that cave before midday. Then the work begins.' He rubbed his hands together, sounding as excited as a kid.

Archie set the pace, with the others following. Viv was so grateful for the mercy of good weather, the sun shining, no wind, only the sounds of the sea, the odd gull or oystercatcher. Viv stared directly at the sun and blinked then sneezed, sneezed again and then again. The weather could so easily have been miserable.

'So what would you have been doing if you hadn't had to come on this little ad-ven-ture?' Archie stretched out the last word, sounding slightly camp.

'Work probably. I'm a hairdresser and Saturdays are busy days, so I'd have seen clients all day yesterday, and today I'd have gone for a run or for a swim. Got that covered.' She smiled at him. 'What about you?'

'Hairdresser? And I don't think.'

She sighed. 'Oh God, you're not one of those, I-have-to-have-people-in-neat-boxes-types?'

'There's no way. Why would they invite a hairdresser on one of these courses?'

'Because this hairdresser likes to poke her nose into other people's business.' She'd said more than she ought. 'Never mind that, what about what you do on the weekends?'

He looked suspicious but responded. 'I'd have watched sport with the boys, then seen my folks.'

Viv shot him a quizzical glance.

He leapt to his own defence. 'What? Saturdays are for the boys and Sundays are for my mum and dad, brother and his family. We always have a traditional Sunday lunch together.'

Viv was genuinely surprised. 'Really? Every Sunday?'

He laughed awkwardly. 'What's wrong with that?'

'Nothing's wrong with it. It's just that I haven't heard of anyone doing that kind of routine for years. I mean, even as a teenager I'd have found an excuse not to go.'

'I suppose my parents let us know early on that it wasn't a option to miss it.' He hesitated. 'I like it. It's a ritual. Keeps us together. And my mum's a great cook.' He patted his belly. 'Preparing me for my own family life.'

'You sure you like it? Sounds like you're super-ego led.'

'What's that supposed to mean?'

Viv grinned and shook her head. 'It means that you're still toeing a line that childhood authority figures laid down for you. At some point most of us snip off those apron strings and go it alone. Which means, if you wanted, say, to watch porn in your boxers all day on a Sunday and not go to the family lunch, you'd feel okay about it.'

He snorted. 'You saying I'm still a kid?'

She pushed him gently. 'Sure you are.'

A shadow crossed his face, then self-consciously he pasted on a smile and nodded. 'Probably some truth in that. But aren't we all?'

Archie was a big guy. But he didn't strike her as a gentle giant, in fact she'd caught an edge to his voice, not menacing but on the way there. Why so defensive? Viv guessed he'd played rugby so asked him. 'What sort of sport are you keen on?' Safer ground.

He said. 'Rugby of course, but almost any.'

His build, accent and demeanour said it all. 'Did you play?'

'Yep, for the Accies at county level. Had to have surgery so didn't make the Scottish first team.'

She heard his sadness. 'That's tough.'

'Yeah. Shit happens.' Now she knew he was joking.

Chapter Nine

Davie caught up with them. 'What do you reckon, Viv? An hour still to go?'

She shrugged. 'Ask Archie. He probably has a better sense of distances than I do. I just saw that the cave was two fingers width away.'

Archie interrupted. 'I guess we'll be there in an hour if we keep up this pace.'

Davie was already panting. 'Crikey. I'll need a sleep before I get into a canoe.'

'You'll be fine. Although we don't know what the ground will be like. We might all be abseiling off a cliff. With any luck we can scramble down to the shore. Wait and see.'

Davie rummaged around in his rucksack and pulled out a small plastic pack, the sort that might contain tomato sauce or mayo. He ripped the top of it and sucked it clean. 'Energy bar in a pouch.' But didn't offer anything to the others.

He was prepared even if they were only one night away from civilisation. She reflected on what Archie had said about his weekends and how different a childhood could be, based on what your dad did for a living, if you had one. Her dad always worked weekends. Shifts weren't kind to family life. She could hardly remember a Christmas or New Year when her dad was around. A dad who was a detective had its romance but not at meal times.

Viv wasn't hungry. The coffee with the powdered milk and sugar was still swilling around in her belly. 'Archie, you were right about that coffee this morning. How much sugar did you put in it?'

'Builder's formula: milk 'n' two.'

Viv shuddered – the thought of two scoops of white sugar was even worse than the idea of powder that had never met a cow in its life. But it had kept her going.

After about twenty minutes hiking, Viv stopped and removed her fleece. The mist had cleared and the heat of the sun intensified. Gordon and Archie also peeled off their tops, momentarily exposing slices of the grey-white skin peculiar to Scottish men with indoor jobs. Archie had a long fine scar running down the centre of his torso. Perhaps his injury hadn't been a torn ligament as she'd imagined. Although both guys could do with a bit of sun they kept their tee shirts on. Both wore Rohan type trousers with plenty of zips and pockets, and hiking boots that were beyond the spec needed on this trip. But who was to know how easy they'd be having it?

Davie wasn't as tall as Archie and Gordon but had a cyclist's build, slender and sinewy. He puffed along at her side wearing a lightweight grey jacket, the kind he'd wear to the office, white trainers and a dark blue tee shirt. His rucksack looked more capable of an Everest adventure than a weekend in Scotland. Apart from his weather beaten face he didn't strike her as the outdoor type.

'So Davie, what would you be doing this weekend if you weren't with us?'

'Work. Definitely work.'

'So no big family lunch on Sundays for you then?'

'No, until recently there's just been my dad and me, but he's about to marry a woman who is younger than me and who doesn't know whether she should flirt with me, or him. So lunches aren't exactly fun.'

'You must love your work, though.'

A spark of excitement flickered in his eyes. 'Love it. Have always tinkered with machines and electronics. Now I get paid for it.'

'Really always? When was your first foray into computing?'

'Well it wasn't so much computing. I'd build bits of electrical equipment in my dad's shed.' He giggled. 'Until I blew it up.' He wiped sweat from the tip of his nose with the back of his hand. 'Crikey, the woman next door called the cops. Nothing that exciting had ever happened in our street before. Can you imagine, a council estate in Dunfermline with police cars blocking each end of our street, an ambulance, the bomb squad van.' He giggled again. 'God, was I kept in. "Grounded" as people over here call it.'

Viv laughed. 'Oh we got "kept in" as well. But how old were you when you posed a threat to the neighbourhood?'

'Eleven. Maybe twelve. First year at secondary school.'

Viv shook her head. 'Your mum?'

'She died four years back.'

Viv didn't pursue this. 'But going into work every weekend, d'you never get bored?'

He looked around as if checking for the boss. 'I don't spend every minute working. But what I discover on computers is my life.'

Archie interrupted. 'He hates sport. Have you ever met a man who hates sport? Well you're looking at one.' He pointed to Davie.

'It's no crime.' Viv defended him.

But Davie said, 'Oh no, it is, Viv. At school I almost got killed for not liking football.'

'Quite bloody right.' Gordon said, catching them up and making his first contribution to the conversation. 'Sport's about building allies and I bet Davie hasn't got any mates to draw on – if he'd played football or even just supported a team he would have.' He glanced at Archie. 'And at a push that goes for rugby as well, although they're more likely to be pansies.'

Viv couldn't believe she was hearing this. 'What's with the political correctness by-pass?'

Gordon snorted. 'Can't be arsed with all that crap.'

'It's not crap. It's essential. People with prejudices . . . bigots have to be put right.' Viv felt the heat rising up her neck and across her cheeks.

'Yeah, so they're free to have their voices heard and I'm not?'

'Not if your voice is talking bullshit.'

'Who decides? You? Since when did you become the PC police?'

This was dangerous territory for Viv, who was inches from telling him to go fuck himself but expected he'd love that. It would add fuel to his fire. How the hell did he ever get a job at the NTF? Was he taking the piss?

Davie said with a grin, 'Well, I'm quite happy with my own company. While you lot have "mates", he did air quotes, 'whether you want them or not. You stick together like Velcro. At Watsons it was pathetic.'

'Watsons!' Viv and Archie said in unison.

Davie grinned again. 'What are you lot like? Just because I lived on a council estate in Dunfermline doesn't mean I didn't have access to private school. I travelled through to Edinburgh on the train every day. Love that rail bridge as if I'd built it myself.'

Viv was astonished, although his accent did have shades of Edinburgh south. Archie, on the other hand, was posher, more nasal, less clipped, difficult to describe, but definitely different. She'd guess that Gordon was either a Royal High boy or maybe a Herioter. She'd find out soon enough.

Chapter Ten

Frances straggled behind, stopping every now and then to take a photograph. How the phone had survived the swim she had no idea. Viv had left her tech, nervous of getting it wet. Frances looked much better now; her colour had returned and her eyes were bright. She must have sorted out her medication. How weird to sleep walk without knowledge of what you'd been doing. There was a famous historical case of somnambulism in Edinburgh, where a man killed his wife with a meat cleaver and got away with it because he was asleep. Nice work if you could get it. She smiled. Also been studies where sleepers were filmed walking around their homes, their gardens, eating stuff from their fridges and freezers, then when awake denied the whole thing only to be shown the film footage. One woman had even gone out to the local shop and they had it on their CCTV. So much for 'know thyself'. We've all got bits of ourselves that are buried, not always a bad thing, but in the main it's surely better to root them out and befriend them.

'Come on, Frances, catch up.' Viv called over her shoulder. The testosterone around her was becoming claustrophobic.

They waited and Frances caught up. She raised her phone to photograph the group but Archie shouted, 'Oi, you don't have my permission to do that.'

The rest of them looked surprised. It wasn't as if they were naked or in a compromising situation. What could he possibly object to? Viv hated having her photograph taken, but couldn't be bothered arguing about one snap.

Davie said, 'Chill. She's not going to post it on Facebook or anything.'

Even his tone was more of a command than a casual observation. Were they all photo-phobic?

Archie said, 'Could you delete that please?'

Frances shrugged. 'No problem.' She turned her phone towards him and deleted it. 'Better?'

'Thank you.'

They marched on in silence until Davie said, 'Look.' And pointed out to sea.

They stopped and stared at the calm water. Nothing.

'What are you staring at?' said Viv.

'Shhhh!'

Then a seal bobbed its head above the water only a few metres from the shore. Viv wondered if it was the same one. She started singing the Skye Boat Song. The others stared at her as if she'd lost the plot. The seal began to duck and dive and then bobbed its head up again and stared back at them. Viv was thrilled and sang the next verse. It did the same routine then stopped again to stare at them. Davie, Gordon and Frances wandered ahead, still watching the seal.

Archie laughed, a deep bellowing sound. The seal disappeared.

Viv nudged him. 'See what you've done.'

'I didn't mean to.' He playfully pushed her back. 'Hey maybe we could get a drink sometime?'

Viv couldn't take her eyes off the horizon but smiled. 'Maybe.'

They stood for another few minutes, Archie a little too close for comfort, but the seal didn't reappear.

'You spoiled its fun.' Viv said, disappointed.

Frances dropped back. 'Look.' She passed her phone to Viv.

There it was, a video of the seal playing before her eyes. 'That's fantastic. Could you send me that?'

'Sure. No worries. I'll get your email address before we leave.'

They continued along the edge of the cliffs, Viv's eyes peeled on the water, in the hope that the seal had followed. No luck.

Eventually they stopped and she laid the map flat on the ground again, checking for specific contours and landmarks. By her calculations they should be almost directly above the cave. She lay flat on the ground and stretched over the cliff edge. There were a couple of options on how to get down. There was a chimney that they could climb down, but further on they might more easily scramble to the shore. They walked on.

Gordon stopped and sat on the edge, draping himself over. He scrambled down sideways, making light of the descent. 'No probs. We'll be down . . .'

Half way down, about thirty-five feet from the bottom, he had to turn around. He lost his footing and grabbed at the rock, just managing to secure himself. Still unable to see where to place his feet, he froze. He was stuck. Amazed at how quickly his confidence evaporated, Viv checked the cliff further on for a way that she could join him. She'd tried free climbing in her youth but much preferred using a rope. Without that option she carefully slipped over the edge.

By the time she reached him he was soaking with perspiration, his fingertips white, as if he'd become rooted to the rock. Viv climbed to where she could get a good hold about a metre to his right. He was teetering with one of his large booted feet on a tiny ledge.

'If you move your right foot a short distance further to the right you'll be fine.'

He glared at her. Sweat dripped off the end of his nose. She could smell his panic. It wasn't a difficult move at all, but he'd entered that zone where everything was distorted.

She scanned the rock assessing the safest way to get below him. Free climbing was precarious even at ten feet from the ground and they were much higher than that. She gripped a fissure and stretched her foot down until it settled on a fine ridge, but as she tested it with her weight it gave and she lost her grip. By sheer fluke her fingers held her weight until her foot found a crack, which prevented her from coming off. She took a long breath and slowly but steadily managed to climb below him until she was a few feet from the shore. His right leg was shaking uncontrollably. 'Look, you'll have to trust me on this. Just stretch your right leg out to the right and you'll feel a large ledge. If nothing else it'll give your leg a rest.' Adrenaline was a wonderful thing if you wanted to sprint or do the high jump. But when you're convinced you will fall to your death, unless you're super efficient at mind over matter, adrenaline was not your friend.

Gordon stretched his shaking leg and almost got to the ledge but pulled back. 'Fuck!' His fingers were gripping too tightly to a large fissure. No point in telling him to relax them, it would make matters worse.

'You were almost there. Next time just another few inches and you'll do it.'

He stretched again. The silence from the others above spoke volumes. He managed to place his foot. Putting his weight on the ledge meant he could shake out his arms one at a time. If he continued to move to his right there was an easy way to the shore. Viv waited until he was confident enough to make eye contact with her.

She nodded. 'If you continue right, there's a huge crack that you can get your feet and hands into.' Viv knew that if need be he could make a fist and hang off the damn thing, but she could see he was in no mood for theatrical moves.

He blew out another long breath then glanced toward the crack she'd described. 'Thanks. I think I can manage the rest of the way.'

She continued to down climb onto the pebbly beach and watched as slowly and deliberately he made his way to meet her. It wasn't graceful but he made it.

He brushed himself off as if he'd got dust on his trousers. 'Thanks.'

She could see that this had cost him, so she just nodded and called up to the others. 'Just follow the root down this crack, don't get creative, and it'll be a piece of cake.'

Gordon raised his eyebrows.

'Well it was, wasn't it?'

He stood back from the cliff and shaded his eyes. 'It does look like a piece of cake from here but when you're up there . . .'

'I know everything's out of proportion. Let's see if we can find the cave.'

They set off to the right along the shore. There were a couple of possibilities. Viv crouched on the ground and guarding her eyes from the sunlight, squinted into the darkness. She could make out shapes that might be canoes. 'This could be it.' She sighed, surprised that they'd been set such a feeble challenge. 'Not much of a challenge, is it?' She turned to look at Gordon who by the horror on his face clearly thought he'd had plenty to challenge him for one day.

The others joined them, Frances first then Davie and Archie.

Archie said, 'This is a piece of cake, Viv. D'you think they've got some belter waiting for us round the bay?'

'No idea. Let's do one thing at a time. Who wants to crawl inside and push the canoes out?'

Davie volunteered and he and Archie hunkered down beneath the gloomy entrance and adjusting their eyes to the cool dark interior, edged their way inside. Archie, although bent double, caught his hair on the rough damp roof. Davie was on his knees, his slight wiry frame making light of crawling over the slimy rocky floor. The depth of the cave was difficult to gauge but it didn't matter since the canoes were only a few metres beyond the entrance. They pushed them one at a time out into the sunlight, where the others waited, eager to pull them onto the beach. Each canoe contained a double paddle and a lifejacket.

***

The last canoe was the furthest in and sat at an odd angle.

Archie gasped. 'Wait! What . . .' His voice echoed around the low chamber.

Viv hunkered down and flicked her pocket torch on. 'What is it?'

Archie pointed to a boot sticking out at the back of the last canoe.

'Oh my God.' Moving as quickly as she could, Viv crawled her way to the body. She checked her pulse. It was the dread-locked woman from the centre. She was alive but her skin was ice cold. There were no signs of blood but she had a dark purple swelling on her forehead. They had to get her out of the wet cave. 'How are we going to move her?'

Archie backed out, allowing Davie and Viv access.

Viv said, 'Davie, quickly, take hold of her feet. We have to get her out of here.'

Archie said, 'But what if something's broken?'

Viv stopped. 'I think we need to get her out. She's freezing. It's a risk . . . What do you guys think?'

They all nodded unhelpfully.

'What does that mean? Shall we move her or leave her here until we can get the coast guard or someone from the centre?'

Davie said, 'I say we move her.'

A general nodding of heads. Davie crawled to the woman's feet and Viv struggled to get her own arms fixed beneath the shoulders.

Without ceremony they heaved the woman inch by heavy inch to the front of the cave. Once they had her in full sunlight Viv took her pulse again. She hauled a fleece from her sack and wrapped it round the woman's torso, saying, 'Frances. Is your phone working?'

'Nope. It's out of battery.' She looked sheepish. 'I should be able to send an emergency text.'

'Send an SOS to Mac.'

'Who?'

Viv sighed. 'Marconi. Tell him to get back round here as soon as.'

The bump on the woman's head looked much worse in the sunlight. It looked like there could be internal bleeding. Not sure what to do next, Viv checked her pulse yet again. It was still weak. Her icy skin wasn't helped by her damp clothes. How long had she been there? When had the canoes been dropped off? Viv tried to remember the sequence of things. She chewed her lip. It would take too long for Mac to get to them.

'I wonder if we should just try to get her back to the centre by canoe?'

The others looked down at the woman, then at Viv.

Archie said. 'I think it's worth waiting for Marconi. She might have other injuries and we've no idea how long it's going to take us to get back.'

Gordon nodded. 'I'm with Archie on that.'

Viv replied, 'Yeah, I get that. But every minute that we waste here she's getting weaker.'

Frances said, 'The text hasn't even gone yet. There's no telling how long it could take. It could sit on some server. I say we get her into a canoe and get moving.'

A couple of the canoes were designed for two people.

Davie chewed at the inside of his cheek. 'I say we get going.'

Viv nodded. 'Any volunteers?'

Archie looked around and since no one else was offering he shrugged. 'Okay, I'll take her, but someone else will have to take my rucksack. The canoe isn't big enough to take that as well.'

Davie said, 'Pass it over here. I can manage it, my sack's pathetic.'

'Settled,' Viv said to no one in particular.

Archie had serious upper body muscle, but after his reaction to the swim Viv wondered about his endurance. The Corryvreckan must surely influence the currents in this bay and would make the paddle back hard going. Viv and Davie lifted the woman, no lightweight, into the canoe, while Archie held it steady in the water. Easier said than done.

'Frances, could you send Mac an update? Delete the last text if you can.'

'No can do. But I'll send an update and hope he gets it before he acts on the first one.'

Viv and Davie pushed Archie off from the shore, then grabbed their own canoes. Frances hauled hers away from the water's edge and stepped into it. Viv, Davie and Gordon followed – Davie opted for the other large craft. Perfect conditions. No wind, a high sun, every canoeist's dream. Frances quickly paddled out to the front, with Gordon then Davie following. Davie overtook Gordon and paddled alongside Frances. Viv was keen to stay with Archie but held back until they were in clear water before she came alongside. him. 'You okay?'

'Sure. What could be nicer than this? I mean chances of me charming a woman to come to sea with me are pretty remote. But she's not making a fuss.' He chuckled. 'Best kind of woma . . .' Catching Viv's raised eyebrows he changed course, 'I mean . . .'

'I know what you mean and it's probably better if you don't go that route. You done this kind of stuff before? I know you said you'd played rugby but this?' She glanced around her. The coastline from the water was magnificent. It gave a whole new perspective to the landscape. She spied another couple of places where it would have been easier to descend, but hey ho they were fine now.

Archie said, 'I did a bit of sailing in my youth but it wasn't really my thing. I like contact sport.'

She nodded. What was it about big burly men and rough and tumble? Were they hanging onto their youth? Continuing behaviour that was sanctioned in the playground? She could think of nothing worse than a scrum.

Archie said, 'Wonder how the family lunch will be today? They'll be delighted to have the golden boy to themselves. Taking on the family firm, married his school sweetheart, now got an heir and a spare. Perfect, fucking perfect.' He glanced at Viv and gave a slight grin as if he'd just noticed that she was his audience.

Viv looked away in the hope that he'd continue.

He did. 'You know I've never done anything right. Well, not as far as they're concerned. The bro. He's toed their every line. Usually in families the prodigal son, you know the one who pisses off, does his own thing, then returns, is greeted with open arms and a large slice of the inheritance? Not my parents. They've rewarded him for being dull. Really, he's allowed them to manipulate him. He's even been forced to take my father's place in the ar . . .' Suddenly he stopped. Said too much. He laughed. And in a much lighter tone continued, 'Families, eh, you've got to love them.'

Viv was intrigued. Surely his father was too old to be in the army? How was she going to tempt him to finish his sentence? She said, 'I have a sister who seems to be doing a similar kind of thing. She's married and has produced the first grandchild.' Amanda had toed as few lines as Viv, but he didn't need to know that.

'Why is that?' Archie said. 'Is it not a child's desire to forge their own way? Stray from the family line?'

Viv hadn't noticed that he was doing any of that if he was still pitching up every Sunday for lunch. So what else had he been up to that had made him unpopular?

'D'you get on with your brother and his family?'

'To an extent, although they seem to think I'm judging them for being goodie-two-shoes, which of course I am. Even their kids are perfect.' He sniggered. 'Bound to come apart at the seams sometime, eh?'

'Bound to. Perfection is a myth in my book.'

He stared at her. 'You strike me as pretty perfect.'

'Me? You've got to be kidding.' She shook her head. 'What do your dad and brother have in common that you couldn't care less about?'

He hesitated.

She continued, 'You see, my sis has a life dominated by fashion. You know – must have the latest high-end superficial crap.' They paddled on at a gentle pace.

He laughed. 'Doesn't every woman?'

'You're on very shaky ground, mate. And need to get out more. Find yourself some different women. Amanda, my sister, she'd never be seen dead without the latest label. Me? Couldn't give a toss.' This wasn't entirely true.

'You look pretty good.'

'Piss off. I wasn't fishing for compliments. I'm just saying there are women who have other things that interest them. So what about your dad and your brother?'

'Well, they have the law for a kick off. Then there are all the societies that go with that. Like the Spec.'

Viv said, 'What's that?'

'A debating society for fogies.'

She nodded, remembering that Spec was short for Speculative Society, a society that had recently been in the press. They used rooms in Edinburgh University's Old College, rooms that hadn't changed since R.L. Stevenson had graced them. But the university powers were trying to get rid of them. The difficulty was that the Spec had owned the site since before the University was built and the rooms were theirs in perpetuity. They'd originally exchanged their own building, allowing it to be demolished and a new quad, now the 'old quad', to be built on their site. So the land belonged to them and the University could do nothing about that. And since many of their members were lawyers, the Uni was on a hiding to nothing. If the Spec moved it would be because the members had voted to, not because some outsider told them what to do.

'So you're not a fan of the Spec, then?'

'Don't know. Never been invited.' He couldn't keep the edge from his tone. 'Nor do I get invited to dinners for the High Constables, and definitely not the Archers.'

Viv had a vision of Ambridge but swept it aside knowing that this could be important. 'Wow, so your dad's an Archer?'

'Sure. As will my brother be . . . oh never mind them. Who wants to protect the Queen anyway?'

An odd thing for someone to say who had signed up to do exactly that.

Viv shot him a quizzical glance. 'Well we all would if it came down to it, right?'

He raised his eyebrows. 'I suppose. But surely it would depend on the stakes?'

'Yeah. Yeah. I guess.' This was not Viv's understanding of the forms she'd signed for Ruddy.

'Just wait 'til I have my own kids . . .' He stopped and turned toward the rasping sound of an engine crossing the bay.

It grew louder and louder until a huge gin palace, possibly the one she'd seen from the chopper with Ruddy, passed by at top speed causing a wake that tested their ability to remain in their canoes. All five of them yelled out in response.

Archie bellowed, 'Whoa!' His canoe banked and took in a wave.

They steadied again and Viv regained Archie's side. 'You both okay?'

'Yes. But she'll be really soaking now.'

They were going at a fair pace so Viv couldn't ask him to crank it up further. But said, 'This pace okay for you?'

'I'm fine.' His voice a tad high for that.

Viv glanced inshore. They were a good, three, maybe four hundred metres from the craggy edge. 'We could go ashore for a rest, or stop here for a bit.'

'I'm fine.' He sounded irritated, his tone still a fraction high.

'Well, let me know if you're flagging.'

They continued round towards the end of the peninsula, seabirds skimming over the water and a slight wake from a boat too far away to see, enough only to disturb their paddles slightly.

Chapter Eleven

At the furthest point they made their way back along the coast of the inner sound. Viv heard another engine. She squinted into the horizon and saw a rib racing towards them. The tone of its engine changed as it slowed about fifty metres short of their canoes.

Mac shouted, 'What's happened?'

Frances shouted back. 'We found the woman from the centre. She's unconscious.' The skipper of the rib manoeuvred the craft alongside them as their canoes bobbed precariously close to each other.

Mac turned to Viv. 'So where was she?'

'In the cave with the canoes. She's had a nasty bump to the head. There's no blood but the swelling on her forehead is serious. She's still unconscious. And maybe hypothermic, but I've no idea if she has any other injuries.'

As if the woman had heard, her eyelids began to flutter.

Archie said, 'She's coming to.'

Mac spoke to the skipper. 'Let's get a harness on her.'

Mac and the skipper began the precarious task of putting a series of straps beneath her and attached to a hoist on the rib, before removing her from Archie's canoe. No mean feat.

Before the final hoist Mac said, 'The rest of you keep going. We've got this covered now.'

Gordon looked skyward and shook his head. Davie shrugged. Frances looked disappointed that she wasn't getting to see the hoist on the rib in action, but paddled off with Gordon and Davie tailing her. She called over her shoulder. 'Last one home's a rotten egg!'

The effect was immediate. Both Davie and Gordon began paddling furiously. The rest of them laughed. Even Mac raised an eyebrow at how easily men became boys. It took a few attempts to lift the woman, whose name turned out to be Becky, and as soon as they had her secured they gunned the engine and turned the rib towards the centre.

Archie said, 'Well, I'm glad that's done. She's not my type. Hate dreads and I don't get all that piercing.'

Viv didn't either but shook her head. It wasn't a singles weekend. The sea did strange things to sounds and Archie's voice was amplified. How odd.

The sun was hot, but Viv's hands were numb after so long on the water. Once on their way she shot Archie an enquiring glance. She just wasn't getting the measure of him. The more info he gave about himself the more conflicted she was. What kind of man was he really? He yo-yoed between one state and another without warning. If he wasn't a patriot what was he doing in this job? Were he and Gordon mates? There was something going on with him that she just couldn't get to grips with. Maybe she'd get a bit more info on the next leg of the journey.

Once the rib was well on its way Viv followed Archie's canoe, but could see that he was pulling ahead of her and she had to work hard to keep up with him. Was he responding to Frances' challenge? Worried about being regarded as a rotten egg? Viv decided to slow down and take in her surroundings and the birds. She thought she saw a puffin but it moved so quickly she could have imagined it. Cormorants and gulls dived around a tiny inlet, their screeches piercing the clean still air. They were feeding, but on what she had no idea. As she drew closer they rose and scattered then returned to bomb into the sea.

She paddled along, finding a steady rhythm and enjoying the sun on her face although she still couldn't feel her hands. The others were now like dots on her horizon, occasionally being lost from sight, when a wave carried them out of view. She stepped up her pace and within a few minutes she was closing the gap.

Davie held back so that she could make up. 'Come on, you. We're supposed to be a team.'

He had obviously been in a canoe before, since he turned and reversed it effortlessly – a skill that Viv hadn't mastered.

She said, 'I just thought, I'll probably never be in a canoe on this coast ever again, so I'd better make the most of it. Well, at least now the injured are off our hands.'

'It is amazing, isn't it? I didn't think I'd remember how to use one of these.' He gestured to the canoe. 'But all that outdoor education at school is coming back to me. I bet I could roll it.'

Viv hoped he wouldn't, because if he failed she'd have to rescue him. 'Going to wait 'til we're nearer base. Then I won't have to get wet. I mean wetter. I can't feel my hands any more.'

'Me either. But it's still beautiful. So much for preferring being in the office. I'm having a great time. Amazing what you learn about folk when you have to do things that you don't normally. Like you, who'd have thought that building a fire would come so naturally to you. The rest of us just stood gaping. At home with the flick of a switch we've got heat, light whatever we need. It surely can't last.'

He was enthusiastic and Viv was keen to hear his chat. 'Not worried about being a rotten egg, then?'

'No way. One of the bonuses of not being a rugger bugger, or a football lad. There's little that anyone could throw at me that would be an offence, "rotten egg" is the least of my worries.'

'I can't imagine you having worries.'

'We all have something to worry about. Makes you get up in the morning, doesn't it?'

They paddled on at a gentle pace, spoiling the stillness with their chatter. Viv wondered how far their voices travelled. Did the sound make it to land?

'So, Davie, what exactly would keep you awake at night or make you get up in the morning?'

'Solving the latest cyber attack.'

A reminder, if she needed it, of why they did what they did. Who among them was trying to sabotage this work? She had to keep her wits about her. No conversation was benign. 'Not missing hours of *Candy Crush* then?'

'No, I've never really got into gaming.'

'How about hacking? I bet that's another thing.'

He looked at her blankly. 'Hacking?'

'Come on. My life wouldn't be worth living if I couldn't trespass into worlds I shouldn't.'

He looked shocked. 'I could report you.'

'Be my guest. I think that's why they ask me in. They know I'll poke around and they don't want your reputations to be sullied, whereas mine already is. They pass the buck to an outsider anytime it suits them.'

'You really think that?'

She nodded. 'Indeed I do.'

He laughed. 'I might have had a peek at the odd thing. Nothing serious. No porn.'

She hadn't considered that. But now she did. Yes, she thought, I bet you have.

The computers in the office were swept too regularly for it to be worth doing anything really bad. But Mac had once called her in on a case where kiddy porn was involved. So anything could happen.

'So you and Mac an item them?'

She almost tipped into the sea. 'No. Who the hell told you that? No way.' She heard her own protest and realised it was a touch too adamant. 'Not that he isn't a good man and all that, but no. Who told you?'

He gestured ahead. 'Gordon. I just thought there must be some truth in it. No smoke without fire and all that.'

'No smoke and definitely no fire, this time.' She smiled at him. 'You got a partner?'

He hesitated. 'Not really. Nothing that I'd tell anyone about.'

'Fair enough.'

He lowered his voice, enough for her to just catch. 'Too scared to wish.'

Viv felt her heartstrings being played and didn't respond. They were almost back to where they'd originally swum ashore. Now all they had to do was paddle across the bay and they were home if not dry. She recalled what Archie had said, about a 'belter' waiting for them sometime. Maybe they'd bypassed the 'belter' since they'd rescued Becky. Although she agreed with Archie that the tasks so far had been light on risk. Maybe the purpose of getting them together was simply so that Viv could elicit information in an informal setting. Surely that wasn't all that Mac expected?

Frances and Gordon had taken off over the bay but Archie waited for her and Davie to catch up.

Archie said, 'By the way, I was kidding about that Queen and country thing.'

'Sure, no worries,' Viv replied, wondering why it should be playing on his conscience.

Davie said, 'Have I missed something?'

'No,' Archie said quickly. 'Viv and I were having a conversation about life. So nothing major.'

Viv, seeing Davie's surprise, said, 'We've both got siblings that are a pain in the arse. You, not having any, won't have that issue.'

Davie smiled. Appeased. 'No, you're right there. Being an only child has its complications, though.'

Viv wondered what those might be, beyond his stepmother making a play for him.

Chapter Twelve

They headed back across the bay. Halfway over, Viv slowed and screwed up her eyes. 'Do you see what I see?' she whispered.

Archie and Davie slowed and stared in the same direction as her.

Archie said. 'I think I might. Is it that little black head?'

She nodded. 'Yes. Is it the seal?'

She paddled slowly towards what looked like a seal's head, but it didn't move. It was a buoy. But what was the use of a black buoy? Viv trailed her hand through the water and touched the top of it. It was the size of a football. She tried to push it with her hand but whatever it was attached to was pretty secure.

Davie said, 'How weird. A black buoy is about as much use as a . . . chocolate teapot.'

Viv smiled. 'If you're gonna use a cliché at least pick a newer one than that.'

'Ouch!'

Viv shook her head. 'It's not exactly designed to draw attention, so I wonder what it's for?'

The other two circled the buoy and each touched and patted it, trying to work out its purpose.

Archie said, 'It might have something to do with lobster pots, or maybe it glows in the dark. It has got to be here for some reason. We can ask at the lodge when we get back.'

Viv thought lobster pots was a good idea, then Davie said, 'It could be marking a change of boundary or a rock hidden beneath the surface.'

Also good ideas, but she had a niggling suspicion that it wasn't to do with either of their suggestions. Surely if a fisherman was marking his pots he'd want them to be as obvious as possible.

Both Archie and Davie were looking overly pink and she wondered if she would be as burnt as them, although so far she didn't feel any discomfort. 'Come on, let's keep moving. I've built up an appetite.'

They continued paddling, with the sun beating down on their heads. A breeze was getting up and the sea had a slight swell. As they reached the rocky shoreline the others were standing around with hands on hips, waiting to greet them.

Frances said, 'Joint rotten eggs.'

Viv snorted. 'Not too worried by that, but Archie might be.'

'Am I biffo,' Archie replied, as snippily as he could manage.

Davie shook his head. 'I'm happy to claim the rotten egg title. I've been called so much worse, it's almost a compliment.'

Viv plonked herself down after struggling with her canoe up the pebbly beach. She turned and saw Davie do the same. He had been more of a team player than the others. Although she conceded that Archie's providing food for everyone was a big deal. Davie's canoe caught on a big boulder so she jumped up and pushed it out of his way, at which point he also collapsed and lay back on the beach. 'That's the hardest work I've done all day.'

Viv pointed to the horizon. 'The day is not over. Check that out.'

Archie said, 'Where the hell did that come from?'

A curtain of dense, dark rain clouds had gathered out at sea and was moving in their direction.

'We're going to get pissed on big time,' Davie said. 'Let's go.'

Without the help of the others Viv and Davie took an end each of their canoes and lifted them up to the shed, where a bearded man with a polo shirt bearing the same motif as Becky had had on hers, said, 'Thanks, guys. I'll hose them down before we stack them.'

They grabbed their rucksacks and walked back to the front door of the centre.

Viv said, 'Christ, I can hardly move I'm so stiff. Who'd have thought a couple of hours in a wee boat could be so demanding?'

Davie smiled and stretched his arms above his head. 'Know what you mean.'

Viv, Davie, Archie, Frances and a member of staff, who hadn't introduced himself, stood inside the refectory and watched as the storm approached. Gordon sat at the table, scowling as if he'd had bad news. When the wall of water hit land, hail began to fall in balls the size of Pan Drops. The room, that minutes before had been bright and welcoming, was transformed into a damp gloomy hole not unlike the cave they'd pulled Becky from. Then rain and darkness fell as if someone had turned a hose on and switched the lights off. Someone did put the lights on, but no sooner had the group sounded their approval, with a collective 'ah that's better' than the lights flickered, then flickered again.

The member of staff laughed. 'Looks as if we'll lose power. Nothing unusual out here. Dodgy generator.'

Viv said, 'What does that mean?'

'It means there'll be no hot showers and a creative dinner.'

Viv scampered toward the stairs and took them two at a time. She'd rather have half a hot shower than nothing at all. Salt was drying all over her skin and she felt like clawing it off. It was almost as bad as tiny shards of newly cut hair sticking into her pores. She ran the shower as she pulled off her kit. Standing beneath the hot stream she relished the sensation of salt and sand, wherever that had come from, dissolving and running down the drain. She even managed to shampoo her hair. She stepped out of the shower and, as if on cue, the lights went out. She fist-pumped the air. Job done. Monsoon style rain continued beating against the window as she pulled on clean underwear, trousers, a tee-shirt and a fleece.

There was no sign of Mac so she assumed that he'd gone off with Becky to the nearest clinic. Had Becky simply bumped her head or was there more to it? She lay on her bed and looked out at the sky, which was getting heavier by the minute. She didn't mind if the electricity was off, she was clean. For the first time since she'd arrived, her thoughts turned to Robbie Ritchie the minibus driver, who hadn't made it across the bay. Where was he? And why hadn't he turned up? She couldn't imagine an adult in the NTF not being able to swim. And that was the only reason she could think of for Mac letting him off the hook. She could be wrong. Her belly rumbled. If they had to do tasks in their pairs she'd now get the chance to speak to Frances. What kind of person hides an illness like diabetes? No one had had a second thought about taking the food from Archie. He must have known that doling out food would afford him a few favours. Why did he need favours?

Should she head down stairs or lie here relishing the solitude of the room? It wouldn't be long before Frances would take up her space. She lay a bit longer. What Archie said about 'Queen and country' kept coming into her mind. The NTF were taking a chance if they had a republican in their midst. You didn't have to declare yourself as a royalist but they wouldn't employ anyone actively anti-monarchy. Let it go. She knew that the best way to reason was to let her thoughts have space. She closed her eyes. It didn't take long for her to fall into a deep sleep. It wasn't until the door squeaked and Frances crept into the room, flashing the walls with the beam of her head torch, that she stirred. With the room no longer in total darkness and the sound of rain still beating hard against the window Viv sat up instinctively, raising her arm to protect her eyes against the glare of the beam.

She snapped, 'Oi! Get that off!'

Frances immediately turned her head away and fiddled with the torch. 'It's supposed to have three settings, but it's stuck. She ripped it off and tossed it over to Viv. 'See if you can get it onto another setting.'

Viv had her own torch, which she set on the windowsill, with its beam splaying up over the stark white surface. 'No sign of any electricity coming back on, then?'

'Nope. Candles all round downstairs. Looks romantic and they've lit the wood-burner. Apparently it'll boil a kettle on the top. Dinner's not far away. We drew straws. You either had to cook or tidy up. You got tidying up. The cooks didn't have to do much.'

Viv shrugged. 'Fair enough. What time is it anyway?'

'Seven. Well five to. Wish I'd had a shower. I can hardly stand to be in the same room as myself.' She sniffed her armpit to make her point.

Viv grinned. 'I couldn't stand the grime. I would've had to get it off even if there hadn't been hot water.'

'I've had enough water to last me a lifetime . . . Thanks, by the way.'

Viv screwed up her eyebrows.

'For saving me in the bay.'

Viv nodded. 'No worries.'

'I'm actually a pretty good swimmer. But I was so cold. I could feel the cramp, ever so slight to begin with, but it was too late for me to go back. I had to keep going. Fucking agony. You ever had it?'

'Sure. Strangely only ever when I've been in bed. Or maybe once when I was running in a relay race for the school. That made me really popular.' She snorted.

Frances went into the bathroom. 'I'll just get a wash – army bath at best.' She shrugged.

Viv said, 'I'm going to join the others.' A lie. Frances was already closing the door.

Chapter Thirteen

Did Mac have evidence that Frances was the mole? Was it just a hunch? It would be unlike him to go on hearsay, but not impossible if he'd heard enough. If Frances was sneaking about the office trying to hide her diabetes, getting tetchy when she needed insulin, Viv could see that she'd become an object of interest at the very least, but why so unpopular? Nobody likes a sneak, but what about the others? Who was most likely to have a grudge against the NTF? Viv glanced at Frances' things lying on her bed. She hesitated, then lifted the head torch. Frances' phone was on the bed. She nudged it and it sprang into life. 'Shit.' The sound of water running and splashing continued, so she decided it was safe to scroll through the messages. The splashing stopped. Viv flipped the phone over and tiptoed from the room.

She stood outside the door and counted to ten before bursting back in as Frances came out of the toilet rubbing herself with a towel. 'Managed to get that torch onto a different beam. Not brilliant but not quite as Gestapo-like.'

'Great. Thanks.'

When Viv entered the refectory the others were sitting at the long wooden table. Candles flickered in quirky ceramic holders in the middle. If she didn't know better she could imagine they'd just ordered dinner and were waiting for their drinks and a basket of bread to arrive. The wood-burner was ablaze and the walls ran with condensation. A smell akin to sweaty socks hung in the air. The rain had more than dampened the environment. She glanced at

Gordon and wondered why he was staring into space like a man doomed.

Her face felt hot but her inner temperature was definitely lower. Davie waved her over and tapped the bench at his side. She stepped over it and sat down. Archie, Gordon and Davie's usually pale faces were crimson from exposure to the sun. Gordon had white marks where his wraparound sunglasses had been. The others' eyes were swollen and half closed. None of them looked as if they'd moved from the room since they got back, the skin on their faces still bearing traces of salt. Yet they were all wearing fleeces. A large empty Strathmore bottle stood in front of Archie and each of them had a glass with water in it.

'We dry?' she said.

'Fucking temperance house this,' Gordon said.

She bristled. His defensive tone was irritating. She wondered if he was always like this. The one time she'd met him at Fettes he had been. What was really going on with him? Fear is our biggest drive but what was *he* so scared of? She'd have thought that after the climbing debacle he'd feel relieved that they were on the home straight.

'Want a drink?' Davie asked, tipping the dregs of the Strathmore into a spare glass and handing it to her. He shook the bottle to emphasise that it was absolutely empty.

The gesture reminded her of a boy she'd been at primary school with. Jimmy Robinson used to do that same thing with the little bottle of milk they each got each day at playtime. He'd been unconvinced that he had finished it so quickly. Jimmy's family were so hard up and he relied on the milk, every drop counted. She wished she'd realised that at the time, since he was constantly teased for not being a sharer. Whatever he had he scoffed the lot, not because he was particularly greedy, but because he was starving, under-nourished. She looked across at Davie and wondered what it was like for him to be a bursary boy at a school where most pupils had rich parents. He was a survivor.

'Cheers!' She raised her glass and chinked it with Davie. Archie joined in but Gordon didn't move.

'I'm not smelling great aromas from the kitchen. Does that mean we're on bread and cheese?'

'You'll be fucking lucky.' Gordon, obviously not in the mood for speculation, barked. 'Cheese. Don't make me laugh. Apparently we're vegans for the night. Alfalfa and mung beans with . . .' Whatever he had in mind he couldn't remember what it was called. He snapped his fingers. Then he said. 'Nut fucking roast.'

'But that would have to be cooked and we'd have had a whiff of it by now.'

Gordon didn't want to hear this. 'Christ.' He thumbed in the direction that the member of staff had gone. 'As he said, it's not unusual.'

Archie sighed. 'You know what, Gordon. We're here now and there's not much we can do about it. So why don't you . . .'

Gordon interrupted him. 'Why don't I what?' His glare made Archie smirk, which didn't help matters.

'What the fuck have you got to laugh about?' Then he spat, 'Pansy.'

Viv snorted in disbelief. Was she in a boy's public school? 'Pansy? Who in God's name says that these days?'

'Who rattled your fucking cage, Miss Prefect?'

'I think you've got the wrong gal. Prefect me? I don't think so.'

Davie said, 'Okay, guys. We'll all be happier once we've had some food. Vegan or otherwise.'

Gordon stretched over the table and jabbed his finger at Davie's chest, almost touching it. Then through gritted teeth said, 'And you can shut the fuck up.'

Davie leaned back out of reach of the offending finger, almost overbalancing onto the flagstone floor. Viv caught him and helped him back upright.

Archie tried to push Gordon back onto his seat, but got an elbow in the face for his efforts. If only Viv could have filmed the whole scene. She watched wide-eyed as the situation escalated into a brawl. Archie leant over the top of Gordon with his arm pulled back, hand balled into a fist, ready to plant it on Gordon's face, when the man who'd told them about the generator walked out of the kitchen carrying a tray laden with food. He grinned, 'Bit early for show time. No?'

Archie stalled with his arm in mid-air. Gordon was about to roll off the end of the bench but managed to grip onto the rough wall behind him.

The staff man laughed. 'You've done well. The hackles usually rise way before now. This nosh should help.' He placed the tray at the end of the table and pushed it into the middle. 'Help yourselves.'

It occurred to her that withholding food might be intentional. People become total divas and dragons when they're hungry. Being here was forcing them into detox. No red wine, no coffee that she could see, not even real tea. They were all in the deprivation zone. Including her. Clever move if it was part of the plan. Although there was no way they could have planned the storm. Nature's revenge.

There was enough food to feed a dozen people, but now they were hesitant to tuck in. Viv was the first to head over to a stack of shelves where crockery and cutlery were in orderly piles. 'Anyone want a plate or cutlery?'

Davie and Archie raised their hands. Davie said, 'Me thanks.'

Gordon remained sullen. But once Viv and the others started to eat he got up and helped himself to what he needed. Sharing food was an ally-building exercise, but she didn't see Gordon thawing any time soon. If they hadn't been told that the food was vegan, they'd never have known. Everything was delicious. Frances joined them, her hair still wet, and squeezed in next to Gordon, chivvying him to budge along the bench. He shifted silently and Frances gave Viv a questioning look across the table.

Viv shook her head. 'This food is so good. Who prepared it?'

Frances raised her hand and elbowed Gordon at the same time. 'We were supposed to but they let us off the hook because the electricity's off. It wouldn't have been this creative if we had.'

There were different kinds of dense wholemeal and seeded breads, oatcakes, and other sorts of crackers. Hummus, tapenades and other bean-rich dips sat alongside a curd, which although not dairy you'd never have known had Gordon not told them. There were, as Gordon had predicted, mung beans and alfalfa, thick slices of beef tomatoes and cucumber, celery sticks and a dish of artichoke hearts. The rhythm of gratitude rose and fell, rose and fell as they each got a taste of something more delicious than the last. Viv watched them eat. It was telling. The tension in the room dropped with each mouthful consumed.

A deep rumble of thunder ran directly overhead, then seconds later a stunning fork of lightning lit up the bay and the room. The windows streamed with water – no sign that the rain would let up. This torrent hadn't been mentioned in the forecast. Scots were wired to anticipate changeable weather, so she was prepared for rain and wind, but this was something else.

The man from the kitchen came through bearing another tray with large catering flasks on it. 'Hot water? Teas, or infusions? Whatever floats your boat.'

He must have seen all manner of behaviour in this place, and wasn't in the slightest bit fazed by catching Archie about to throw a punch at Gordon's head.

Frances bottom-shuffled along the bench to Viv. 'You get the feeling we interrupted something?' She grinned.

Viv sensed Frances beginning to relax as they neared the last leg of their weekend. 'You okay after . . .?' Not sure how to put it she left the blank for Frances to fill.

'My insulin levels are influenced by all sorts of things including temperature. The hot journey in the bus followed by the cold water had me yo-yoing. Fine now, hopefully. I should have known better.' Although she was smiling she didn't sound entirely convinced.

Viv stood to get herself a mug from the shelf. This time she raised it in a gesture to Frances, who shook her head. Viv didn't offer the others – she'd done enough mothering for now. There were coffee substitutes on offer, but she wasn't keen. She filled her mug with hot water and dunked in a peppermint tea-bag. Then, with hands wrapped round the mug, she tuned into the chatter around the table. Gordon was still nursing his wrath, his jaw set like a Bash Street Kid who hadn't got his own way. Was he pissed off that he'd needed Viv's help? A high achiever in the office was bound to feel humiliated needing help in the outdoors. What was this outing really about? Had Mac already made up his mind about who the mole was? How come he had gone off with Becky? Why not let one of her colleagues take her? Actually Viv didn't know for sure that that was where he'd gone. Better stop crystal balling.

The tension round the table began to rise again when Frances said, 'So, Gordon, what's wrong with your face? It's been tripping you all day.'

He glared at her. 'What's it to you? You've not exactly been the life and soul of the team. Almost getting yourself killed out there.' He thrust his chin toward the windows.

Frances sighed. 'At least I was gracious in defeat. Have you even thanked Viv for rescuing you off that cliff?'

Viv wasn't looking for thanks, but was interested in how he'd react. She glanced at him.

His jaw tightened and his eyes bore through her. 'She didn't need to interfere. She should have left well alone. But no, she goes sticking her nose in where she thinks she has expertise. She's a fucking mole.'

Interesting choice of description. Should she defend herself?

Just as she opened her mouth to respond, Archie beat her to it. 'What an ungrateful bastard. What is your problem?'

And there they went again. Gordon jumped up at the same time as Archie. Toppling the bench that they'd been sitting on. They began pushing each other back and forth until Gordon stumbled back onto the table with the crockery on it and the man from the kitchen came to the rescue. 'Take it outside, guys. If you need to vent, here's not the place.' He pointed to the door and the torrential rain beyond. Neither seemed too keen to continue. Gordon stomped off towards the men's quarters. His parting shot, 'I'm not listening to this wankery.'

Viv couldn't contain herself and bursting out laughing, spilling her tea in the process. The others also managed to see the funny side, although Archie was peeved.

'Wankery. What a terrific word. Never heard that before. Love it. I bet it'll make it to the *OED*.' She snorted, shook her head and went to get a cloth to clean up her spill.

She scanned their faces, looking for anything that might give away a desire to taunt Gordon or to goad one of the others into doing it for them. But no, they all seemed passive, in the circumstances. Was that the nature of the cyber-beast? Were they at their most passionate discovering algorithms? She wouldn't be in the hacking game if she wasn't interested in people's behaviour.

She said, 'Thanks for trying, Archie. But I wasn't looking for gratitude. Just glad he didn't go head over tit or we'd have been in real trouble. One body was enough to bring home pillion. We should all be thanking you. You did the work. How are your arms after canoeing for two?'

Archie stretched his arms over his head. 'Not bad so far. Tomorrow will be the test.'

Those who had drinks raised their mugs. 'Well done, Archie,' they chimed in mock posh accents.

He grinned as if he'd won the cup. No notion that he was being sent up. He was a loveable big laddie. Viv wondered about his romantic life. Not that it was any concern of hers. No sign of a girlfriend, seeing his folks every weekend, big praise for Mummy's cooking, what did that add up to? Don't make leaps, she thought she said to herself, but Davie said, 'What was that, Viv?'

'Oh, nothing. Just thinking out loud.'

Archie intoned, 'Succedere incipiet regnare.'

They all turned to stare at him. Candlelight flickered over his large red face. His strong, square jaw made him look more like a medieval knight than a twenty-first century cyber analyst. Viv thought it must be the way his hair had flattened along his forehead, as if he'd just taken a helmet off.

Davie said, 'My Latin's a bit rusty. You'll have to help me out.'

Archie grinned, clearly dying to inform them. '"To succeed is to reign". Family motto.'

Was he boasting or just informing, as if it was still a novelty to him? Viv suddenly saw him in a different light. How many families at her school had had mottos beyond "eat yer dinner, or there's nae puddin"? And why was he telling them about it? He must have known he'd sound like a toff. Or did he want them to believe that he was? In Viv's world real top-drawer didn't need to boast, just oozed privilege from their core.

Before she realised, she had said, 'Now why would you say that? Are you referring to your tussle with Gordon or your success in bringing back a damsel in distress?'

He missed a beat before regaining his composure, but not before it registered with Viv that that had simply been a bubble of false bonhomie. He opened his mouth to continue, but his eyes flicked towards the door and he turned. They all turned.

Chapter Fourteen

Mac stood in the doorway, dripping onto the flagstones. He scanned the room. 'Too late for food, I expect?'

Within seconds three of them were scrambling to their feet and moving toward the shelves to find crockery for him.

Viv's eyes widened. 'I'm sure DI Marconi can get himself whatever he needs. No brownie points for sucking up to the leader.'

Frances said, 'No, but I might get rewarded in heaven.'

Viv shook her head. 'Planning ahead, Frances? Everyone likes a planner.' She shifted along the bench to make space for Mac, who shrugged off his wet jacket and hung it by its hood on the top of the kitchen door. He gripped the window ledge and proceeded to tussle with his waterproof trousers.

Viv said, 'Need a hand getting those off? Sit here, since we're all coming to the rescue.'

He sat and Viv pulled his wet trousers off by their hems and laid them over the back of one of a pair of wooden chairs placed to face the plate glass window and the view of the bay. Binoculars lay on the sill. It struck her that they'd probably had a voyeur all day.

'Cheers,' Mac said. Rivulets of water ran down the sides of his face until he rubbed his hands up and over it into his hair. 'Good day, then?'

Davie spoke first. 'Interesting. Not sure we've bonded in the way that we were expected to.'

Mac picked up his wet kit and wandered into the kitchen. 'Must get these into the drying room. Who said you were expected to bond?' He disappeared for a few minutes, returning without his kit. Then he said to Davie, 'Well?'

Davie shook his head. ' I just thought . . .'

Frances said, 'I've had a better day today than yesterday. No complaints here.'

Archie asked, 'What's happened to . . .?'

He snapped his fingers.

Viv said, 'Becky?'

He continued, 'Yes, Becky. She okay?'

'Not sure yet. They were worried about her temperature. She'd been lying for hours in the dampness.' Mac said, 'That bump on the head was pretty suspicious. It's not as if that was her first time in the cave . . . I mean what was she up to?'

Viv interrupted. 'Now, now, she was doing her best.'

'She might well have been, but say you guys hadn't found the cave and she was out there for another night. She'd have been even more in the shit than she is already.'

'You'd have sent someone out to find her, though, wouldn't you?'

He shrugged. 'Doubt it. We'd have thought that she was still waiting for you guys to pitch up. There was no reason for us to think that she'd be hurt. Hypothermia is a killer, make no mistake.' He shot a glance at Frances. 'There's nothing more that we can do. Although I wouldn't mind having a look inside that cave.'

There was something irritated in his tone and Viv said. 'Do you believe her story?'

He hesitated and sighed. 'No reason yet to believe otherwise.'

'That'll be a no then,' Viv countered.

'No that'll be a, we have snippets of a story which we, as yet, have no reason not to believe.'

'But?'

He didn't respond.

Viv could tell he was holding something back. After her helicopter trip she had more reason to be suspicious than Mac. Since Ruddy had subtly implied to keep her recce to herself, she kept her mouth shut.

'Right, mind if I tuck into what's left?'

'No, no, go ahead,' was the collective reply.

The room stank of garlic, which was fine when fresh, but Viv dreaded to think what it would be like seeping out of pores the next morning.

'Where's Gordon? Already thrown in the towel?'

Frances said, 'Eh, he's gone to bed. I think.'

This got Mac's attention. 'You only think? Or he has gone to bed?'

Viv said, 'No idea. He stormed off earlier. But he was going in the direction of the men's quarters and we've not seen him passing.' She checked with the others. 'He'd have to pass us to get out? There's no way out the back. Anyway, who in their right mind would go out in this?'

As she spoke she stared out at the torrential rain and blackness and wondered if Gordon was in his right mind – whatever that might mean. Another rumble of thunder directly above made her think it was worth checking. 'Anyone want to volunteer to go see that the beast is in his lair?'

'Why am I getting the sense that all is not well with Gordon?' Mac said, between bites of bread. Maintaining a persuasive picture of calm.

Davie prised himself out from the bench and said, 'I'll check.' Off he headed to look for Gordon.

Mac glanced at Viv, then at Archie, who had become captivated by his empty mug. 'Care to fill me in?'

Archie sought out Viv's eyes, but she shook her head. 'I've got nothing to say. Floor's all yours.'

Archie remained silent.

Mac said, 'If there's anything to report now's the time . . . No one will be going far. We couldn't get the minibus down the track. A culvert at the top has collapsed and the water is pouring like a river right down to the shore. Unbelievable. I've never seen a flash flood. Could easily have swept the bus into the peat bog. Robbie has taken himself to the nearest village to see if there's anything we can do to get the culvert fixed. Meantime. Snakes and Ladders or Charades?'

Viv sighed. 'Shit. I don't think this lot will be too keen on the Snakes and

Ladders idea and I'm guessing Charades have already been happening.'

Mac said, 'Tell me more.'

'You'll find out for yourself.'

'But I'd like you to tell me.'

Archie stared at Viv, as if willing her not to speak.

Mac turned to Archie. 'You want to fill me in?'

Archie stood up and climbed out from behind the table. 'Knackered. Could do with a early night.'

'Ah, Glen, how have they been behaving?' Mac said.

The man that had provided the food had come in and now had a name. 'Oh, no worse than any other group. It hasn't helped not having power. Here. I've brought replacement candles and if anyone wants a hot water bottle . . .'

Viv laughed. 'Scotland. The only country in the world that has hot water bottles on the menu all year round. I'll have one.'

Glen pointed to a cupboard. 'Bottles are in there. I've filled up all the flasks. Watch yourself – it's boiling.'

Viv was about to go and fetch a bottle when a look from Mac made her stop.

He said, 'You'll not be needing one quite yet.'

She sat herself down on the opposite bench and said briskly, 'Right. What's all this really about?'

'You know, Viv, I thought I had it covered, but the incident with Becky doesn't smell like the kind of incident that she thinly described. There's something that doesn't add up. How many times do you think she's been in that cave and never bumped her head?'

Viv shrugged and raised her eyebrows. 'Plenty, I guess.'

'You got it. How did you get on with the troops?'

'Well, I managed to piss two of them off big-time. Frances seems to have thawed but Gordon is a touchy sod. Oh and Archie said something that might be nothing . . .'

'Spill.'

'Well, he said something about not dying for Queen and country. I thought that was an odd thing for someone who'd signed the OSA, a declaration that he'd do exactly that. But what was more interesting was the fact that he was nervous that he'd said it, and immediately started to back pedal. Could be nothing.'

'We managed to sweep all of their consoles back at Fettes. None of them look as if we have anything to worry about. I can't help thinking that we should have had you in on the sweep instead of sussing them out here when they're out of their comfort zone.'

'Now you tell me. Now that I've made enemies. I've got the feeling that Frances is putting on a fabulous act, and Archie swings between being gentlemanly and a bruiser. He and Gordon have had a couple of scraps. But he's got to be doing some serious acting too. I can't believe the amount of bad faith . . . oh forget it.' She batted her hand to brush the vision away.

'And Davie?'

'He's had a voyage of discovery this weekend. Seems to have enjoyed being pushed physically and he could fairly handle a canoe. Surprised himself, since he'd not been in one since he was at school.'

'So what happened with Frances?'

'Well, you already know that.'

'Humour me.'

'She got into trouble crossing the bay and I brought her to shore.'

'Yep, I got that. Nothing more?'

'No. Nothing more.' Viv was convinced that whoever the mole might be it wasn't Frances. Mac had probably based his suspicions on her surreptitious behaviour in the office. Sneaking off to inject herself with insulin was no crime. He had nothing, no reason to suspect she was up to anything else that Viv knew of. Since they'd arrived the 'incidents' with Frances had both been insulin-related, and as far as Viv was concerned that was Frances' secret to tell. Although it was in her interest to tell it sooner rather than later.

'Look, Mac, unless you've got something on her that you're not willing to share with me I'd say you're wide of the mark. Sure she has issues but they don't run to worrying anyone about National Security.' She snorted. 'I fucking hate that phrase. It is so meaningless, a generalisation designed to scare people. No evidence equals "National Security".'

He raised his eyebrows. 'It's not a joke, Viv. There's chatter. There's something in the offing and our job is to intervene. Stop it from becoming a bigger threat.'

'In that case you'll have to let me have access to their consoles.'

'I told you they'd been swept.'

'Yes but you didn't say by whom or how creatively.' She nudged his arm and winked. 'You need someone unorthodox to take a peek. Go on, you know you want me to.'

He sighed. 'You've no idea of the ear-bending I'm getting. When we get back we'll go straight into HQ.'

She smiled. 'Now you're talking. You mean the real HQ, not Fettes?' She was definitely warming to the idea of snooping around in cyber-space. There was nothing more exciting than breaking into places that were thought to be unreachable. 'Can you get me clearance or are we under the wire?'

His eyes almost popped out of his head. 'You are going nowhere near that HQ. And as for clearance! You're kidding, right?'

'Okay. Okay. Keep your shirt on.' She grinned and punched his upper arm. 'Things are looking more like my kind of thing all of a sudden. I've had quite enough babysitting for one weekend.' She was about to tell him about Gordon's cliff scare when he walked in. A look of disgust swept over his face as if he'd witnessed some kind of atrocity and not two colleagues sitting chatting in the candlelight.

Viv asked, 'How are you doing?'

Mac was Gordon's boss and Viv watched as he tempered his response. 'Fine, thanks to you. You've no doubt filled him in.' He nodded in Mac's direction. Borderline insolence. Unlike Viv, Mac was a team player, but he was no lightweight. Viv waited for his reaction.

'She hasn't said a word about the weekend apart from the bit when Frances almost killed herself. But I already knew about that. So how about you? You get on okay?'

Viv imagined Gordon flushing, but his face was so sunburned it was difficult to tell. He turned his back to them and filled a mug with water from the flask. He stirred the teabag as if it were a work of art. Eventually he raised his head and glanced at Mac. 'I didn't enjoy it much if that's what you're asking. I hate swimming, I hate climbing, and I'm not a big fan of canoeing. So all in all it's been a bit of a nightmare for me.' He poked his own chest. 'Me. I'm a dry land creature.'

Viv thought he was certainly right about the 'creature' bit. He'd been a proper pain in the butt.

Mac said, 'You don't get any sense that you've stretched yourself, then?'

'No I fu . . .'

Viv's eyes widened. He was seriously pushing his luck. Insubordination was a sackable offence in the NTF, and just because they were away from the office didn't mean the hierarchy evaporated.

He didn't finish that particular line. 'I don't feel stretched. It's just been wet and a waste of everyone's time. The sooner we get back to the city the better. In fact, any idea when that might be?'

'Well, there is the small matter of the minibus not being able to get down the track until we find someone who can do a temporary repair on the culvert. In the morning, if the rain's gone off we'll either find a way of fixing it ourselves or we'll walk out and catch the bus at the main road.'

Gordon bit his lip, physically and metaphorically. He sighed, shook his head, and left the room.

Chapter Fifteen

Mac turned to Viv. 'He's behaving out of character. Although I've never seen him away from the office . . . oh no, that's a lie, I played football with him once. I didn't make it to the post match booze up, so I haven't seen him socially. But he's usually an affable bloke.'

Viv replied, 'He was helpful when Sal and I had to . . . well you know about that. I mean he was peeved that I could go places that he couldn't, well at least not in work time. But he let me use his console to . . .'

Mac interrupted by putting up his hand. 'Best I don't know.'

'You think we'll get home tomorrow?'

'Don't see why not, although the track was dodgy. Huge stretches where it's been washed into the ditch. It wasn't hard going for me because I was walking down hill. But you lot marching up hill in the morning after so much exercise today . . . I'm not so sure.'

'You laying down another gauntlet?'

'No. I'm just saying that there might not be a track left.'

'On that jolly note I'm going to hit the hay.' Viv stood and mock saluted him. She gathered up the remaining food and took it to the kitchen. Archie's bulk loomed before the open fridge. He stared into the dark hole, bare apart from a couple of half empty jars of pickle in the door. Everything else in the room looked soft with candlelight flickering over it. The work surfaces, pots and pans, the deep Belfast sink could all have been part of a movie set.

'Still peckish?'

He hadn't heard her come in and looked guilty.

She handed him the tray. 'Here there's some bread and stuff left. Tuck in.'

He screwed up his face. 'If we ever get out of here I'm having steak tartare for two.'

Viv laughed. 'Did you hear what Mac was saying about the track?'

He shook his head. 'No, why? What's happening?'

Viv wasn't convinced. 'He doesn't think we'll get the bus down or whether we'll be able to make it to the road. The rain has washed sections of the track into the ditch.'

'Christ, that's all we need. I think he underestimates our desire to get out of this place. I'll be walking come what may.'

Viv thought, we'll see. 'Night.'

'Night.'

Chapter Sixteen

Viv woke the next morning with the sun streaming through the bedroom window. She looked across at Frances tangled in her duvet, only her hair visible. Viv pulled back her own quilt and slipped over to the window. The bay was a more tranquil sight than she could have imagined after the drama of the storm. Wall-to-wall blue sky, the sea like glass, and barely a ripple as tiny waves crept onto the shore. Dark brown seaweed was banked up on the pebbles, evidence that she hadn't simply dreamt the wild weather. Where had it all come from? She was glad it hadn't been floating beneath the waves as she swam across the bay, nor when they'd paddled back. She pulled on her kit and squeezed silently out of the room.

She wasn't the first up. Glen was sitting on one of the wooden chairs, with binoculars up to his eyes.

'Hope I'm not eating into your precious time?'

'No, you're all right. I'm waiting for the urn to heat up. I don't trust it on its own. I'd rather be out there.' He pointed to the beach. He handed her the binoculars. 'Take a look at that.' He grinned. 'Go on, go down to the beach and check out what our seals are up to this morning. They love the calm after a storm.'

She wandered down to the shore, taking up a position on a large boulder. She stood in the cool still air staring out into the bay. She caught sight of two seals ducking and diving over each other. She grinned, transfixed at how at home they were in their watery environment. It was like watching ballet.

Occasionally both heads would rise and they would stare at each other before continuing their dance. She drew in a long breath and released it slowly, as if allowing herself a guilty pleasure, and relished the silent sea air for the first time this weekend. Eventually the seals swam further out to sea, getting smaller and smaller as Viv watched.

She turned her sights inland. The weather had ravaged the track as Mac had said. To her left near the shore a pile of rubble and sand had washed down leaving huge gouges where the track had been. It wasn't only the culvert that would stop the minibus getting here.

'Hi.'

She turned to see Mac standing in the doorway wearing a tee shirt adorned with a faded figure in an impossible yoga posture, and light coloured trousers with pockets everywhere. 'I can hardly believe we're in the same place. I see what you mean about the track. No vehicle will be going up that for a while.'

'You'd be amazed how quickly they'll fix it with the right machine. Coffee?' He held up a mug and handed it to her.

'Ta.' She sniffed the steaming mug. 'Is this real?'

He nodded. 'Secret stash.'

'Excellent. It's unbelievably beautiful when it's like this. Blue sky as far as the eye can see. Seals in the bay.' She nodded in the direction of where they'd been. 'Mind you a weekend's plenty.'

Mac laughed. 'I'm grateful that you came.'

'What, even if it was a total waste of time?'

'But you wouldn't have got to see the seals. They have to be worth it.'

'Maybe. If I had another day I'd be able to do a bit more digging. Meal times are always revealing. Although I haven't enjoyed being Gordon's scapegoat.'

'What exactly has he been up to?' He laid his mug on the ground and performed the most amazing salute to the sun.

Viv's jaw dropped. 'Since when did you start doing yoga?'

'Six months. Got to get these muscles in shape.'

She shook her head. She'd never seen Mac anything other than super-fit. Perhaps there was a woman involved. She was about to ask but couldn't. She continued. 'Gordon's just lost the plot. His ego's punctured. I can't think that it's anything more than that. And since I came to the rescue for Frances and then him, he's tarred me as a smart arse. Ungrateful shit. He also thinks that you and I,' she pointed in disbelief, 'are an item, but he's been saying that since the get go. I've tried to put him right but he's persistent and it's definitely affected the others.'

'How?'

'They're doubtful.'

He nodded. 'He doth protest too much. I think he's jealous.'

'Spare me. No way.'

He finished a few more stretches as Viv looked on, incredulous that he'd become so supple in just six months. 'The power's back on so there should be a hearty breakfast. I heard Archie in the kitchen last night foraging for leftovers.'

'You mean when I took the stuff from the table into the kitchen or later?'

'No, I mean during the night.'

'How did you know it was him?'

'I watched him slink along the corridor. He stopped at the other bedroom doors and listened before tiptoeing downstairs.'

'I'm impressed, Sherlock. Had the weather calmed by then?'

'Yes. The rain was much lighter and the wind had died down. Why d'you ask?'

She laid her coffee on a rock, lifted the binoculars and scanned the bay. When she spotted what she was looking for she handed them to Mac. She stood behind him and pointed. 'See if you can see what I see.'

It took him a few minutes to focus but he said, 'The only thing that I can see is a little black head.'

She nodded. 'It's a buoy. Now what is the purpose of that? Surely a buoy is only useful if it's highly visible. It's supposed to be a marker for some kind of hazard below the surface is it not?'

'Yes, makes sense. But where are you going with this?'

'Not sure. When we canoed back I spotted it and went to see what it was. It's secured to something incredibly tightly.'

'You thinking it could be a drop point?'

'Exactly.' She hesitated, not wanting to mention her trip with Ruddy. Then continued. 'I know I'm making a leap from someone with a bump on the head, but it's got me wondering.' She grinned at him. 'I've been reading too many smugglers tales. Well, drug trafficking thrillers if I'm honest.'

'Wow, Viv, I could say you should get out more but you might be onto something . . . what led you from Archie stuffing his face in the kitchen to smuggling?'

'I had a vision of him in the pitch dark flashing a torch at someone out to sea, like a baddie in an old black and white movie. Not *Whisky Galore*, more Margaret Rutherford to the rescue.' She laughed at the look of doubt on his face. 'Okay. I can see it's a stretch, but to my mind the point of a black buoy can only be as a pick-up. It's got to be a marker for someone with its exact GPS. It's no good to the uninitiated.' She shrugged. 'It could be for a lobster pot. But I'm not getting that Thermidor sensation in my belly. Besides we should give fishermen more credit. I'm sure their buoys are bright pink or orange.'

Mac stared at the buoy. 'Unless, as you say, there's an obstacle out there you've got to wonder why it's there at all. Come on, let's get some breakfast.'

'Wait!' She grabbed hold of his arm. 'Look, Mac, I'm sorry.'

He looked confused. 'What do you mean?'

'Well, I've failed this weekend. I haven't delivered.'

'You don't know that yet. Besides I see things differently to you. That's why we make a team. Come on, let's eat.'

'No, let's check out that buoy.'

His eyes moved along the beach to the shed. Hers followed. She could see where this was going, and they both took off at the same moment.

'I'll get my ears chewed off if this doesn't turn out to be anything.'

She grinned. 'Nothing ventured and all that.'

They had to untie the rib and roll it down to the water's edge. She had no idea how it worked, but Mac seemed to know what he was doing. Once they'd pushed it away from the shore he dropped the engine into the water and pulled the starter cord. Nothing. He tried again. Nothing. She stared back towards the bunkhouse to see if anyone was watching. They didn't seem to be. As he tried one more time she ran to the back of the shed and searched until she found a can of petrol. She held it up and Mac nodded, gesturing for her to bring it. Five minutes later they were motoring out to sea and circling the buoy.

'You know we might as well hang for a sheep as a lamb. Let's check out the cave.'

He hesitated. 'Okay, it'll take us twenty minutes to get there. Hope we've got enough petrol.'

He gunned the engine and the rib sped round the point. Viv's hair whipped out behind her and a fine salt spray covered her face. She scanned the horizon for any other boats. Nothing. Odd, since it was a beautiful day for cruising. They pulled up on a short section of pebbly beach and tied the rib to a rock. It bobbed and bumped until its wake calmed and they felt safe to leave it. Mac hunkered down and went in first. Viv followed. She pointed to where Becky had been lying. It hadn't occurred to her to check this as a crime scene, but that's exactly what Mac seemed to be doing.

'There won't be much chance of finding footprints since at least three sets and a few hands and knees have been over the space since Becky was here. People always leave evidence. No crime scene is completely clean however careful the criminal is. Is that what you're thinking?'

He nodded. 'Difficult not to jump to some kind of conclusion. A well trained outdoor teacher bumps her head in a low-ish cave. Unbelievable, don't you think?'

'Yes. I see what you're saying.' Viv crawled further into the cave and picked up a couple of damp cigarette butts. 'You think Becky's a smoker? These haven't been here long.' She held them to her nose. The smell was vaguely familiar. She had smoked once but never properly got the hang of it. Her dad, however, never had his pipe out of his mouth, so she knew that the smell was foreign. It reminded her of Balkan Sobranie, one of her dad's favourites but difficult to come by.

Mac pulled out a plastic bag from one of the pockets on the side of his trousers, and handed it to her.

She smiled. 'Always carry evidence bags with you?'

'You never know when they'll come in handy. Anything else down there?'

'Not that I can see. Wish we had a torch.'

A beam of light flitted over the area she was searching. She shook her head in disbelief. 'Did you know we were going to come here or are you always uber prepared for breakfast?'

He grinned. 'I'm a cop. Never leave home without one.'

'I'm not seeing anything else. Pretty careless of someone to leave these if they had anything to do with Becky's crack on the head. I mean we're not talking sophisticated crime, are we?'

'Nope. But sometimes people just get lazy or complacent. Depends how far up or down the chain they are.'

This made sense to Viv. A relief that Mac thought the same thing. Had he already been briefed on the illegal goings on in the area? If so why had Ruddy asked, implied, she keep quiet? Perhaps he didn't mean Mac, just the others.

'Let's get going. I definitely want to check out that buoy now.'

She lifted her face to the sun as soon as she exited the cave. 'Wow, it really is cold in there. I wouldn't want to lie on that damp floor, especially not if I was unconscious.'

Mac didn't respond, just untied the rib and jumped on. He held out his hand but she ignored it and swung herself over the side, landing with an ungainly thud. Mac shook his head.

He cut the engine as they pulled alongside the small black buoy. Viv grabbed it and tried to rotate it with both hands. Nothing happened. Mac pulled on some latex gloves and his hands stuck to the wet buoy like Velcro. She steadied the rib with the steering wheel as best she could as Mac continued to jostle, pull and push at the buoy. Nothing appeared to be happening. But one last serious yank caused a huge splash behind them and made them both topple to the floor. Mac caught the wheel and helped her to her knees. They stared wide-eyed at a large silver pod shaped like a horse's head floating in the water about twenty metres from the boat.

'Well lookie here.' Mac grinned. 'What d'you reckon is contained in that?'

She shielded her eyes to get a better look at it. 'Holy shit! Someone has a sense of humour. Different sort of mule from the usual sort.'

Mac sniggered. 'You're quick. I hadn't thought of that.'

'What should we do with it?'

'Try and get it to shore. Pass me that, would you?' He pointed to a bright orange rope coiled beneath a shallow bench.

She handed him the sodden end and watched as he made a lasso. Impressed, she tried to gauge exactly what he was doing, since she hadn't paid much attention in knotting class at Girl Guides. His first attempt to snare it was way wide. He tried again and again until eventually on the fourteenth time the loop slipped over the head.

Viv punched the air and cheered.

Mac looked towards the shore. 'Keep it down. If this has anything to do with them,' he nodded to the bunkhouse, 'they'll be ready to run. Although the track will make life difficult for anyone trying to get to the road.' He chuckled. 'And no one's going anywhere in the rib.' He struggled but managed to slowly pull the horse's head toward the boat. 'It's heavy. I think we'll have to drag it behind us.'

'Why, what did you think we'd do with it?'

'We should bring it aboard.'

'What if it contains . . . explosives . . .?'

He blew out a breath. 'What exactly have you been reading?'

As they approached the shore two members of staff stood with their hands on hips.

'Welcoming committee,' Mac said to Viv, who was hanging onto the horse's head as if her life depended on it.

Glen, who'd given Viv the binoculars earlier, said, 'So what have we got?'

Mac said, 'Not sure, but whatever it is probably isn't legal. We'll have to get the local guys round here.'

A look passed between Glen and his colleague before he replied. 'Shouldn't we take a look at it first?'

Mac snorted. 'We won't be taking a look at anything until your local guys get here.'

Viv jumped ashore and said, 'I'll go and ring them. You'll need the muscle to get it up the beach.'

Mac frowned but she took off back to the bunkhouse. She rang the local station then had a quick snoop at the office computer. Keen to find out what qualifications were required to become an outward-bound instructor, and how long Becky had worked there, it didn't take long to locate a few emails with the info she needed.

By the time she returned to the beach the rib was back onto its trolley and the sound of an engine could be heard in the distance before they saw a boat race round the bay.

Glen said, 'Boys in blue have an alternative mode of transport. Must've heard that the drive's out of commission.'

Mac explained who he was but the local sergeant wasn't impressed and demanded to see his ID.

Mac showed him it. 'Look we've no idea what's inside . . .'

The sergeant interrupted him and in a sarcastic tone asked, 'Where exactly did you find this, Sir?'

Mac pointed out to sea. 'There's a black buoy out there. We hit it on our way back. Then this thing appeared and we thought we'd better bring it back.'

The sergeant shook his head. 'You had no business moving it . . . Sir.' He ordered his constable to take hold of the rope attached to the silver horse's head then tied it to the police rib.

'We'll be wanting to speak to you, Sir, so don't go far.'

'We're going back to Edinburgh today.'

The sergeant began to protest, but Mac raised his hand to stop him.

'I said we're going back to Edinburgh. You've got my name, you'll find me at Fettes HQ after 5 pm today.'

Without as much as a glance back the two local cops turned and took off back across to where they'd come from. Viv, Mac and the two members of staff stood speechless on the beach until the police rib rounded the northern peninsula.

Glen said, 'Well, that'll be that, then.'

Viv shrugged and glanced at Mac with knitted eyebrows.

Mac shook his head. 'I'm guessing they've got some idea what's inside. I wouldn't be surprised if we'd . . .'

'We'd what?' Viv glared at him.

'I'll find out later. Meantime let's eat.' He strode up the beach but turned and waited at the threshold for her to join him.

It was frustrating not knowing how much to share with Mac, but she decided to keep quiet. The smell of cooking soon had her salivating. The sounds of pipes humming and floorboards creaking above were signs the others were up and about. She hoped moods had improved after last night's debacle.

She said, 'I wonder what would have happened if I hadn't come? I mean, I know it was about info gathering but if I hadn't pitched up would one of the others have rescued Frances? Or what? They are all really unfit. Aren't police meant to be fit? And Gordon, would he have managed to . . . oh never mind. I've not managed to do what you asked.'

'I'm sure you have more in that head of yours than you're making out . . . we'd never have taken a look at that cave again if you hadn't shown me the black buoy. Pretty good call I'd say . . .'

'I notice you didn't give them the butts.'

He shot her a what-do-I-care look, and before he could continue Frances appeared. 'Hey. Everyone sleep okay?'

Viv and Mac nodded.

Frances threw them a humorous wide-eyed look that questioned their sleeping arrangements.

'You were in quite a tangle when I came up,' said Viv, 'and I don't think you moved much in the night.'

Frances rubbed her hands together. 'Looking forward to getting back. Hot date.'

'Anyone we know?' Viv said.

She hesitated. 'Doubt it. Only been out a couple of times. Nice guy.'

To describe a hot date as 'nice' wasn't a great start, but Viv continued, 'Where is he taking you?'

Frances grinned like the proverbial cat that got the cream 'It's a surprise, but I'm hoping the Timber Yard.'

Viv nodded. 'Nice!' Her sarcasm lost on Frances who was no doubt already planning her outfit.

Mac had a look on his face that said he wasn't getting involved.

Viv pushed. 'Come on, tell, who is the lucky guy?'

Frances, not to be drawn, tapped the side of her nose and wandered off to the kitchen.

This made Viv think that he could after all be somebody they knew, otherwise why the big secret? She didn't push any further.

Mac had been right about the breakfast. Everything that you could imagine going into a real Scottish fry-up was available, only without meat. Mock bacon, beans, hash browns, mushrooms, tomatoes, veggie sausages, lashings of toast – obviously made by the staff and not the cooking group.

Viv sat opposite Mac and they tucked in. Only noises of appreciation disturbed the quiet in the room.

Gordon pitched up but brooded in silence.

Frances returned from the kitchen with a modest plateful and sat next to Mac. She said, 'Saving myself for tonight.'

Viv was mortified at the amount she had on her plate versus what Frances had on hers, but it didn't stop her from eating it. She was making up for two days of meagre pickings.

Gordon didn't sit with them and instead headed for the door with his breakfast.

Viv glanced at Mac who shrugged in response. 'He's a grown-up. He'll work it out.'

Frances said. 'What? What are you talking about?'

Viv smiled at Frances' complete lack of observation and marvelled at how she became a cyber analyst at all. They were joined by Davie who brought with him a blast of coconut. His freshly shaven face was shiny with moisturiser, so much so that it might slide off. He was pumped up for another day of activity. His shorts, tee shirt and sandals looked as if he'd just cut their labels off.

'You do realise we're going home today, Davie?' Viv said.

'Yes. But since I'd bought some kit to come here I thought I might as well get some wear out of it.'

His face and arms were bright red from yesterday's sun but everywhere else was an unhealthy bluish shade of grey. His thin legs seemed insubstantial, although he must be relatively fit since he cycled to and from work every day. He was solid around the waist and he stooped. A 'scribe's posture', so called from days when men sat hunched all day in poor light painstakingly writing or copying manuscripts. Davie, a modern version, did the same hours leaning over his computer. Viv wondered if it was also to do with not wanting to stand tall. She'd come across tall guys who never straightened up so that they didn't transcend the crowd. She glanced at Mac; he looked taller. His posture had improved. It must be the yoga. All she knew about it was the idea of an invisible thread, secured to the top of the head, and from this thread the whole body hung in the posture that it was designed to. She shifted on the bench, rolled her shoulders back and down and immediately felt the space in her diaphragm where her lungs should move unobstructed.

Mac said. 'Better?'

She screwed up her face. 'What? Are you the posture police?'

He shook his head. 'You were the one making the effort to change your position. Looks much better.'

'Piss off. I was fine the way I was.' She did feel better but he didn't need to know that. 'What time are we walking out?'

'Soon as.' Mac said between bites. 'We'll have to walk up hill with over the knee heather all the way. Still, it'll help work off this grub.'

'We,' Viv pointed to the others who, between words, were deep into their large cooked breakfasts, 'have already got a few calories to make up for never mind work off. You sure the bus will be at the top of the track?'

'I'm sure. I have to be back in Fettes by 5 pm.'

'Well, if *you* have to be back then it's a sure thing.'

'Easy with the sarc. You don't want to hang around here any longer than you need to, so why don't you get going and pack.'

'I don't have to pack. I didn't really unpack.'

That wasn't entirely true because she had left her phone and a few dry clothes out, but she travelled light and was pretty much ready to leave.

Archie wandered into the room yawning and scratching his exposed belly. He looked rough, lips swollen and cracked from too much sun and his unshaven face bright red – could just as easily have been from a boozy night.

Mac said to Archie, 'You had better get a bend on if you want breakfast before we leave. Ten minutes at the front door.'

'Shit. What's the hurry now?'

Viv smiled and took her plate and mug to the kitchen before heading to her room.

Chapter Seventeen

Mac was already waiting when she came out.

She gazed at the sea. 'There won't be any of that when we get back. Edinburgh will still be heaving with Festival crowds, the stench of beer and cooked onions spilling out from air conditioning units. Oh Joy!'

'Nice image. You could always stay on here. See what's going on with that buoy.'

She shoved him. 'I don't think so. Whatever it is won't be our business as soon as we get up that hill. Unless he's involved.' She nodded indoors to where Archie was still guzzling breakfast. 'Sometimes I think we've become too paranoid. I mean, we always see a potential crime before anything else. And that buoy could actually be completely innocent yet we're off down the criminal route.'

'That's why we're good at what we do, Viv. Suspicion isn't a bad thing.'

Her mind wandered back to Dawn. If only she'd been more suspicious, or willing to follow the intuition that she'd actively ignored. 'Should we get going?' She pointed to the steep brae, a serious scramble to start their journey to the road.

'Yes. We'll just give the rest a minute.'

Once the others joined them they set off, Mac marching up front with Viv, Archie and Frances close on their heels, and Davie and Gordon lagging behind.

Viv said, 'So what happened to Robbie?'

'I said he could help at this side.'

'Dare I ask why?'

'First up he couldn't swim. And second he's had stuff going on at home.'

'None of which he knew before we left?'

'What can I say, Viv? Some people lie their way into jobs . . . He's a great analyst.'

'What will happen to him?'

He stared at her with incomprehension. 'Happen to him? It's not school. Nothing will happen to him. They all came of their own accord.' He pointed his thumb at those behind.

'Like fuck they . . . we did.'

'Ah, well, apart from you.' He grinned.

The ground was rough and their breathing laboured. Mac's strides were so long that Viv had to trot to keep up. She was grateful for a breeze that kept her hair off her face. She wished she'd tied it up but couldn't now be bothered faffing around for a band in her sack.

Archie caught up. 'Looking forward to getting back to the big city then, Viv?'

'Sure. You can get too much fresh air. It can't be good for you.'

Archie said, 'But you're a natural. Swimming, canoeing, rock climbing, a veritable all rounder.'

There was an edge to his voice, an indication that perhaps he wasn't really impressed. Mac obviously caught the tone as well. He glanced at Archie, who was puffing along to keep up. 'So she's done well this weekend? Who would you say comes second?'

Not expecting this Archie said, 'Oh, I'm not sure. But not Gordon. He's been an arse. Davie's been on form.'

'Not putting yourself in the running then?'

'God no. I thought I'd die swimming over that bay. I'm so unfit.'

Although he'd vomited when he'd finished the swim, Viv didn't believe he was as unfit as he was making out. 'What will you do when you get home?'

'Eat. Then eat a bit more and probably a bit more still.'

Viv said, 'That breakfast we had was enough to feed an army on the hoof.

You can't grumble about feeling hungry now.'

'It's psychological. Unless it's meat it doesn't count.'

'Christ, Archie, it must be difficult being a carnivore. I bet if you hadn't been told that there wasn't any meat you'd have been perfectly happy. I'm stuffed.'

Archie screwed up his eyes. 'And by the way, why would you be interested in what I'm doing when I get back? Or care about my eating habits?' He glared at her.

Mac chipped in. 'I'm interested, though. Because the meat thing is something I've been toying with the last few months. My yoga teacher says our digestion, our inner health, is better if we eat vegetarian. But bacon butties get me every time, even those flaccid efforts that sit for hours under lights in the canteen. Can't pass them by.'

Viv said, 'Neither of you have enough will power. Pathetic.' She strode on ahead. She wanted to prove her point. Mac caught her up, but Archie stayed behind with the others.

She said, 'Something has riled him and I don't think it's just food deprivation.'

Chapter Eighteen

One by one they made it back to the road, where the mini-bus waited. Gordon and Frances came last, and in no hurry. They clambered aboard, taking the seats that they'd had on the journey there. Such territorial creatures, it was more than simply habit. The mood had shifted, lighter now that the end was in sight. The chat turned to what they were doing when they returned. Frances, eyes glued to her phone, appeared to be checking out her 'hot date'. Viv caught a glimpse of a photograph of a man. It was difficult to see what exactly the attraction was, since he was huddled in a scarf that covered his mouth and had a tight woolly hat pulled down to his eyebrows, but Frances was excited. Davie was wound up like a tight spring, dying to get back into the office. Gordon was also keen to get back to work, but not before having a hot bath to rid himself of the smells of the sea. Archie didn't say much but stared out of the window, occasionally adjusting his rucksack, which was doubling as a pillow. He grimaced every time he moved. She guessed he must be stiff from the exertion of the weekend.

Viv remained alert. She still had work to do.

They stopped for a comfort break at the Green Welly again. Viv wasn't desperate so stayed put. Archie got up but did a comical double take between Viv and his rucksack before reluctantly deciding to leave it. Viv, inevitably suspicious, wondered what might be in it that he was concerned about. As soon as everyone was out of sight she took a quick peek. She slid the zip along, releasing the smell of worn clothes with sweaty deodorant clinging to them.

She rifled around, found nothing suspect and closed it. The large side pockets had lots of slips of paper, receipts all from the same place, Coral, so he was a betting man. Multiple used Irish lottery tickets – no winners – a business card for an Italian restaurant on Leith Walk, an empty packet that used to contain Tic-Tacs. Nothing that Viv could see he'd need to protect. But his hesitation had indicated otherwise. There was another pocket along the top, but it only contained toiletries, too many for one weekend, but that wasn't a punishable offence. She headed off the bus just as the driver returned. Better use the facilities after all.

She arrived back before the others and wondered how to get more info from them before they reached Edinburgh. It was a tall order but she'd have to try. Once they were on the road again she said to the whole bus, 'So did any of us learn anything this weekend?'

Gordon shot back, 'What the fuck is it to you?'

Frances replied, 'Nice, Gordon. I see the weekend's improved your manners. I learned that I can't swim as well as I thought.' She stared and mouthed 'thank you' to Viv. 'But also that veggie food can be delicious if you take time to prepare it. Which is never going to happen in my flat – I like sausages too much and my flatmate is a good cook. I'd have to battle with the gourmet smells she produces. What about you guys?' She nodded to Archie and Davie.

Davie said, 'I suppose I thought I was a landlubber, but I really enjoyed being in that canoe. My school experiences had obviously been contaminated by horrible boys who never . . .' He looked out of the window and continued. 'It helped that the weather was fair. I'd like to have another go. Oh and I learned that it doesn't help to judge people.'

Viv couldn't stop herself and said, 'What do you mean?'

He hesitated. 'Well, I thought Frances was a bit of a twit taking on the swim. Putting someone else in danger. Having to be rescued.'

Viv could see Frances' colour rise and she was about to interrupt when Viv knitted her eyebrows in Frances' direction, enough to prevent her butting in.

Davie continued. 'But then I got to thinking about what I would have done. Any one of us could have got cramp, or just over tired. But I also thought that Frances recovered really well and didn't let that spoil the weekend for the rest of us. I mean she could have used that to become the centre of attention but she didn't.' He looked around him, and realising how attentive the rest of them were, he shrugged.

'Bravo, Davie! I agree,' Viv said.

Gordon ostentatiously turned his back when Viv spoke – a brazen attempt at silencing her. It worked. She wondered how the others would react.

Archie said, 'You must have learned a lot, Gordon. We both collapsed after that swim and couldn't have rescued Frances if our lives had depended on it.'

Gordon stared out of the window nursing his angst.

Archie continued, 'If Viv hadn't . . .'

Gordon spun round. 'Miss fucking goodie two shoes there,' he stabbed his finger in Viv's direction, 'should mind her own fucking business.'

'Oh yeah, and leave you to fall off the cliff?' Archie goaded.

There was something going on between them that Viv had ascribed to lack of meat and caffeine. Perhaps she'd missed the mark.

Archie said, 'Honestly, Gordon, if you were a grown up you'd be grateful that she was there. Or would you rather have broken your neck? Or that Frances had drowned? Which she could have if Viv hadn't jumped in.'

Gordon responded. 'Are you quite finished arse licking the boss's pet?'

At this Mac, who had clearly decided to stay focused on the road and not interfere, raised his head but didn't say anything.

However small his gesture, it didn't go unnoticed. In turn the others shifted in their seats as if suddenly remembering this was still work. Silence fell and the journey was completed without further comment.

The minibus made good time and pulled into Fettes just before 4 pm. They'd only had the one break at the Green Welly and now everyone stretched like waking caged animals. Viv bent over to help pull bags from the hold, but stopped in her tracks when she caught a glimpse of Sal at the other side of the car park. A woman that Viv didn't know was rubbing a proprietorial hand up and down Sal's arm and Sal was laughing in a way that Viv would describe as coquettish. Viv's colour rose as she became aware that not only was she staring but she had halted in an awkward mid-crouch.

Mac's voice broke her concentration. 'Right, Doc, grab this.' He threw her a bag, which distracted her for a moment. Sal hadn't registered them. The woman, taller than Sal, an Emma Watson look-a-like, elfin, stunning with short fair hair, tanned skin. She wore torn jeans and a pale blue tee shirt. She leaned in and kissed Sal on the cheek, then skipped off and jumped into a silver BMW Cabriolet parked a few cars up from Sal's Golf.

Viv glanced away, trying to look busy. Sal got into her car and drove off, oblivious to her audience.

Viv turned to Mac. 'Did you know?'

Mac stared. 'Whatever I say is going to be the wrong thing, so cut me some slack. I could see there was something in the air but I didn't know what exactly.'

'You could have said.'

'What could I say? "Oh, Viv, there's something going on with Sal", to which you'd have replied, "And your point is?", or words to that effect. Besides it's only been a couple of weeks.'

Viv swung her rucksack over her shoulder and headed towards her car. The others called cheerio but she just waved her hand and kept walking.

Irrational though it was, she wasn't ready for anyone else to have Sal, especially someone as beautiful as the woman she'd just seen. She was just about to turn on the Rav's engine when she heard someone call her name. Ruddy's driver stood on the steps at the entrance to the building and began walking towards her. Mac was already making his way over and they fell into step.

'Seems you've made a little impact over there on the west. He wants to see you both.'

She glanced toward Mac. Their eyes met briefly and they both began to speak at the same moment.

'No, no, you first,' Mac said with no small measure of sarcasm.

'No, no, after you.'

The driver raised his eyebrows. 'He's in session room four.'

Peevishly, Viv took off into the building, but halted abruptly as she realised she had no clue where room four was. Mac caught up and gestured for her to follow him.

Room four was in a section of the basement where Viv had never been. Ruddy greeted them with, 'Okay, okay, so I didn't want either of you to know what the other knew for good reason. If I'd told you both what I suspected was going on over there it would have been your only focus and Mac had other fish to fry. Good job done, though. I've heard from the local constabulary over on the west coast. They're waiting for an explosives expert to show up.'

Now Viv and Mac did stare at each other. She blurted, 'Explosives expert? What . . ?'

Mac rubbed his hands across his face. 'Shit. I really jumped the gun. I assumed drugs. Never gave anything else any real consideration. Thanks to Viv we didn't pull the container aboard.'

Ruddy nodded. 'I'll let you know when we receive information about what's inside. Oh and they did find a microchip GPS on it, so whatever it turns out to be is being monitored from somewhere, which also means the owners know that it's no longer where it should be.' He grinned and nodded at Viv. 'How did you find it?'

'Just lucky to spot the black buoy. A black buoy isn't much use for making anything obvious.'

'Good job. Oh and we'll need whatever you got on the woman who bumped her head. I assume you did get something?'

Viv nodded and sensing Mac's discomfort said, 'Mac sent me to ring the local guys so . . .'

'Don't need details on how you're covering his arse.' Ruddy nodded again, this time a 'that'll be all' nod.

But as they walked away he said, 'By the way there's been more chatter on the Queen.'

Mac raised his eyebrows. 'I'll get right on it.'

As they made their way back to reception Mac said, 'So there was a mission from on high.'

She nodded. He sighed, but seemed satisfied with that as an answer, and she turned back to the Rav. 'Cheerio. No doubt speak soon.'

Chapter Nineteen

Viv arrived back in the West Bow earlier than she'd anticipated, but still couldn't shift the vision of that affection between Sal and her new friend. She needed a distraction. She checked her email. One from Mac said, 'You need to come back to HQ.' Yeah, sure, HQ could wait. She rang Ellie. 'Hey you, how're you doing? How's about we have that night out?' Ellie hadn't met Sal, but Viv had hinted to her about their affair.

'Sure. When were you thinking?'

'Tonight. Like in a couple of hours or so?' Viv's voice was too high. Forced joviality.

'You okay?'

'Never been better . . . I'll fill you in when we meet up.'

'It's Monday night, a school night.'

This was code for no-can-do-I've-got-work-next-day.

Viv pressed. 'How come you've got a job so quickly?'

'Just helping a friend out. I suppose . . .'

'Excellent! That's settled then. I'll meet you in Copa Cabana at half seven.'

Ellie sighed. 'Copa what?'

'Cabana. It's at the top of Leith Walk near the cinema. Come to think of it we could see a movie.'

'Look, Viv, I'll pass on the movie but happy to hear what's on your mind.'

Viv put down the receiver and caught up with her other messages. She replied to clients, apologising for her delay, and deleted most of the others.

'Thank the Lord for cutting hair.' She blew out a breath and reminded herself that seeing hair clients was what kept her grounded. She shook her head, still unable to shift that image of Sal. The more she thought about the scene in the car park the more she thought there was something familiar about the new friend.

She tossed her grubby clothes from the weekend in the washing machine and looked for something to wear. If they went to the movies it didn't matter what she put on so long as she was comfy.

Viv wandered up Victoria Street through a stream of tourists, skipped over George IV Bridge, and took a right onto the Royal Mile. She'd put on a pair of cream cord jodhpurs and a black linen shirt, and slung a jacket over her shoulders, but a nippy wind had got up and she pulled the jacket on. Everything she needed was in her pockets.

Ellie greeted her with a huge hug. 'Soooo good to see you properly. We going on a bender?'

Having cooled off, both metaphorically and physically, on the walk down, Viv was less desperate to get hammered. She grinned. 'Not exactly, but the idea of sitting brooding wasn't on the cards.'

'I've never known you to brood, well not for long.'

Viv hugged her again and rubbed her arms. 'Oh, I can do brooding. But I'll be fine. Good to see you too, though. You look less stressed than on Friday.'

'I'd just got off the plane . . . well almost. It's so nice to see my folks.'

'How are they doing?'

'My dad's as he ever was, cheery, definitely getting old, though. God! Talk about slow.' She shook her head. 'It's doing my mum's head in – she's still energetic. Got a real shocker though, she's stopped dying her hair. Looks much better. Less Cruella De Ville. She's completely white. It suits her skin much better.'

Viv nodded. 'I encourage women to avoid harsh dark shades unless they're willing to wear a ton of make-up. As we age everything gets paler – hair and skin. Dark tints are counter-intuitive. There's nothing worse than white regrowth and black ends. How many badgers does the world really need?'

Ellie let go a belly laugh. 'My mum's too vain to let roots show for long but I know what you mean. How's your mum?'

'Chuffed to have a grandson. Mand's secured her position at the top of the favourites list. Not that I was ever in the running. But James is a wee cutie. Now, he could make me properly broody.'

'No way.'

Viv nudged Ellie's elbow. 'Just kidding. But he is a cracker. Let's order a drink.'

There was a card with a list of cocktails on the table. 'Fancy one of these?' Ellie nodded. 'Why not? Let's have a look.'

Viv already knew what she was having, and once Ellie decided she headed off to the bar. As she waited for the barman to give up his conversation with two athletic youths at the far end of the bar she thought she saw a familiar form. She stood up on the brass footrest to get a better look, but she'd missed him. If it was who she thought it was, what was he doing in here?

She ordered two strawberry daiquiris and while the barman gave them his meticulous attention she hoisted herself onto the bar again to check whether she'd been seeing things. If it was Archie, he had made a quick exit or had disappeared into the back corridor where the loos were. She took the cocktails over to the table and said to Ellie, 'I'll just be a minute. Got to check something out.'

Ellie was about to object but flipped her hand at Viv to take off.

Loos for all genders were in the same internal corridor at the back of the pub. With no access to natural light, the pub owners had over compensated with bright LEDs: harsh after the soft tones in the bar. There was no one in the corridor, but as Viv passed the door to the men's a guy came out, revealing a brief view of Archie up against the sinks with a young man leaning on his chest. The door swung shut. But the shock on Archie's face had left Viv in no doubt that he hadn't wanted to be seen. She waited, and within a few seconds the young man came storming out and shot Viv a filthy glare. She waited. No sign of Archie. She waited. Still no sign. She pushed the door and there he stood rubbing his hands over his face. Distressed or frustrated? He obviously hadn't been home, since he was wearing the same clothes as on the mini-bus. She said, 'You okay?'

'Sure. What the hell are you doing here?'

She smiled. 'I could ask you the same question. But since we're both here it's probably safe to say that our reasons are sympathetic.'

His shoulders eased. 'I don't get it. I thought you and Mac were an item.'

'You shouldn't listen to propaganda. Besides why would it matter if we were? There would be nothing to stop me from drinking in here.'

He snorted. 'No, but you'd be labelled a fag hag.' He raised his eyebrows. 'Or maybe you can . . .' he rocked his hand back and forth, 'eeksy peeksy?'

She laughed. 'You learn that from your mum?'

He nodded and smiled.

'Me too. It must have been a generational get out clause. I'm not one for labels. As soon as someone pops me into a box I spring right back out.'

He rubbed his hands roughly over his face again. 'I don't want anyone to know.'

'Fair enough. But why would you . . .?' She brushed the question away. 'The police have a great gay . . .'

He shot her a don't-even-go-there look. 'This had better not go in your article. Or was that just a cover?'

She raised her hands. 'It's okay, your secret's safe with me. I sure as hell hadn't guessed.' She turned to go.

'Can I really trust you?' His eyes screwed up and jutted his chin out. 'You seem pretty pally with the bosses.'

She snorted. 'I'm not any more pally with them than with you. Work it out for yourself.'

'Why was Gordon so adamant that you and Mac were an item?'

'You'd have to ask him that. But I'm guessing his ego was bruised at not managing the swim very well, then he topped that by having a wobbly on the cliff. Gordon's okay. He'll be fine when he's back in his comfort zone.'

'But he was already pissed off with you on the bus. What was that about?'

She shrugged, gave him a small wave, and returned to the bar. Ellie was sitting with two men who'd obviously decided she needed company.

As Viv approached Ellie smiled. 'See, told you I was with someone. But thanks for looking out for me.'

They got up and looked Viv up and down. 'Nice. Been together long?'

Viv was about to put them straight, but Ellie said coyly, 'Not long enough.'

The men laughed and went over to the bar.

'What the heck?'

Ellie replied, 'I was only taking the piss. Relax. It'd be like sleeping with my sister.'

Viv raised her eyebrows. 'That bad, eh?'

Ellie punched her upper arm. 'You! So, what's got you hopping back and forth to the loo? Still got that hand-washing thing?

'Piss off! I don't do compulsive washing.'

'No? The ways you have of dealing with stress have always been odd.'

'Not that odd.'

'Not how I remember you. As a teenager you wouldn't go anywhere without a polybag and pockets full of tissues. What was that about?' She sipped her drink and continued. 'Get more than you bargained for on that job?'

Viv was alarmed by Ellie's observations. It hadn't occurred to her that showering had become pathological, a symptom. Well not so as anyone would notice. And she did remember the tissue phase. She'd just swapped one neurosis for another, then another.

Since Ellie had seen Ruddy's car pull away outside the pub, she said, 'You mean the car outside the . . .?'

Ellie nodded enthusiastically.

'Oh, that. No, that was fine. But when I got back I saw Sal in the car park at Fettes with her . . . I'm not sure what to call her, girlfriend I suppose, too new to be partner.'

Ellie nodded. 'Okay. I get that you weren't ready to commit after that debacle with Dawn. But every time Sal asked you to make a plan you had an excuse not to. A woman can get bored waiting.'

'I know, I know. It was just odd seeing her, that's all. I don't know who the new girl is or what she does, but she's good looking.'

Ellie raised her eyebrows. 'And your point is?'

'Just saying. You know on the way here I was thinking how difficult it is to shift stuff. Even Dawn still lurks in the recesses of my head, waiting for the next opportunity to trip me up. It's like having a tiny stone in my shoe. There's no getting away from her. Speaking about it makes me feel stupid.' She gave a huge sigh and stared out of the plate glass windows onto the street. 'I hated that I loved her so much. I'll self-destruct if I don't get it out.' She rubbed her heart with her knuckles. 'She's still right here like a log that I can't shift . . .'

Ellie stretched over the table and rubbed Viv's arm. 'You'll get through it, Viv. You know you're probably revisiting other stuff. Stuff about your dad as well. And if you're not ready, then you're not ready. You'll just have to wait. It will come right . . . I'm amazed, though, since she treated you so badly. You'd think it might be easier to move on.'

'That's just it. Couples who have the most fractious times seem to take longer to . . . it's as if arguing was their sport . . . Just because she wasn't the most honest of partners didn't stop me from falling head over heels. I mean the fact that she was reticent made her a challenge. I'm not blaming her. I just need to find a way to stop her from leading me from the grave.'

Ellie nodded earnestly and Viv laughed. 'Stop that, you look like a nodding dog on the back shelf of a car.'

Ellie shook her head. 'Self-deception is the new black.'

Viv laughed again.

Ellie continued. 'Listen, talking about self-deception, how about Dawn's brother-in-law? What's happened to him?'

'It's not been to court yet. My lawyer assures me he'll do time. I'm not convinced.'

Ellie gasped. 'The sod had better. Who's representing him?'

Viv snorted. 'Oh, he's got good Counsel. Elliot.'

Ellie shook her head knowingly. 'Yeah. He's a ticker.'

'For sure, and he's not got many ticks, if any, in the debit column. Still, I've got to do something about this Dawn stuff, or at least stop beating myself up about being such a poor judge of character – even my frickin' dreams are haunted by her.' She rubbed her hands over her face and up into her hair. 'It's weird, though. I always dream that things were much better than they were. It's like I harbour a fantasy that I was wrong. Maybe I was. Maybe things weren't as bad as I made them out to be.'

'How can you think that, Viv? She was a proper bitch. She had women in every port, kept you dangling with false promises.'

'I suppose that's what's difficult.'

'What bit of it?'

'The bit where I was naive enough to hope; to want the bad stuff to be a figment of my over active imagination. But I was also arrogant enough to believe I'd be able to win her over.'

Ellie shook her head. 'You can't believe that. She was a monster to you in the end.'

'It could be the money. It could be that she entrusted me with everything.'

'She didn't entrust you. She encumbered you. Dumped a whole load of family politics in the form of land and trusts right in your lap. Don't start rubbing out her wicked intentions. She had no good intentions and you know it.'

'Yeah, you're right, but I still don't know what to do with it all. Although I think I had a breakthrough at the weekend, a moment when I did think about her without feeling pain.'

'Great! It's the beginning of the end. You don't have to do anything. Just let it sit there until you feel an urge to buy an estate in the Highlands.'

They giggled at the notion of Viv moving to the country. Both had been brought up on the streets of Longstone, a suburb of Edinburgh, and were suspicious of soft ground beneath their boots.

Viv stretched. 'Sorry to dump on you. I guess seeing Sal with someone brought all the shit back. Let's get another drink.'

Ellie laughed. 'I think I owe you. My shout. Same again?'

Viv nodded and grinned as Ellie slipped out of the booth and sashayed across to the bar. The men she'd been speaking to parted and let her in. The Copa had had a short but mixed history. The man who'd taken over in the last year had made some changes. Before, it had been a gay men's bar with the odd women's night as a gesture. Now it was completely mixed, with a club in the basement that attracted straight and gay because of the new DJ. The stairway to the basement was cordoned off with a thick red rope capped at each end with heavy brass hooks, as if it were a country house and the owners' apartments were below ground. The loos were the measure of any pub for Viv, and she was impressed with what they'd done here, otherwise she wouldn't have come back – well at least not as a patron.

When Ellie returned she said, 'Those guys recommend *Spy*. You know – the film with Melissa McCarthy? They said we'd pee our pants it's so funny.' She began checking her phone for a screening next door.

'Oh all right, I could handle that. How about you?'

'Sure. Not had a belly laugh for a while. But here, we've got these to drink first.'

Viv accepted the fresh glass of strawberry daiquiri and sipped. 'Mmm. He's particularly good at these.' She nodded to the barman. 'Do you need something to eat?'

'Nah. This has enough calories for one night. Besides a bucket of popcorn will keep us going.'

Viv almost gagged at the idea of popcorn and wondered if she could sit through a whole film with the smell of it right next to her. She'd soon find out.

They chatted for another half an hour then moved next door to the cinema. In all the time they'd been blethering Viv hadn't seen Archie leave, and wondered if he'd used an emergency exit. Even if he'd been having sex back there it wouldn't have taken that long.

'Give me another two minutes.' She wandered back to the corridor with the loos. No sign of Archie. She pushed open the Gents. No sign. She went back to the bar and said to the barman, 'Is there another way out?'

He hesitated. 'Sure. You want to use it?'

'No, I just wondered. Thanks. Your daiquiris were ace.'

'Cheers. Any time.'

Chapter Twenty

Viv was in luck, since there was a long queue for the popcorn, and Ellie was too impatient to wait in it. The film was an excellent antidote. By the time *Spy* was over they were both aching with laughter and happy to head home. They sauntered arm in arm up to the top of Leith Walk where at the first bus stop on Princes Street Ellie caught the bus to her parents'. Viv jogged over the Waverley Bridge, up Market Street and took the steep steps leading to St Giles' Street. There were even more people out and about now than there had been earlier. Festival fever. What a relief to close the door of her building, and rest against it for a moment before taking the stairs two at a time to her flat.

Inside, she noticed a piece of paper that had jammed in the brushes of the letterbox – unusual since every flat had its own pigeonhole in the passage at the bottom of the stairs. All it said was, 'I didn't mean to offend you. It wasn't what you think,' signed A, with a doodle of a smiley face. Interesting but which A was it from? She guessed Angus, since he was closest, and knew where she lived, but what did he mean?

Her brain was unsettled and she found herself Googling Angus again. For a millisecond she felt a twinge of guilt at trespassing into his life, but it passed. There were lots of entries. His career was 'illustrious'. She was annoyed that she hadn't heard of him. With so much to read she tucked one foot beneath her butt and scrolled. One photograph, of him in an embrace with a female, caught her eye. The caption read, 'Angus Buchanan with Samantha Jones'.

Jones was the woman she'd seen with Sal. Well, well. Did Angus know about Jones' relationship with Sal? And if he did, was that his motivation for speaking to her?

Now that Viv knew who Sal's girlfriend was, she turned her attention to finding out everything she could about her. Viv said out loud, 'Sam Jones. Sam Jones.' Why did she think she knew the name? She laughed. She'd been in a meeting recently with Mac, Sal and Red and someone remarked on how like a sheep dog trial it sounded. She laughed again. They could easily add a Sam to their pack. Although in Viv's world, to shorten someone's name or call them by a nickname was likely a sign of affection. She wasn't sure if Samantha would qualify. Viv was almost falling off her seat with tiredness, before she stopped scanning the info on Sal's new love interest, who'd had a significant number of public love interests herself, all men. Viv was suspicious. It wasn't that a woman couldn't change her preferences, but it was odd that Samantha had left a string of good-lookers in her wake. Or was it? Samantha had attended an all-girl, Catholic school, which had its consequences for a girl's sexuality. Nymphomania became common, as did the inability to look a man in the eye let alone get between the sheets with one. Samantha's behaviour with Sal had struck Viv as overtly 'out', yet there was no evidence of this in her public history. Viv rubbed her hands over her face. What could that mean? Wanting the world to know who you were in love with was one thing, but being all over someone like a rash was just in bad taste surely? 'Christ, listen to yourself.'

She closed the laptop lid and took the computer to bed. With no intention of sleeping, she began a new search for Archie. With the number of old articles about his rugby prowess, he'd obviously been going places before the accident, but one particularly caught her attention. A photograph of a group of guys looking the worse for a hard game, with their filthy strips and knees, swollen eyes, and mouths still wearing gum-shields. Archie was at one end, clinging round the shoulders of a much smaller stockier player. The look in Archie's eyes wasn't euphoric like the rest of them – he appeared distracted, screwing up his eyes, seeking out something or someone beyond the camera.

Apart from rugby there wasn't much else to go on, so, as a shot in the dark, she scanned the police's gay web pages and was surprised to find an image of

Archie taken during a charity walk – so much for not wanting anyone to know. Still, none of what she'd read added up to much. In fact, the more she read about him the less she knew.

She quickly flicked through Festival flyers but saw nothing of interest, unless she planned to attend a knife-swallowing show tomorrow. Time for sleep.

Chapter Twenty One

Viv's first client, Marjory Cook, was a part-time GP who lived life at 100 miles an hour. Her Victorian terraced house in a cul-de-sac in Newington looked as if it was stuck in the land that time forgot, complete with Virginia creeper climbing up the walls. Drainpipes, windows and doors painted in a foreboding dark green. Inside, although more Parker Knoll than Philippe Starck, it was tidy, every item functional, without consideration for style or coordination. As she approached the gate a downstairs curtain twitched – Marjory ready and waiting. She didn't even have to ring the bell, but braced herself for the smell of cats. Marjory opened the door and ushered her into the kitchen, checking her watch as she walked. Viv, a stickler for punctuality, didn't dally with any of her clients. Her hair days were tightly scheduled, with routes between clients meticulously worked out in advance. The festivals made driving slower, but rarely interfered with Viv's work.

'Hello, Viv. Glad you're on time. I've got something else on in forty minutes.'

'No problem.' Viv quickly moved to the spot in the kitchen that she always used to set up her floor cover. She plugged in her dryer, selected the scissors she would use, pulled out an unforgiving heavy Ergol chair that could do with a cushion and, placing it in the centre of her cutting mat, she indicated to Marjory to take a seat. Marjory was prepared. He wiry fair hair was damp from an earlier wash.

Viv swept a gown round her narrow angular shoulders and clasped it loosely at the nape of her neck. Marjory hated the sensation of anything near her throat. Viv sprayed her hair with water from a small misting bottle. 'Now, what are we doing with you today?'

Marjory seemed agitated, but Viv put this down to the tight time slot.

'I'd just like it trimmed. The usual, really. If only I could get a little bit more height on the crown.'

'I'll see what I can do.'

Viv snipped in silence, until she noticed Marjory's shoulders tighten and a tear escape down the pale skin of her papery cheek. She batted the tear away with the back of her hand. Viv continued, hoping that Marjory would get herself together. No such luck. Marjory suddenly curled forward in the chair and pushed her fists into her eyes. She cried, proper crying, silently into her knees with shoulders heaving. Viv had never seen Marjory in anything other than super-efficient mode, and although she realised that everyone was bound to crash sometime she wouldn't have expected her to let it happen when anyone else was around.

Viv filled the kettle. No intention of making anything, just to give Marjory space to do whatever she needed to do. Viv was used to clients crying. People underestimate the intimacy of having their hair cut. Having someone right inside your personal space, making gentle physical contact with you was rare and could trigger an emotional flood.

As the kettle came to the boil Marjory sat upright, pulled a handkerchief from a pocket and said, 'Sorry. Okay now. Can we continue?'

Viv raised her eyebrows, but not within sight of Marjory. She continued cutting into the layers on the crown in the hope that undercutting would support the longer lengths and give her the height that she wanted. Viv knew that Marjory's hair regime was minimal and if she wanted height on the crown she'd actually have to use a hairdryer now and again. Unlikely, Viv thought, but at least she'd covered all bases.

As she began the blow-dry Marjory was back to her usual tense self. Her blotchy face and a handkerchief being tortured between her hands were the remaining signs of her distress. If she had wanted to talk to Viv about what was going on she would have. Viv tidied up her things while Marjory went off to write a cheque. As Viv was leaving she gently touched Marjory's shoulder. Big mistake. Her eyes filled again and she retreated so quickly that she caught Viv's kit bag in the front door. Experiences like this reminded Viv that everyone was carrying a history that no one else knew, and the more swan like the exterior the more they were paddling like fury beneath the surface. Marjory was an unusual woman, because despite being a regular and long-term client their relationship had remained formal. Marjory's husband, on the other hand, was an open, sometimes too open, academic – his wife's polar opposite. It took all sorts to make a nation, and she wondered what was going on for Marjory. She tossed her kit into the back of the Rav and glanced back at the sad exterior of the house.

Her next client was the antithesis of all that was wrong in the world. Jinty lived in Royal Terrace, a few doors away from the ferocious Edinburgh Bridge Club. On days that they were playing it was impossible to park, but today Viv had sailed into a space right outside Jinty's front door. Jinty greeted Viv with a warm hug and a couple of air kisses, and already had coffee on the go. It was always a joy to see her. She had good things to say about everyone and had a fabulous head of hair that was one of Viv's best advertisements.

'How are you, girl?' Jinty asked, as she turned down the gas on a pan of warming milk and pulled out a jar of homemade biscuits from an overhead cupboard in one continuous sweeping gesture.

'Great. Just been on the west coast.'

'That's not like you. I see you as an urban animal.'

'Oh, I am, but this was a work thing. Got the chance to swim with a seal.'

Jinty swung round. 'What a seal seal with flippers and . . .what else do seals have?'

They laughed, neither knowing quite how to describe a seal.

'Help yourself.' Jinty pushed forward the jar of biscuits. 'Made them yesterday. Ginger cookies. Not bad for a first attempt. Posh do on at Holyrood tonight. Queenie and all. No idea why we're invited but hey ho, no hardship since it's a hop, skip and jump from here.'

'What's the occasion?'

'Something to do with the Archers' centenary. I've probably got that entirely wrong. But we've been summoned and the jewels are out.' She snorted. 'Well the mockeroos are out.'

It was Viv's turn to laugh. She was sure that Jinty had jewellery enough to please a gathering of royals, but she was happy to wear paste.

'So what's happening to your hair?'

'Exactly as you did last time, and the time before, and the time before that. Do you know, I even get stopped in Waitrose? People, well women usually, although I have had comments from men, ask who does my hair. It gives me great pleasure to say that you are unavailable until someone dies. Itching powder, that's all I want off.'

Viv laughed again. 'You know this is money for old rope.'

'If my husband hears you calling me old rope he'll agree with you and adopt it as his own. Let's go up.'

Viv drained her coffee and they took the stairs to Jinty's bedroom on the first floor. The paintings on the way up were a stunning mix of Victorian portraits and landscapes. One portrait of a young boy had such detail on his necktie that Viv gazed at it every time she passed. In the bedroom Jinty had an outfit lying on the bed. Still wrapped in a moth protector. Viv could only see the exquisite embroidery on the hem.

'Can I have a quick glance at the . . .' She nodded to the bag.

Jinty hauled off the cover to expose a cream silk jacket, the sort of thing Viv imagined Nehru could have worn. Crewel work, tiny raised fronds of foliage with small flowers clinging to it as if their petals might at any minute close, glimmered on pale golden silk.

'It's old. A family thing. Had it tailored to fit. Think they've made a decent job of it. Designed, of course, to be worn in candlelight. It shall positively sing in the royal dining-room tonight.'

'What will you wear with it? I mean do you have to have a skirt or trousers beneath?'

Jinty pulled out a pair of cream silk palazzo pants. 'They don't match, but in a dim light what does it matter?'

This was one of the things that Viv loved about Jinty. She could wear a paper bag and look fabulous with the natty turn-up of a collar or knot of a scarf.

'Come on then, let's get that itching powder off.'

The unspoken aspect of Viv's job was to keep the secrets of her clients. Many of them knew each other and had come to her through personal recommendations, which made this more difficult than it sounded. Jinty was Viv's number one fan and had sent her lots of clients, some Viv wished she hadn't, but others who Viv enjoyed almost as much as she did Jinty. Once her hair was completed and payment made, Viv skipped back to the car.

Her next client was five minutes' drive from Royal Terrace, and she was tempted, since she had a parking space, to walk. But the weight of her kit banging against her calf in the heat of the sun made her think otherwise. Easter Road was fast becoming the bohemian end of town with its lovely wide streets where there were no parking restrictions. This was fine most of the year, but in August, with so many visitors looking for free parking for the duration of their stay, this area was manna from heaven. Viv sympathised with the residents. She cursed as she circled for a parking space. When she eventually found one she still had to walk a fair distance to reach Annabelle's flat. She rang the doorbell. No answer. Not good. No sounds from inside. She rang the bell again. Same, nothing but the chime echoing in the hallway. This had happened before, but Annabelle had eventually appeared, flushed from her basement studio, having lost track of the time. Not today, though. Viv took out her phone and rang her number, hearing it loud and clear on the other side of the door. No one made any attempt to pick up. The answering machine kicked in. Viv left a message saying she hoped everything was okay and would she ring her back. She called her next client, and in a rare stroke of luck he was in his office and could see her early. She made her way back to the car and drove to York Place. The client, a solicitor, had parking at the back of the office, which she had permission to use if there was space. There was.

When she entered, Carol, his snippy receptionist, smiled an unconvincing smile and said, 'Take a seat. I don't have you in the diary for another forty-five minutes.'

Viv was about to speak when Carol lifted her phone and stabbed at the unsuspecting buttons.

'The hairdresser is here. Would you like me to get her coffee?'

He must have said 'send her through' because Carol, evidence of anger crawling up her neck, gestured with a jerk of her head for Viv to go in. What was it with receptionists? They were the first greeting point for the firm, were supposed to put people at ease. She behaved like a eunuch, sleeping on the floor outside his door.

Viv smiled. 'Hey, Gerry. Thanks for changing the time.' She set up her floor mat and plugged in her drier.

Gerry brought a chair over and tried to secure the gown. 'Oops. You'll have to do this.' Viv took it from him, and once he was seated she wrapped him and the chair beneath it.

He said, 'This suits me really well. I've got tickets for a show later, but I've a notion to go and sit on George Street with a large latte and watch the world go by.'

'Sounds good to me. Does Carol know you're on your way to . . .'

He grinned. 'No, she bloody well does not. I'm sure she's getting worse. Anyone would think that our citadel was worth storming.'

Viv sprayed his hair with water and began cutting. 'Why don't you send her for some training?'

'Oh God. You should hear the fuss. "If I'm not good enough etc etc." The stuff of high drama. She only has two years before she retires. I swear she's got a genetic predisposition to torture.' He snorted. 'But today I'm off to play hookie and she doesn't know.'

Gerry wasn't the only client who was afraid of his secretary. Was it because receptionists had so much information stored in their heads that it wasn't worth the hassle of trying to replace them? Two years seemed an awful long time to put up with someone who was beyond a pain in the neck. His hair took Viv twenty minutes to cut and less than five minutes to dry. Gerry was one of a few men who were phobic about going to a salon, and he frequently asked what he would do if anything happened to Viv. Her response was always the same. Why worry about something you have no control over? If only she could put her own rhetoric into practice. The huge office had windows facing onto York Place. The firm had amalgamated and another name had been added to the inscription on the window. To Viv's eye, the calligraphy had been done by an artist determined to show the inferiority of the original; the result a modern colour combination that did nothing to enhance the old discreet names. Ferguson, Smith and now Cameron. The 'Cameron' brash, like Walter Scott's idea of tartan against the subtle plaid of an old clan.

'New partner?' Viv nodded at the window.

He drew in a deep breath. 'Needs must. We apparently should have an in house matrimonial solicitor.' He huffed.

'Surely that means an anti-matrimonial solicitor?'

He laughed. 'You're right. I'm not impressed. We've been conveyancing solicitors since the beginning and never had to contend with too much strife. Now we're dealing with warring parties who once shared the same bed. It's obscene.'

Gerry was a bachelor. Not, as is often the case, a euphemism for a gay man in the closet, but a real live bachelor with old school values, braces, cufflinks and an embossed pinkie ring – style. Viv imagined him wearing a bowler hat until the ridicule became too frequent to bear.

Chapter Twenty Two

The following morning Viv decided to start the day with a run. As she was leaving the building she received a text from Ruddy. She locked up, jogged up Victoria Street and turned left towards the Mound. As she reached the junction with the Lawnmarket she looked right toward St Giles' High Kirk. A metal barrier was set up along the edge of the pavement holding a crowd of people behind it. All eyes were peeled on the doors of the Kirk, which dominated Parliament Square. She stopped and said to a woman holding her phone aloft, 'What's going on?'

The woman replied in a Texan accent. 'Queen Elizabeth. We've never seen the Queen.' She grinned.

Viv stepped behind her and waited.

The sun shone and the expanse of cobbles immediately outside the Kirk's doors glistened from an earlier downpour. The air was fresh and tourists were in high spirits. A row of black saloons waited, their engines idling, their drivers capped and gloved, ready to move at the slightest nod from a soberly dressed official with an ear-wire, legs apart and hands clasped behind his back.

Viv had watched a clip with the Queen and the First Minister on the late news last night. They'd been snipping some ribbon or other, the Queen sacrificing days away from her beloved Balmoral.

Within the huge edifice of St Giles', the Queen and her Knights of the Thistle had a private chapel. Becoming a KT was an honour bestowed on a select few who liked that sort of thing. For this visit High Court judges, a number of High Constables and the Royal Company of Archers. They had not been called out for any other occasion this year. If the Queen was actually under threat these would be the last men who would be able to protect her. The Constables and Archers made up an army of about 100 men, many of them too old and too overweight to fit into their eighteenth-century style uniforms. Viv stared at them and felt a giggle rising, as it occurred to her that clothes used for the preservation of rank, could, over time, have the opposite effect. This lot had become like caricatures.

There were so many people behind the barrier that they were squashed against the shop fronts of the Royal Mile.

Viv looked up to the roof of the building behind her on the corner of George IV Bridge and spotted two marksmen. So she did have real protection. People began to clap and cheer. Viv spotted a tiny figure dressed in lilac exit the church's vast double doors flanked by men in stiff, dark green uniforms, none of whom looked fit enough to make it to the next bus stop never mind defend their monarch. Their hats, with great slim feathers extending up into the air, and ornate longbows were assurance of the ceremonial nature of the job. She spotted Jinty's husband looking very upright and uncomfortable, but in true military fashion they marched her to her waiting car, not her usual one with the glass bubble on the top, but a black saloon with dark tinted windows that was bound to belong to Edinburgh council. No walkabout today then.

Just as Her Majesty was stepping into the car a skinny youth broke ranks from the crowd and charged into the line of Archers. There was a collective intake of breath as one of the most elderly Archers was hurled to the ground. It all happened in seconds. Two other Archers rushed to his aid. A strange look passed between them as they half-heartedly tried to lift him. He roughly brushed them aside. Meanwhile the door of the saloon closed and the vehicle was driven off in a swift orderly manner, with the Queen safely inside, leaving her Archers trying to keep a grip on the offender. The watching crowd let go of their breath as soon as the Queen was safe, but the Archers seemed unsure of who was more important, their ancient colleague still kneeling on the ground, cocooned in his uniform, or the skinny young man being swung round by one of their number who had had the wit to grab his tee shirt. The young man wriggled efficiently out of it and bolted into the crowd, swerving as people tried to grab him. No shots were fired from the rooftops.

She thought she saw him turn left into a close, so pushed through the crowd and raced towards St Giles' Street, a dead-end for cars but with steps leading onto Market Street. If the young man had taken any of the closes on the left side of the High Street he'd end up in Cockburn Street and Viv might have a chance to cut him off. Knowing Edinburgh's Old Town, full of nooks and crannies, increased her chance of success.

She was breathing hard when she turned into the bottom of Cockburn Street and crashed head on into the tee shirtless young man. He side-stepped her but she stuck out her foot and sent him head over heals. She was on top of him in a second. He was around the same height as her, both of them slender and fit, so it was an equal fight. She managed to pin one of his arms to the ground with her knee and forced the other arm behind his back. Purplish bruises on his upper arms and old yellowing bruises on his back looked as if he'd been held by force before. Just as she pulled out her phone, a plainclothes security guy came puffing down Warriston Close. He looked right and left before settling an astonished look on Viv sitting astride the young man on the pavement. He ran to them and cuffed the man before even opening his mouth to Viv. Passers-by stopped and pointed their phones. Viv turned her back to them.

'How did you know to do that?'

She caught her breath and shook out her limbs. 'Watching crime on telly.'

She stood with her hands on her hips, still with her back to the increasing crowd, and watched the security guy, or whatever the royal household's minders were called these days, haul the man to his feet. He spoke into a tiny mouthpiece. 'Assailant apprehended. Request backup vehicle on Cockburn Street.'

Viv was intrigued by the formality of his language. 'So what happens now?'

'We will need a statement from you, Madam.'

Viv walked away a few paces, took out her phone and rang Mac. 'Hi. You'll never believe it.'

Mac interrupted her. 'Try me. You've just witnessed an attack on the Queen?'

'Yes, but if it was an attack it was pretty ineffectual. I'd say it was more like a decoy. What has been running along your ticker tape?'

'Two minutes ago it came over the wire that a young man had attacked the Queen.'

'I saw it. He didn't actually attack her. He ran at the Archers but didn't get to touch her or anything so that doesn't constitute an . . .'

'Whatever, Viv. What are you doing?'

'I apprehended the guy.'

She could hear him almost choke at the other end of the line.

'What the fu . . . You mean you chased him?'

'What else was I supposed to do? Did you think I'd just spectate? Look I'm not sure what to tell them. Should I keep quiet about our stuff or will they already know?'

'Some of them will know but who is with you? And listen, what were you doing there?'

'I was out for a run. Hang on, you speak to him. It'll make life easier.'

Viv turned and strode back to the cop who, with his hand protecting the man's head, was guiding him into the back of an unmarked car. Now that Viv could see him clearly he was definitely more boy than man; looked about sixteen maybe seventeen years old. One thing that struck Viv about him was the absence of tats.

Once the door of the car was closed she said to the security man. 'What's your name?'

He bristled, his jaw tightening. 'I am the one asking the questions?'

She handed him her phone. It would be difficult to explain what her role was since she wasn't clear what it was herself.

He took the phone and looked at it before putting it to his ear. Mac must have said who he was and asked for his name. 'Parker. I was going to take him to St Leonards . . . okay . . . okay. We'll bring him.' He stared at Viv as he spoke to Mac. 'Fettes it is.' He handed Viv back her phone. 'You have to come along for the ride.'

She'd thought this would be the case and she followed him to another unmarked car with a driver. He opened the back door but she took a seat in the front and watched Parker raise his eyebrows.

'I get car sick.'

'And your point is?'

'I'm not on a power trip. I genuinely can't sit in the back.'

He put his hands up and got in behind her. The driver, a young man with the beginnings of a beard, smirked. Viv smiled then turned round in her seat. Parker was good looking, despite a nose that had clearly been broken, clean shaven, greenish brown eyes, kind of rugged but unassuming. His thick coarse curls had been cut so short that they had no way of expressing themselves other than through his wayward hairline. Viv guessed he'd have to have it cut every three weeks to keep it contained. 'I wonder if someone got his tee shirt?'

'That's what we're about to find out.'

A voice from the radio cut in from the other car. 'Arrived at HQ. Shall I wait or hand him over? There's a welcoming committee.'

Parker leaned forward and pressed a release button. 'If it's DCI Marconi hand him over. No one else.'

They were only a few minutes behind the other car and as they swung into Fettes' car park Viv spotted the young man being 'unloaded' at the far end of the building. She was intrigued to see what happened next and walked towards them.

Parker called out, 'Excuse me, Madam, that's a restricted zone.'

She gestured to the end of the building. 'I thought I'd take a look over there.'

He shook his head. 'Please follow me.'

She shrugged. If she wanted to see down there she'd find a way.

She nodded to Billy at reception and he grinned, giving rise to a grunt from Parker.

'Who are you? And why is he reacting to you as if you're the tooth fairy?'

'Maybe I am. All you have to do is believe.' And over her shoulder as she walked in the direction of the downstairs interview rooms, she threw, 'I did catch your criminal, after all.'

He quickly stepped in front of her and opened the door to let her through.

'Thank you. I'm a big fan of gentlemanly conduct.'

Their steps echoed on shiny grey vinyl tiles as they walked down a barren greenish corridor. The public were not permitted down here unless they were cuffed.

They met Marconi coming toward them. He shook Parker's hand and said, 'He's being processed. Good work, Viv. I'm sure that wasn't coincidence.'

'You know how I feel about coincidence.'

He nodded. 'Still, it'll be interesting to find out what he thought he was up to. I can't imagine he doesn't realise how grave it is to attack HM. Probably thought it'd be a laugh. Well, he's just about to find out about the sense of humour failure the royal household is having about this. Not to mention the Archers and the High Constables.'

'Christ, Mac, they are a total farce. There's no way that lot should be given duties, even ceremonial. In fact delete that unless completely static. They need to do a clean sweep and recruit a whole new army under forty.' She snorted.

'For God's sake. The Archers are equivalent to the Beefeaters at the Tower of London. They're not meant to really guard the Queen. They're decorative.'

Parker stood in silence, until Viv realised he thought they were talking about his lot.

'I'm talking about the coffin dodgers with the dark green uniforms and the guys in the toppers. Not . . .'

Parker interrupted her. 'I get it. What I don't get is how you got the heads up on a possible threat.'

Mac jumped in. 'Viv's one of us. If she was in on it she was for good reason. She doesn't need to justify herself.'

'Look do I really need to be here?'

'Yes,' The two men said in unison.

She sighed and stared at Mac, trying to size up how much to say in front of Parker.

He nodded his understanding and said, 'Coffee? She won't function without caffeine.'

Parker spotted it. 'I get it. I'll go and see how he's settling in while you two have your little tête-à-tête.'

Parker walked off toward his colleagues and Mac said, ' So how come you were in the right place at the right, or was it wrong, time?'

The fact that he was asking the question meant that he doubted that it was simply a coincidence. 'Luck.' She shrugged and turned at the sound of a door opening further down the corridor. Sal stepped out and stopped in her tracks. She looked as if she was weighing up her options. She closed the door gently behind her and waved an acknowledgement but walked off in the opposite direction.

Viv stood with her mouth open. She looked at Mac, then back at the end of the corridor where the door that Sal had exited was still creaking on its hinges. 'What the hell . . .'

Mac shook his head. 'I'm not getting involved. I'm only interested in how you knew that something was happening at St Giles'.'

His eyes urged her, but she didn't bite. If Ruddy hadn't involved Mac it was also for good reason, and until Viv found out what that was she'd keep her mouth shut. 'Honestly. I was on my way to . . .'

Her hesitation was all Mac needed. 'Fair enough. No point in my wasting time trying to prise it out of you. But you'll still have to describe what happened for the tape. Come on.'

She grudgingly followed him until they entered an interview room, where he left her with a DS who took her statement. Viv knew the form and estimated that if she played the game she would be on her way in thirty minutes. Sure enough the DS was efficient and obviously recognised Viv as part of Marconi's inner circle.

It wasn't until Viv was back in the car park that she remembered she was on the hoof. She walked briskly into Comely Bank and turned left toward the busy shopping area of Stockbridge, a village within the city, which valued its autonomy. Good coffee houses and charity shops heaved with middle-class bohemians who either lived in a nearby district called 'The Colonies', or were camping with friends for the festivals. She perused the shelves of the Oxfam bookshop, always a must, then, seduced by a waft of real caffeine, retired to a café to luxuriate in an espresso and read her purchase.

Viv slipped her fleece over the back of the first vacant chair and scanned the room. The tables by the windows were full. This was as close as she could get to a view. She wondered what was unique about Stockbridge. There were many hamlets within Edinburgh. The Grassmarket, Bruntsfield and the Shore also had their own identities, but she was pushed to tease out exactly what they were. Eventually she decided it was the people. It could only be the people who frequented the shops, bars and cafés. 'Suits' didn't make it as far as these villages unless they were walking through them on their way to somewhere else. George Street was for them, with their leather shoes that made feet look much longer than they actually were.

The West Bow relied on a population of tourists, students and staff from the university and the art college, and at the weekends, hen and stag parties – more evident at night than during the day. She glanced round as the waitress brought her espresso. Most people were reading something, palmtops, even the odd book or newspaper. This made her smile. Trees were not out of danger yet. At the Oxfam bookshop she had picked up a second-hand copy of *Darwin's Worms*; she'd lent her first copy to someone and never got it back. Phillips was her go-to non-fiction writer and she had to drag herself away from his tantalising prose. As he says, 'We are always relaxing in the killing fields', a reference to nature, and the beauty of what we see as only being a fragment of the whole picture. For nature to flourish things must die. He was so on the money about that. She closed the book and went to pay her bill. The walk home would only take twenty minutes, as long as she didn't get distracted.

She'd barely gone ten paces when she caught a glimpse of Sal's familiar and unique upright walk. Viv stared as Sal tried and failed to compete with other pedestrians on the pavement. She was clearly in a hurry, but couldn't get moving for window shoppers. Eventually she skipped onto the road, round a parked car and back onto a gap on the pavement. Viv considered calling out to her but didn't, and was relieved that she hadn't when she saw why Sal was in such a rush. Just before the bridge over the Water of Leith Viv spotted the female from the car park. She scooped Sal up in an unequivocal embrace before they marched off along Henderson Row, arms round each other's waists.

Viv felt a lump rising in her throat. She swallowed, tucked her book and bookmarks into the waistband of her Ron Hills and jogged up Frederick Street, over George and Princes Streets then up the Mound, easier to navigate than the Playfair Steps. 'You'd better get used to it' was what she kept telling herself. She wished she had taken the time to do a bit more research on the new woman. There was definitely something familiar about her. But there again, in Edinburgh lots of people looked familiar.

As she closed the door of the flat, her mobile rang. She looked at the display – it was Mac. 'Hi . . .'

'Where are you?'

'At home. Why?

'He's escaped.'

'No way! How the hell did that happen?'

'Trying to find that out. But it was Parker's men who were looking after him.'

'Shit!'

'Hitting the fan as we speak.' They were cut off.

She continued pulling off her trainers hopping down the hallway into the sitting-room, and slumping onto the couch flicked on the television, as if that would somehow explain what Mac had reported. How on earth could a young man escape from police custody so quickly? It had to be an inside job. She rang Mac back. 'Hi. It has to be someone on the inside. CCTV?'

'Yes. We've thought of that.' His tone irritated.

'Don't get at me, matey. I wasn't the one who lost him.'

She heard him sigh. 'We've got footage of two figures in hoodies. They knew the lay-out of the building. I'll let you know when we find them. Oh and Viv, I'll get you to take a look at the NTF consoles after all. How soon could you get back here?'

She sighed and checked her clock. 'Within the hour.'

'I've arranged an emergency meeting. This is definitely an emergency.'

She was about to answer but he was already gone. She pictured the chaos at Fettes and chewed on her lip. Would now be the best time to check their computers? She knew a way of doing it from her sitting room, but there were other things she could find more easily if she were in situ.

She packed a few bits and pieces, including an entry card, and headed for the Rav. She wondered if HQ suffered from SAD; it was so dull and uninspiring. She continued past the car park and stopped on the side road outside Fettes' College. The more discreet she was the better. She hoped there were no smokers lurking at the entrance, although since the ban they shouldn't be anywhere within the building or grounds. Still, good to see one or two who'd ignored the memo. Once inside she acknowledged the duty sergeant on reception again and headed down to the basement. There were people in the corridors but she hoped the cyber-hub, as they were supposed to call it, was empty.

She slid the card into the entry slot and the door hissed open. There was a plan for an iris recognition system but the software still had to be fully loaded with the identities of users. She guessed that by the time they got round to putting it in something equally morbid would have been designed to take its place. How odd that all staff's unique eyeballs were on a database somewhere. Viv stood for a minute, visualising where each of the analysts sat. Mac's meetings were notoriously quick. So she set to work. Her main task was to find what personal stuff they were doing from their work consoles. If they had wisdom they'd be doing very little beyond the occasional game of solitaire in their breaks, but most analysts liked a bit of risk.

Viv settled at the first console, which was where Frances worked. The hum of too much electricity coursing round the room was not the most reassuring sound. She could tell a lot from the way people organised their desks, and worried more about those who were uber-tidy than those who were shambolic. The doodles on a pad at the side of her computer were fascinating. Lips, lots of lips; full, thin, coloured in, not coloured in. Telling. She noticed that there were a few who'd ignored the no-wet-substances-at-your-desk rule and there were one or two mugs, half-full of coffee, defiantly in sight of anyone who cared to complain. No bad thing, she thought.

Frances' computer sprang into life as soon as she nudged the mouse. Viv scrolled through the history, clicking here and there to clarify a site. Frances played in work time, she ordered stuff online and was a fan of Lara Croft, making it easier to build her profile. Her spending habits were erratic.

Recently she'd been on a cosmetics spree. Viv would never have been able to tell from the weekend away. Her concern about cellulite was costing her dearly, although there was no evidence of her having any. Viv whistled at one purchase for face cream costing over £100, which made Viv's own beauty regime look like a pauper's. Frances hadn't struck Viv as a girlie girl who would spend her hard earned on miracle cures, but she'd bought a box of hair crayons and that wasn't a sign of sanity. Her reading habits were no surprise: a thriller binger. Once she found an author she liked she bought the canon. Viv could empathise with that; she was partial to binge reading herself. Apart from clearly having trouble with her drains, since she'd bought multiple packs of an industrial cleaner, Viv couldn't find anything untoward – although the Amazon algorithms must have gone awol, since they were targeting her for babies' nappies. Weird.

Finally she checked deleted emails, feeling slightly bad that she might now work out whom Frances was dating. Viv uncovered emails from a dating agency, one with recommendations for how to behave on a first date. She became engrossed in details like whom they should tell where, when and with whom they were going. She laughed at the 'no bed on first date' rule. After a bit more digging she discovered the most recent date. It had been set up in the last month. She hacked into the man's details. He wasn't familiar and although quite pleasant to look at he wouldn't have floated Viv's boat – his hobbies included curling – 'What's that about?' she said aloud before realising she was the only one listening and the hum of electricity still the only other noise. He worked in 'horticulture', suitably vague, which could mean anything from working on the tills at a garden centre to clambering round the Himalayas collecting plants. Frances' frequent activity on the site justified her expenses in the body makeover department.

The next console was Davie's. She smiled. His mug, half full of cold milky coffee and with the words 'Don't Mess With The Best' printed on both sides, sat at the side of his keyboard. 'Good man,' she muttered. Then wondered who had bought him the mug. No one would buy that for themselves. Did Davie have someone in his life that thought he was 'the Best'? Could be an old mug, although it didn't look over used. His desk was just the right degree of shambolic. He probably knew where every item was, so she had to be careful not to shuffle them. He was a pen chewer. Since returning from the west coast he'd wasted no time in joining a couple of chat rooms for canoeists, and his buying history indicated that he was serious about taking it up as a hobby; he had ordered a dry-suit. All in work time. His unopened emails were endless. She had scrolled herself into a kind of trance when a telephone rang and she almost leapt out of her skin. The phone, on another desk, rang and rang and rang until she shouted at it, 'No one's in!' and it stopped. She wiped her hands on her thighs and blew out a breath. Her heart rate now higher than when she'd arrived.

The consoles were all at the same level, on a continuous desktop. No drawers, only the large stationery cabinet at the back of the room. No one could secretly stash a bottle of Bell's for the odd tipple.

Satisfied that Davie's station didn't have anything incriminating, she moved on to Gordon's. Too tidy. No mug, not a chewed pen in sight, and ordered piles of paper. So much for a paperless office. Already Viv could feel her judgement shift into overdrive. What kind of person was Gordon, really? Viv believed that stress and/or alcohol didn't bring out the worst in someone, but magnified characteristics they already had. Gordon's sarcasm began on the bus, so had he been stressed about the weekend before the start? Having his flak directed towards her had not been much fun. All groups need a scapegoat, but he had got into it early and without any good reason that Viv could discern. Still there must be a reason. What was he afraid of? A safe enough assumption since fear was our greatest motivator.

Gordon was big on music. His buying history was mainly downloads from iTunes. Surprisingly folksy stuff, even the Corries. Viv also sympathised with him about a few of his emails from his sister, who was giving him grief for not seeing enough of her kids. What was it with siblings? They want to get on with their own lives, but as soon as that life includes kids they want everyone else to share them. His buying history included super cleaner for alloy wheels, seat covers for inside the car. Must be for those pesky nieces and nephews. She laughed. Then on hearing a noise at the door she jumped up and went into the kitchen, hoping that the person entering wasn't Gordon or his nearest neighbours.

It was Mac who stuck his head through the door.

'Christ, Mac. I almost lost my skin. What are you up to?' She laid her hand on her heart acknowledging its extra effort.

'Just thought I'd give you the heads up. We'll be done in about ten minutes.'

'You said . . .'

'Too bad. You've got ten minutes tops.' And he disappeared.

Stop getting too involved in what people are buying, girl, and get the job done. There was one item that caught her eye from Gordon's recent Amazon purchases, a blow-up double bed. She wondered if he was having guests. She quickly moved on to Archie's console. His was another story. No Amazon account. Who in the world today didn't have an Amazon account? This was the first strange thing. Next were the emails from an online gambling consortium, not quite of the knee-capping variety, but close enough. She found other emails with details of debts he'd run up. Not good. Could this explain the absence of an Amazon account? She clicked on a few keys and whispered, 'Bingo.' His credit rating was so far into the negative as to scare even her. No wonder he'd relaxed at the weekend. No one could touch him while he was in the wilds with a bunch of cops. There was one conversation in his emails which Viv thought worth tracking. From it she worked out that there was another email account with a further conversation. She dug deeper. Nothing. Archie, judging by the mess on his desk, wasn't remotely meticulous so there was a chance that he'd made a mistake somewhere and left a trail on which she would discover the account she was looking for. Nothing. She tried another tack. She checked the time on the screen. They'd be back in the next couple of minutes. She persisted. Still nothing. She heard voices and made a few clicks that would disguise what she'd been looking at. The screen was still live. Nothing she could do about that.

The door hissed open and Gordon and Archie entered, with Gordon holding onto Archie's arms. The conversation they'd been having outside the door came to an abrupt halt. Gordon screwed up his eyes. Viv bumped the desk she was leaning on and the other consoles also sprang into life.

Gordon kept his eyes on her then glanced around the room as if looking for someone else. 'What are you doing here?' His tone unwelcoming, but she was getting used to that.

Archie took a seat at his computer. Viv hoped that she hadn't left a sweaty handprint on his mouse. He didn't touch the mouse but shifted a few bits of paper round his desk. Viv thought he was trying to look efficient.

Gordon sat at his place and turned to Viv. 'Cat got your tongue?'

'It seems I've to join you on some work. I'm meeting . . .'

'The blue-eyed boy. Yeah, teacher's pet. I told you, Arch.'

Viv wondered what he'd told Archie and whether 'Arch' meant they were pals.

The door hissed open again and Mac joined them. 'Ah, Viv . . .'

'I told them I was joining them on some work. So now you can let us all in on your secret.'

Mac, a smooth operator, said, 'Well I need to have a quick word with someone first. Leave it with me.' He retreated from the room, leaving Viv with Gordon and Archie.

Viv said, 'What have you been working on that he could mean?'

Gordon grunted back, 'There's nothing going on that he needs to bring you in for. Nothing we can't handle.'

'Well, Mac seems to think otherwise. And if not Mac, someone higher up, or else I wouldn't be here.'

'You shouldn't be here anyway. You should be back behind a hairdryer doing what it is you do best.'

'Really? Is that your beef? You've got a thing about me being a hairdresser?' She snorted. 'Crawl out from beneath your rock. There are people in the world who . . .'

Archie interrupted her. 'You don't have to justify yourself to him. And you,' he pointed at Gordon, 'back off.'

Viv was interested in the way Gordon reacted to this. He coloured, but turned to his screen and began to tap on his keys. The stuff that Viv had been looking at on their consoles could be traced; they were cyber analysts after all, but they'd have to suspect and want to look.

She made for the door. 'I'll check with Mac . . .'

'Yeah, why don't you do that?' Gordon blasted at her retreating back.

The door hissed closed behind her and she took the stairs two at a time. She reached the reception desk and asked the sergeant to page DCI Marconi, but Mac appeared and she said, 'That was close. But one or two things turned up that might be worth looking at.'

Mac's mobile rang. He walked towards the outside doors and spoke to the caller. 'Okay.' He cut the call and turned to Viv. 'I think they've got a lead on Houdini. Walk with me to the car and you can fill me in. I've to check what Parker's lot are up to.'

'Sure. I'll come along for the ride.'

He hesitated. Looked at her through screwed-up eyes and nodded. Then walked towards his car. 'Only if you keep your mouth shut.'

'You know me. Silent as a lamb.' She skipped to keep up.

'I mean it, Viv. Not a word.'

She drew her fingers over her lips like a zip.

'I'm serious.'

'Well, if you're that serious why don't you tell me about it?'

'It's National Secure . . .'

She flinched and yanked the car door open.

'Okay, the attempt on the Queen's life is the most determined we've had for a while. You do know we get them regularly? Well, not me personally, but the Met get them often and when she's up here we get them, fewer but still some. I have to work out how "real" they are . . . since you're involved, by whatever means you got here.' He stared across at her but she didn't bite. 'This particular threat came to light at a different level, I mean the top. You sure it was just a coincidence that you were on the Royal Mile?' He raised his eyebrows.

'How many times do I hear that our "National Security" is at risk? Either I've signed the OSA or I haven't.'

'As you well know, there are different levels of security risk. A threat to the Queen is the highest. There are only a handful of us who have access to that kind of information.'

They stopped at traffic lights.

She turned in her seat. 'You think? When are you guys going to get the hang of the net being like a giant teabag. There's stuff leaking through to anyone who cares to listen at the right keyhole.'

He was quiet for a minute. 'Sure. And that's why we've got the cyber team.'

'Yes. Yes, it is. But if someone on our cyber team is pushing information or doesn't choose to pay attention at the right moment . . .' She left her concerns hovering between them.

They pulled up outside a terrace of Georgian houses on London Street, at the lower end of the New Town.

Mac gestured for her to come. Viv had expected there to be a big police presence, but there was no one around. She followed him to a gate in a row of ornate railings and took the stairs down to the basement behind him. There were thin voiles over the first window, preventing them from seeing in. At the next window the shutters were closed. Viv lifted the letterbox in the door and peered in. Bare floorboards, walls painted in pale mushroom with patches on the walls where paintings or mirrors had once hung.

'Why are we here? And who does it belong to?'

He surprised her. 'It's Archie's flat.'

'Wow! Really? Not at all what I'd expect.'

'No. Me neither.'

She could see a single corridor with two doors off the right hand side and two off the left and one at the far end facing the front door – all closed.

'Does he actually live here?'

'Good question. It's the address we have for him.'

'It looks empty. Unlived in. Although there's no junk mail lying behind the door, so someone's been in.'

'It's a pity we can't get in.'

She stood with her hands on her hips and shook her head. He couldn't ask her to go in but she sensed he wanted her to.

'Now or later?'

'I've no idea what you mean. Let's go.'

They got back into the car, drove up Broughton Street and turned right into Barony Place. This was more like what Viv was expecting. There were three police cars, one with its blue light circling on the top, always a give-away.

Mac headed over towards Parker. 'Found him?'

'Not sure. There's a scared young man inside, but I can't be sure it's our guy.'

'Why not?'

'This one isn't speaking English.' He shrugged.

Although he hadn't said much, the young man had spoken perfect English without a hint of an accent.

Viv had clients who were bilingual. One second they'd be chatting to her in English about the latest theory of thermodynamics, then the phone would ring and they'd slip seamlessly into fluent Greek, Italian or French. It was possible.

'We're not keen to bash the door in if we can talk him out. He must have something to hide if he won't let us in.'

Viv snorted. 'You're kidding me. If you had half a dozen men turn up at your door trying to bang it down wouldn't you want to hide?'

'No, I wouldn't.'

Viv shook her head. 'Well that shows a singular lack of . . .'

Mac nudged her.

'Okay. What's your next move?'

'Negotiator is on her way.'

Just as he spoke a shiny BMW turned into the street and Sal's lithe new girlfriend stepped out.

'This is Jones now.' Parker nodded toward the car.

Viv's belly clenched. The woman looked shocked, her eyes widening. Having momentarily lost her composure, she turned to Mac and Parker, straightening her posture and offering her hand to all three. She was older than she looked from a distance, but there was no denying her outstanding bone structure. Her cropped blonde hair was meticulously messy, each strand placed to look as if she'd just rubbed it with a towel. Viv saw it for the labour intensive artwork that it was. She wore a navy trouser suit with a pale blue tee-shirt underneath, and black patent loafers. Not dressed for trouble, but professional.

'I'm guessing he's inside,' with the hint of a west coast accent. She buttoned her jacket but missed a hole.

Viv instinctively pointed at the woman's navel. 'You've . . .'

Flustered, Jones rebuttoned her jacket and curtly nodded her thanks.

Parker said, 'If you're done with the fashion parade, this way.' He took off towards the building, with Jones keeping up with his stride. 'How many languages do you speak?'

Jones smiled. 'Enough, usually.'

Viv and Mac stayed back and watched as they entered the stair.

'Is he on the ground floor?'

Mac nodded. 'Yes. At the back.'

'Any way out?'

'Yes. Into a courtyard that's shared with properties on London Street and Dublin Street.'

'So why aren't officers posted on those streets?'

He stared at her. 'Because he's still in the building.' He walked over to one of the cars sitting at the kerb and spoke to the driver through the open window. 'Make sure that all streets adjacent are covered.'

He turned back to Viv. 'Satisfied?'

'It's so basic that people forget. If it's him he had the balls to slip out of Fettes.' Viv shuffled her feet on the cobbled road. 'There's nothing for me to do here. I'll take a stroll and come back in . . .' she checked her watch, 'twenty minutes?'

Mac sighed, 'Is there any point in me objecting?'

'No siree.'

Viv wandered back down Broughton Street and along London Street. Have lock picks will enter. She slipped down the steps to Archie's flat and knocked on the door. The sound echoed down the hallway. She went back up the steps and checked the street. Only a couple coming from Drummond Place on the opposite side – nothing to worry about. She returned and began picking. It took a few minutes before she heard the reassuring click she needed, then she was inside. No matter how many times people were warned about the insufficiency of Yale locks they were too lazy to have them changed. By Viv's standards it was almost their fault if they were broken into.

She was assaulted by stale air that had had no place to escape to. The wooden floor in the hall was old oak, its varnish worn at the thresholds. She pushed open a door at the far end and entered the bathroom, small and windowless with all essentials present. It smelled of mould. The greenish black edge on the bottom of the shower curtain was the probable culprit. A mirrored cupboard above the sink was stuffed with items. Bottles and tubs of different antiseptics, bandages, boxes of plasters in all sizes, boxes of Neurofen, scissors, an eyebath, razors, Tylenol painkillers – interesting since they were not available in the UK. An out-of-date pack of Prozac prescribed to Archie, a large tube of KY, half full, and most incongruously a packet of tan coloured tights. Such a significant cache of first aid struck Viv as odd. Why so much stuff to take care of minor ailments?

The next room, painted a warm oriental red, had been a sitting room but all that remained was an old television cable, a typical Scottish 'press' with shelves and a yellowing newspaper. She checked the date. Not as old as it looked. She flicked through the pages, checking for anything that might have caused Archie to keep it. Nothing obvious, but she folded it and slipped it inside her jacket. There were a number of dents in the oatmeal coloured carpet. Signs of a couch, two chairs and slight indents where a coffee table must have been.

Her eyes adjusted to the gloom but she wondered how anyone could live without natural light. She flicked a light switch – nothing. In the next room a double, dark green blow-up mattress lay in the space where a bed should have been. Interesting considering the blow-up mattress in this very colour on Gordon's Amazon history. The bed had been slept in. Four pillows and a duvet all looked as if they could do with a wash. Two glasses sat on the floor, one at either side of the bed – could mean that he was too lazy to roll over to the other side for a drink, or he kept company. A condom packet sticking out from beneath the mattress confirmed the latter. A modern wooden kitchen chair was laden with tee shirts, jeans and boxers. A small gap in the shutters let in a sliver of daylight. How could a man in his early thirties with no dependents, from a 'good' family and with a decent job get himself into this state? She sidled through to the kitchen. Wooden wall and base units were there but no whites, only three gaps where a fridge, freezer and washing machine had once been. She decided she'd seen enough, but patted her jacket to check that the newspaper was secure. She'd look at it properly later. The place was a man cave, a place where Archie retreated to when he needed to hole up. But that didn't make sense, since there was no food and no way of storing it if he had it. Was it simply a safe place to have sex? And what was with all the first aid?

She stopped on the way back up Broughton Street, bought coffees, then joined Mac who was sitting in his car with the door open. 'Here.' She handed him a cup. 'How is she doing?'

He wrapped his hands round the cup and nodded his gratitude. 'The person who reported him thought he was foreign but he "speaks" English with an accent.'

'So who is he?'

'Not sure but it won't be long before he comes out. She's managed to talk him into coming to the station.'

Viv raised her eyebrows. 'So did you know that this was what she did?'

'Yes.'

'And you didn't think to tell me.'

'No. What would be the point? I genuinely didn't know that she and Sal were becoming an item.'

'So is that what they are now?'

He sighed. 'You'd have to ask them. All I know is she's good at what she does. And this might not be the last time you encounter her, so get used to it.'

Viv had already thought of this but didn't care to hear it. At least not from Mac. 'Cheers, buddy.'

'The work you're doing is so far removed from hers I wouldn't get wound up about it. But there are times, like now, that she comes in useful.'

Parker exited the building with a young man at his side. Jones was walking behind them. The young man wasn't cuffed or being held and he got into the car of his own accord. Viv recognised him. He was the young guy who Archie had been with in the loos at Copa Cabana.

She was conscious that Mac would have to know, but wondered if she could invent a scenario that wouldn't give Archie's secret away.

Mac caught her look of recognition. 'You know him?'

'Eh, no. No, I don't, but I have seen him. I saw him on Leith Walk a few nights ago. He was coming out of a bar.'

Mac shook his head. 'D'you think my head zips up the back? I can see you making this up as you go along. But if you are keeping something back there must be a reason. So just when you're ready, Viv.'

She hesitated. 'There's nothing more to tell. I saw him leaving a bar on Leith Walk.'

'And the bar would be?'

She hesitated again. 'Copa Cabana.'

'You still hanging out there?'

An accusation? 'Yes! And what of it?'

He put his hands up. 'Keep your shirt on. What night was it? Was he with someone?'

'He was alone but in a hurry. He looked distressed.'

'Now that wasn't too difficult, was it? Leverage, Viv, that's all we need. A bit of leverage.'

Parker approached them. 'Apparently he's not foreign – speaks something called,' he checked his note pad, '"The Doric".'

Viv laughed. 'For God's sake. Who called this in? The Doric is one of our own dialects. Someone thought he was what?'

'Polish.' Parker smiled.

'So did you really need a mediator who speaks five languages to talk someone from Aberdeenshire out of his flat? Mad or what?'

Mac replied. 'Too late now. All done.'

Viv got into Mac's car. When the engine turned over he hit play on the CD.

She heard a few beats then he switched it off. Viv, intrigued, put it back on. The most beautiful Latin chanting filled the car. She looked at him. 'You've got secrets.'

'Once an altar boy, always an altar boy.'

Religion played such a small part in her adult life that she'd forgotten that as children they'd both been indoctrinated in different ways: Mac to mass three or four times a week, and she to the Band of Hope once a week. At least all she'd had to do was sing. Mac and his sisters would have had to kneel a lot. The music made the hairs on the back of her neck stand on end. There was something hypnotic about pure voices repeating phrases in a dead language. 'What is this?'

'Taizé. It calms me down.'

It was calming her down, but he stretched over and turned it off, leaving the crackling ghosts of the police radio emerging from a mist of insufficient band waves.

They followed Parker back to Fettes, with Samantha Jones behind in her shiny BMW. Mediators like Jones were self-employed and often did their job in conjunction with another one. It was pretty rare to be called in by the courts, police or prisons to negotiate a situation, which if it escalated could begin a media frenzy. So far this was a good result, but it wouldn't give anyone full-time employment. What else did Jones do?

Viv and Mac sipped their coffees, with the police radio hissing in the background. Eventually Viv said, 'There wasn't much inside – a green blow-up mattress, a couple of glasses, a packet of condoms, no electricity.'

'So what do you make of that?'

'Well, the mattress is interesting because Gordon bought that very same one from Amazon in the last couple of months. And Archie had no Amazon history. Who do you know that doesn't have an Amazon history?'

He shrugged.

'Exactly. Everyone we know has one. So if they don't, why don't they?'

'First guess would be that he's making a political statement, or maybe his credit rating is poor.'

'I think it's the latter. I'm guessing Archie has a wee problem with addiction. I found receipts from Coral in his rucksack, and a stack of Irish lotto tickets. At the time it didn't strike me as a big deal, but now, from the way he's living, it looks as if he's got himself into a bit of bother.' She raised her voice, 'Moneylenders, maybe? Loan sharks aren't exactly gentlemanly if you're not paying up. Might lead a man to go into hiding, or do something stupid to save his skin. As for the Queen, I can't imagine him being involved. What would be his motivation?' Before he could answer she switched the radio off. 'Phew. That crackling drives me nuts.'

Mac reached over and switched it back on. 'It might well drive you nuts but it has to stay on. Now what about his motivation? What questions do we need to ask? What would make you take to gambling? And if he has got it that badly, how much debt is he in?'

A voice said from the radio, 'DCI Marconi, we haven't managed to contain news of the attack. Someone has leaked that there's been a citizen's arrest.'

Mac shook his head. 'You're going to be famous. If it has come across our wires then it will be all over the media.'

'Shit! But they don't know my name.'

'I wouldn't be too sure about that. Where were we with Archie?'

She nibbled the inside of her cheek. 'That flat was so sad. I don't get it. According to him he's a family guy. Goes every weekend to Sunday lunch with the whole team.'

Mac's eyebrows knitted. 'Well, that's odd but not . . .'

'You'd think the family would help him out.'

'Maybe they don't know. Or maybe they've helped him out too many times before. These are things we need to find out.'

'I wonder if I should take a look at the other members of his family? He has a brother who sounds like the golden boy. You know, the one who has followed the book of family expectations – gone into the family firm, wife, kids, that sort of thing. Archie on the other hand hasn't exactly toed the line. Do I do this with your permission or what?'

She waited as he thought this through. 'Any time you like, Mac.'

Her phone beeped and a text on the screen said that she had a meeting in forty minutes. 'You'll have to get moving. Something's come up.'

He glanced at her. 'Something that you're not going to tell me about?'

She didn't answer him, but picked at a nail. 'My car is on the back road. Could you drop me there?'

He pulled up next to the Rav and said, 'Be discreet.'

She shook her head. 'Have you ever known me to be otherwise?' She got out of Mac's car.

'Oh and by the way, you don't fancy joining me for a yoga class tonight?'

This was totally out of left field. 'Why on earth . . .'

'Because it's at Dance Base, a stone's throw . . .'

'I know where Dance Base is . . . I'll come and watch.'

'No spectators. Just bring baggy clothes, or tiny shorts and a crop top.' He raised his eyebrows.

'Fuck off. Now I know you're kidding. What time?'

'Seven. That's my girl.'

'If I was still inside that car you'd be for it.' She laughed, shook her head and pressed the fob to unlock her own car.

Chapter Twenty Three

She drove back through Stockbridge until she reached Dundas Street, from where it was a direct route south to the Mound then over and on to George IV Bridge. She parked the car in a resident's space at the top of Victoria Street then jogged the remaining couple of hundred metres back along to the museum on Chambers Street. She missed the fish pools that used to be in the great entrance hall. Her dad used to bring her here when she was a kid to throw pennies into the water. She'd make a wish while the poor fish were being poisoned. She made her way through several cavernous halls to the bird section, a small round room with stuffed seabirds from around the world. Simon was hovering, reading or pretending to read the detail card on one of the exhibits, his hands clasped behind his back.

She coughed. He didn't lift his head to acknowledge her.

'Did you know that the Egretta alba was hunted almost to extinction in the nineteenth century? Feathers for women's hats.'

This was an appalling fact and she was about to ask for details, but remembered her limited time. 'Thanks for the natural history lesson, but if we could just cut to the chase?'

He straightened and winced. She knew he would. Simon was as formal as anyone she'd ever met. The kind of dogmatic man who hated Americanisms, one of Ruddy's recruits whom she'd worked with before. He constantly checked that his shirt cuffs had the correct amount of exposure from his jacket sleeves. His accent was too English, which had led her to believe it probably wasn't his first language – and she'd been right. He wasn't a bad soul, but had seriously outdated ideas about women in the hierarchy, viz, women should be excluded from it entirely. Ruddy had explained otherwise, but Simon was still reluctant to trust her.

She caught a whiff of lavender aftershave. 'You do realise that that stuff leaves an evidence trail.' She flicked the end of her nose.

He clearly had no idea what she was on about and said, 'You'll have to enlighten me.'

'Aftershave. It's a no no on duty.'

He flushed and she suddenly realised that he must have worn it to impress someone.

'I'll remember that in future.'

She said, 'There are times when it's useful as part of a disguise.'

He flinched again. It wasn't her intention to make him quite so uncomfortable, but he'd obviously not read the manual about leaving as little evidence behind as possible, including scent.

He changed the subject. 'I've been sent to remind you to tread lightly on the Queen's attacker.'

'But that's ridiculous. I've no authority on that case . . . Oh, I see. Have I to find him?'

Simon gave an almost imperceptible nod.

'Was that a yes?'

He nodded properly this time.

'D'you know why I've been asked to do this?'

He looked at his feet.

'Okay . . . do I have to guess? Does he have diplomatic immunity? Is he a minor? Is he the son of someone important?'

At this he gave another slight nod.

'Well, this is fun, Si.' He also hated having his name shortened, she noted. 'I'm tasked with finding the young man and what then? Does . . . Control want to see him or do I hand him over?'

'We'll see him first.' He pulled at his elegant double cuffs again.

She smiled. At least her pathological showering habit was entirely private.

'Oh, and . . . goes without saying that it's to be asap.'

She smiled. 'When is it ever anything else?'

'And if you need help you've to call me in.'

'Why thank you, Sir Galahad. I'll bear that in mind. Is there anything else that I should know?'

'No. Only to tread lightly . . . Actually there is something. There's talk of involvement in a cell.'

This last, seemingly casual comment was the nub of their conversation. She raised her hand in a mock salute then retraced her steps through the atrium. Light flooded in from each of the numerous galleries above; she had to admire Victorian ingenuity.

On the walk back she thought about why the boy, or young man, might receive special treatment. Even if he was the son of someone important no one was above the law. Viv had a contact, invaluable when she needed political info. That was as good a place to start as any. She scrolled through her phone, found his number and sent him a text.

It should be easy to find info about the young attacker; everyone had a cyber footprint of sorts.

Chapter Twenty Four

By the end of the day Viv's shoulders were up round her ears. She'd failed to actually find the attacker, but she had narrowed down the options. Mac sent her a text saying he was waiting for her outside Dance Base.

She texted him back saying she had no intention of joining him. She rolled her shoulders back and forward. Then, realising that taking an hour out to do some serious stretching would do her good, she texted him again saying she was on her way.

As she jogged round the corner from the West Bow into the Grassmarket she bumped straight into Angus.

'Whoa! Viv! You in a hurry?'

'Angus! Sorry. My head was elsewhere. Are you okay?'

'Yeah, yeah. Just on my way to a class.'

She ran her hand through her hair. 'Not at Dance Base?'

He grinned. 'Yes, the very place. Is that where you're going?'

'As it happens I am. I'm meeting a colleague.'

Together they walked towards the studio.

Angus said, 'You're not going to pilates, are you?'

'No, yoga. Thought I'd give it a try.'

Mac was waiting in the doorway. 'Hi. Come on, we're late.'

Angus waved and said, 'Enjoy your class.' He hesitated. 'Fancy a bite to eat after it?'

She looked at Mac, then at Angus. 'Sure. That'd be great. See you where?'

They said in unison, 'Bella's.' And both laughed.

Mac looked from one to the other as if unsure of what he was witnessing. But as they walked into the gym he mimicked, 'Bella's, hee, hee, hee!'

Viv slapped him on the back, but was distracted by the number of people already limbering up on mats. By the end of the hour's session Viv thought she would die. She lay on the floor with no idea how she was still breathing. Sweat poured off her forehead and down the sides of her face. She thought she was fit, but being fit and being supple were different animals. Supple, she was not. Holding, then jumping between tricky postures was a combo that required both.

Mac looked equally worked up, sweating as much as her, but not quite as exhausted. 'You ready for your delicious dinner then?' he asked with a grin.

The thought of anything other than standing beneath a long shower was abhorrent to her. 'No way could I eat.' She managed this between gulps of air with her hands on her knees. They were both wiping themselves down with towels when Angus emerged from his class. No sweat.

His eyes widened when he caught sight of Viv leaning against the wall, swigging from a bottle of water that Mac had given her.

'No can do on dinner.' She said. 'I'm not up for anything unless it involves copious amounts of warm water.'

Angus grinned. 'I can sort that.'

She shook her head. 'Not a chance. I mean solo. I had no idea I was in for such torture.'

Mac stepped forward and put his hand out. 'Since the doc here isn't about to introduce us anytime soon, I'm Mac.'

Angus returned the handshake. 'Angus. Most people call me Gus. So are you a hairdresser as well?'

Viv sprayed out the mouthful of water that she was about to swallow.

Mac replied, 'Not exactly. But we do work together sometimes.'

Viv said, 'Look, maybe when I've cooled down we could grab a pizza. It's not as if we've miles to go to get food.'

Gus nodded enthusiastically. 'Sure. I can live with that. How about I see you at Gennaro's in about an hour?'

She looked at her watch. 'That sounds doable. You fancy pizza?' She glanced at Mac.

He automatically glanced at Gus. 'Eh, no. I've got stuff to do.'

Viv grabbed the towels that they'd been using and tossed them into a basket at the other end of the room. She moved as if she'd been in a rugby scrum – grumbling with every step.

Mac said, 'Come three times a week like me and you'll be as bendy as . . .'

'As what? Why do I need to be bendy at all?'

A look passed between Mac and Gus, who both raised their eyebrows.

She shook her head. 'WTF are you like? Come on, Gus, let's get going.' They waved to Mac as they turned back into the street.

She was so knackered that when Gus offered her his arm she took it. 'Yoga is really good for you, but if you'd like something a little gentler come to pilates. It's still a good work out but not as mad as what you've been through.'

'Oh, I enjoyed it. I'm just disappointed with my own fitness. I run and swim, so thought I had fitness covered. Clearly not. It'll give me something to think about.'

When they reached the bottom of his stair he said, 'You could just come up. I've been to Valvona's today.' Valvona and Crolla's was Edinburgh's premier Italian deli. Cost an arm and a leg but nothing ever went to waste. She hesitated. She didn't smell her best. Why did she think that she needed to smell nice? She flushed. 'Actually I really couldn't sit through food without a shower.'

'What if I told you I had a surprise up stairs?'

'I'd think you were a bit creepy . . .'

He looked genuinely injured.

'I mean if you have a surprise for me that would mean that you'd been meaning to bump into me and that this wasn't fortuitous but designed.'

'Oh God. I get it. No the surprise is . . .'

She put her hand up to his mouth to stop him. 'No, don't tell me. I'd like it to be a surprise.'

'Okay. Now I'm confused. Would you like to accompany me upstairs and I can show you what I mean?'

She sighed. 'I stink.'

He laughed. 'I love women who smell as they are supposed to.'

'Yeah. That would be fine if we'd been running for our lives through the bush but . . .'

It was his turn to put a hand up to her mouth. His rough fingertips unintentionally brushed her lips and she flinched.

'Sorry. I didn't mean to . . .'

Seeing how penitent he looked she said, 'Okay. Let's do this.'

She took her time on the stairs behind him so that he was well inside the flat by the time she reached the top. She heard water running and felt panic rising at the thought of being naked with anyone. He came towards her and led her into a room that was bigger than the sitting room that she'd seen on her previous visit. From floor to ceiling the room was covered in tiny mosaic tiles. Running water was coming from behind a curved tiled wall in the far corner of the room.

She couldn't believe that anyone would dedicate a room this size to washing. Her own bathroom was quarter of the size.

She had to raise her voice above the power of the water. 'D'you have a washing fetish?'

'Not exactly. I spent a bit of time in Turkey and thought they had a good perspective on bathing rituals. Here it's perfunctory.'

In her own regime, as frequent as it was, she didn't often languish. She could smell lavender and was reminded of her meeting with Simon at the museum. As the room filled with steam she felt her anxiety rising. She ought to be getting on with searching for the young man. Then Gus handed her a huge fluffy towel, the kind you only get in a hotel at someone else's expense.

Then to her surprise he backed out of the door and said, 'Enjoy! I'll get food together.'

She liked his style even if it was hedonistic. She told herself off for allowing the Presbyterian demons to spoil the moment. Then she stripped off and stood beneath the most amazing rain shower with lights above that changed colour as the power came and went. And the water was definitely perfumed. There must be some sort of filter in the giant showerhead. When she was

ready to get out she peered round the edge of the curved wall just in case he
had thought of joining her. He hadn't. Was she disappointed? No, but he was
gaining Brownie points by the second. She lifted a towelling gown hanging
on the back of the door, held it to her nose and caught notes of lemon –
shaving soap or cologne. She rubbed her hair then slipped into the gown. He
was nowhere to be found in the rooms on that floor. Treading carefully she
made her way into the kitchen. There were letter magnets on the fridge
arranged into a question. Odd. The words, "does she know?". Her belly
tightened. Who was "she"? A newspaper lying on the worktop was open at an
article about the Queen's visit. Why wouldn't he be interested in the news?
She closed her eyes, calmed her breath then took the narrow stairs to find him
in the gazebo. Sunlight bounced off a crystal hanging on a thread in one of
the windows, casting a rainbow over a tray with all sorts of delicious goodies
on it. It made the small space enchanting.

'Well, that was amazing. You must have really loved Turkey to go to so
much effort.'

'I like DIY.'

'What? You did all that yourself?'

He nodded. 'I took my time. But when you're a writer there are huge
swathes of time when you're waiting to hear from editors or readers. So I like
to keep occupied by doing stuff like that.'

'Well the next time you need a wee project just nip over to the West Bow.'

He raised his eyebrows and she flushed.

'Here, take a seat.'

'I hope you don't mind my stealing your gown.'

'Not at all. Makes you look more approachable.'

Surprised, she said, 'Do I come across as unapproachable?'

He laughed. 'Well it's not so much that. It's your forty-metre intimacy
zone. Look, but don't touch.'

She was more shocked. 'God. Do I really give that impression?'

He handed her a plate. 'Come on, help yourself.'

He had slices of sourdough bread on a board. Small colourful ceramic
bowls containing olives and tiny sweet chillies stuffed with goat's cheese. A

platter decorated with a dark blue and gold middle-eastern pattern held a selection of Parma ham, prosciutto and cheeses.

She hesitated, still unsettled by the idea that she was unapproachable. She knew men that she wouldn't let within a five-mile radius never mind forty metres, but hoped Gus wasn't one of them. That her defences had shot up with the mention of Sal was understandable to her but perhaps not to him.

Leisurely he put bread and a few olives on his own plate. 'I seem to offend you easily and my intention couldn't be further from that.'

She stared at him. Tall, tanned and rugged was what she saw, but she sensed that he was another of those swans, paddling like fury to maintain his calm façade. Gently she lifted a slice of bread and to her utter dismay felt herself welling up. He was such a gentleman in the literal sense of the word. He'd touched a nerve. She swallowed and tried to look anywhere but at him. He put his plate down and turned her head up to him. A tear dared to escape and she batted it into oblivion.

'I've no idea what's going on.'

She said, 'I think you've hit something raw with that unapproachable thing. I'd be sorry if you saw me like that.' When she turned to look at him his eyes were also full.

'Oh, my God. I'm so sorry. What have I said.' It wasn't a question.

He rubbed his hands over his face then laughed. 'What the heck's going on?'

She edged closer to him and wiped his face with the back of her hand. 'What a pair we are. That was such a lovely thing you did.'

His brows knitted.

'The shower. It was so unexpected.'

He shook his head. 'It's been a while since I've . . .'

She sat back in her chair and let go of a long breath. 'Let's start again. How about you tell me about yourself.'

He copied her, breathing slowly. 'Okay. I will if you will.'

'Deal.'

'I've only been writing for civvies for about seven years. Before that I was in the army.'

This made sense of the stuff that she'd found online.

'I spent quite a bit of time in the Stans and in Turkey, as you've already gathered.' He gestured towards his wet room. 'After that I needed time to, how shall I put it, heal, recover? Doesn't really cover it. I have difficulty sleeping. Fixing up the bathroom, especially those tiny mosaics, was a good way to keep me occupied in the middle of the night. Tiling is a silent occupation.'

She tucked her bare feet beneath her and nibbled on her bread. She was tempted to get a bottle of red wine sitting on an old blanket-box behind his chair but she didn't want to stop his flow.

'I've had treatment. I mean I've seen people, experts who helped as much as they could. But I find keeping busy with things that require complete concentration works best. How about you?'

'I've had more therapy than you could shake a stick at and I'm still crazier than a bag of ferrets.'

They laughed. He lifted his plate. 'That's good to know. I'd like to free some of those ferrets.'

'Be careful what you wish for . . . Sadly I'm the only one who can set them free.'

'Fair enough.' He nodded his understanding.

She didn't abdicate her own responsibilities. She didn't expect anyone else to sort her. At times this was admirable, but to allow someone to help occasionally was something to aspire to. He'd already pierced through a barrier with the shower routine. 'What made you offer me a shower? I mean you have to admit it's a bit of a weird thing to do.'

A worried look crossed his face.

'Nice weird,' she continued.

He suddenly remembered the wine. 'Shit! Wine. I'm not a huge drinker and I forget.' He poured, they chinked glasses and he returned to his seat. 'Apropos the shower, I suppose it's that business of doing for others as you'd have done unto yourself.'

'So you'd like someone to run you a hot shower . . .'

'Well that or . . . oh I don't know. If someone did I imagine I'd get worried.'

'Worried about what?'

'Well, that they'd want to be intimate.'

This was interesting, since intimacy had certainly crossed her mind. 'So, does that mean that you don't do intimacy or . . .?'

'Oh God, yes. It's just that since I can't sleep I haven't been able to live with anyone.' He stared at her as if weighing up whether or not to continue. 'I scream occasionally.'

'PTSD?'

'Yes. Seems to be a coverall.'

She shifted in her seat.

'Are you getting cold out here?'

'No. Well, yes. A wee bit. It's just my feet.'

He hurried inside and returned with a pair of woolly socks. He knelt on the floor. She unwrapped her legs. He held her foot in his warm hand. 'You are freezing.' He pulled on the socks one at a time. Then returned to his seat. If tension could be sliced, Sabatier were in business. The heat rose by more than a few degrees. He dipped his bread into the dish with olives in it. 'There's balsamic at the bottom. Dig in.'

She did as he suggested and for the next ten minutes they ate and admired the food. Then out of nowhere he pushed the table forward and put a cushion from his chair onto the floor. He didn't ask but she followed suit. So there they were both on the floor without chair arms protecting their personal fortresses. He topped up her glass and they drank in silence.

She laid her glass on the floor and in a move more assured than she felt she straddled him. Then she placed the palm of her hand on his heart and stared straight into his eyes. 'Is this okay?'

His eyes avoided her, flitting right and left. She drew his head into her.

He whispered, 'What a dork I am.' He cleared his throat. 'By the way, I haven't been this nervous before. There must be something in the water.' He kissed her neck. Then gently worked his way up until he found her mouth. He was tentative. In fact, were it not for his stubbly jaw, she might have imagined she was being kissed by a woman. She kissed him back. Tender at first but building. Then, breathless, she pulled back.

He looked shocked. 'What is it? Are you okay?'

'I was just checking that you were okay.' They laughed.

'I can see how this is going to work.'

He pushed her hair back from her eyes. She pulled his hand to her mouth and kissed his fingertips. He closed his eyes. She studied the creases and contours of his face, the tiny white fissures where he'd been squinting in the sun, his eyebrows bleached blonde on the surface, a strong chin with full lips. She bent forward and kissed them. Then she leaned back, took both of his hands in hers and held them. She smiled, got to her feet and said, 'Wait here.'

She slipped downstairs to the bathroom. She ran the hot bath tap and the room filled with steam. Once the temperature was right she climbed back up to the roof terrace where he was still sitting on the floor sipping his wine. 'Come with me.'

He raised his eyebrows but followed her downstairs. He laughed when she led him into the bathroom.

'I couldn't find any bubbles.'

'They're next door.' He pointed to the wall. He pressed a panel and a door that she would never have known was there clicked open. Three steep narrow steps led down to his bedroom. The flat was like a Tardis.

He returned with a small bottle of shower gel. 'This should do.' He handed it to her.

She ran the tap again, pouring the mixture into the flow. Then turned to him and rubbed her hands up and down his arms before gently undoing his shirt buttons then unzipping his jeans. After that awkward moment of him unsteadily kicking off the jeans, he stood in his boxers. She held him, running her hands up and down his taut back. She wondered if he was this tense because of his vulnerability or his pilates. She pulled back. 'Right, in you go.' She returned to the gazebo. She piled the food, wine and glasses onto a tray and brought it down to the sitting room. She knocked lightly on the bathroom door and entered.

He was lying with a halo of bubbles round his head. 'This is so good. It's a pity not to share it.'

She let the gown drop to the floor and stepped in behind him, wrapping her legs round his waist. Brushing her lips against his ear she whispered, 'Don't suppose we can have the power on?'

'Not supposed to be a good idea when there are bubbles in the water. But I've never tried it.' He pressed a button on the rim and jets kicked in. The bubbles expanded and expanded until they could hardly see the other side of the tub.

She squealed, 'Oh, my God. It's going to fill the room.'

They laughed as he tried to find the switch to stop the jets. Eventually he found it and silence resumed.

A real sponge and a loofah sat on a shelf behind the tub. She reached for the sponge, soaked it and poured water over his head and back. She'd not had a bath with anyone for ages and was amazed that they'd made it this far.

He said, 'What had you planned for tonight?'

This punctured her reverie, since she was supposed to be finding 'Houdini'. 'I'm supposed to be working. In fact.' She drew herself up and reached for the towel she'd used earlier.

'Oh shit! I shouldn't have asked. You surely don't have to work. Can't it wait?'

She turned and seeing the disappointment on his face kneeled on the step of the tub and wiped hair off his forehead. She kissed him on the mouth. 'I'm not going far.'

'But I don't want you to go anywhere. I want you to stay right here.' He pointed to the tub.

He made to get out but she laid a hand on his shoulder. 'Stay. It's a waste to get out so soon. How about we make a plan?'

The relief on his face was sweet. 'Okay. Dinner proper . . . or actually I'm having a few people round on the last night of the Festival for the fireworks. Would you come to that?'

'Let's see how dinner goes before you risk introducing me to your friends.'

He nodded. 'Sure. Tomorrow?'

'Sounds perfect.'

He bit on his lip and stared at her as she pulled on the jogging pants and tee shirt she'd left in a heap on the floor. She scrunched her underwear into a ball, hoping he wouldn't notice.

She kissed him, then left, skipping downstairs like a young Giselle as yet unaware of any danger, until she recalled the magnets.

Chapter Twenty Five

Being in his flat was like being in a personal spa, so hitting the busy street was a reality check. And with that she reminded herself of how easily her hormones could get the better of her.

Back in her own flat she settled at her desk waiting for her laptop to boot up. The name the young attacker had given to the police was Roderick Howarth. She thought if he'd made that up it wasn't very creative. He could at least have gone for Roger Rabbit or something. Roderick Howarth sounded real. She Googled it and found a few Facebook entries and eventually one story not on Roderick's own page, but by following a number of tags to other people's pages. Many a trail led to nothing of consequence, but this one tweaked a memory of a news story about a Roderick Howarth, the son of an MSP. Roderick had been caught swigging vodka in the kitchen at Bute House, the home of the First Minister for Scotland. The First Minister's son's school-leaving party had got out of hand – she'd found some lousy, jumpy footage on YouTube. Technology, you've got to love it. She rubbed her hands together. Suddenly life was more interesting.

She emailed Mac, hoping he'd be back in the office, and asked him to forward the CCTV footage with the attacker being brought into and leaving Fettes, and anything they had from Cockburn Street. There was bound to be a camera there, but was it even working?

He responded almost immediately. 'Dinner not a success, then?' He had attached three different files and a huge laughing emoticon.

She didn't rise to his jibe about dinner, but played the footage over and over. A person's gait was like their DNA, peculiar to them. If you tried to change your walk, it was obvious. The time frame that Mac had sent from the Cockburn Street coverage didn't go back far enough. Roderick must have got to the High Street somehow, and that was what she should be looking at. She emailed him again with another request.

He replied by ringing her mobile, 'I've already been through the footage. We have him wandering up the High Street from the Canongate with about fifteen minutes to spare before the Queen exited the High Kirk. What's on your mind?'

'What else have we got from earlier than that? Just wondered if we could follow him backwards. Find out where his journey started.'

'We have an address for him in . . . ' She heard him flicking paper over. 'Royal Terrace. A basement.'

'What is it with guys who want to live underground? Troglodytes! I don't know how they survive without daylight.'

'Not everyone has the luxury of . . .'

She interrupted him. 'Yeah, yeah. I get it. I was just thinking out loud. Could you send me anything else you've got?'

'We're on it, Viv. You don't have to . . .'

She interrupted him again. 'You know me. I'm a nosey sod. Humour me.'

He sighed. 'How come you're not with lover boy?'

'Too conscientious.'

'I guess that's a "mind your own business" answer?'

'You're a good guesser. Send me the stuff if you get a minute.'

Mac was super-efficient and another email arrived within fifteen minutes. On that footage she managed to trace Roderick exiting a café near the old Tolbooth. The quality of the film was poor but something made her continue to watch the café door. Two minutes after Roderick's exit, a man she'd swear was Archie, his build and his funny little limp, wearing a hoodie, exited and followed Roderick up the Royal Mile. What were they up to? Archie turned left onto the North Bridge. She needed more CCTV footage from there. She was pushing her luck but risked it and sent another email to Mac. This time there was no reply so she used other means to find the footage, but the bootleg was worse quality than the last one. As she'd anticipated, Archie turned into Chambers Street and made his way to George IV Bridge. She had to work pretty hard to get access to the next section of footage but she caught up with him at the entrance to Ondine, chewing his nails. Not a good look. He didn't stay there for long. He sloped up to the High Street, and this is where she got really interested, because she saw herself in a frame crossing Bank Street and standing beside the statue of David Hume while Archie, who had failed to notice her, loitered outside the Woollen Mill, which was less than thirty feet behind her. How could he have missed her?

She went back to the original footage to see the view from the east. Frustrated by the poor quality, she screwed up her eyes and drew closer to the screen until she could make him out. Still chewing his nails; not exactly a picture of confidence. But standing a few feet behind Archie was a man that she had also seen recently. She sat forward and rubbed her palms down her trousers. What the hell was he doing there? She zoomed in on his face. Was she seeing things? Was it actually him? 'Shit!' She hacked back into the dating site where she'd seen him but couldn't find his record. She tried Frances' emails again. Bingo. She needed details of times and places where they'd met to build his profile, and she needed access to more CCTV footage. She rang Mac but his mobile went to voice mail. She emailed him instead. He didn't respond. She twiddled a pen on her desk then chewed the end of it, trying to decide how urgent this new info was. There was no way this man's appearance at the scene was a coincidence. She had a number for Ruddy but it was only to be used 'if-and-when'. Was this an, 'if-and-when' time? She tried Mac's mobile again. Still voice mail. His landline was a last resort.

He picked up, out of breath. 'Marconi!' he barked.

'I think I've found something. But I need more CCTV coverage.'

'Christ, Viv, I'm already pushing my luck giving you access to what you've got.'

'You want results? Get me more CCTV.'

'What exactly have you found?'

'I tracked Archie through the footage up the Canongate, North Bridge, back along George IV Bridge to the Lawnmarket. But there's another guy worth checking out – he's standing a few feet behind Archie. He's dating Frances. He was the mystery man that she wouldn't tell us about in case we knew him. Well, I don't know him, but it seems odd to me that he'd turn up in this video.

'Got it. I'll have to go back into the office to view this. Give me twenty minutes. In fact why don't you join me? It would be easier than me sending huge files through to you.'

She guessed that what he meant was that he'd get his balls chewed off if anyone found out he'd passed them onto her and he didn't want to risk any more. 'Okay. I might take a bit longer than twenty minutes. See you as soon as I can.'

Still stiff after the yoga, she thought the only way to loosen up was to keep moving. She pulled on her trainers and clipped on a bum-bag containing her essentials. Once on the West Bow she decided to take a detour. From the Royal Mile she turned left onto the North Bridge. It took this far to find her rhythm but once she had she could have continued for miles. At the junction with Princes Street she ran down to the roundabout at Picardy Place then down Broughton Street and along London Street.

She stopped and leaned against the railings above Archie's flat. A thin shaft of light peeked out between the shutters. She wiped her face on her tee shirt. Should she or shouldn't she? Stupid to even ask the question. She descended the steps and knocked on the door. Footsteps padded up the hall and the door swung back. Roderick stood wide-eyed and tried to slam the door. She was quick and jammed her foot in the threshold.

He said, 'I'm not letting you in.'

'Of course not,' she said as she forced the door open and pushed past him into the hall.

'You can't do this,' he said, as he staggered back against the wall.

Since she knew the layout of the flat she went directly to the sitting room. 'Offer me a seat.'

He snorted. 'Who the hell are you? And what are you doing pushing your way in?'

Before she could answer there was noise down the hall.

'What's g . . .?' Archie entered, wearing the same hoodie as Roderick.

She smirked. 'Hello. I thought I'd drop by.'

Archie shook his head. 'But how did you get in?'

'Easy.' She glanced towards the door.

Archie turned to see Roderick standing with his hands in the pockets of his jeans, who said sulkily, 'She was persuasive.'

Archie looked at Viv. 'So what do you want?'

'I've no idea, but first I'd like to hear your side of things.'

He stared at her. 'What things, what do you mean?'

'I mean what part have you played in the whole charade?'

Archie clenched and unclenched his fists. 'I don't have anything to tell.' He stepped into her space. 'What charade?'

She wasn't in the slightest intimidated but said, 'Don't come any closer. You already know that I'm fitter than you. And I don't think Roderick here is keen to get anymore GBH on his record than he already has. Let's start with whose idea it was to attack the Queen.'

Roderick and Archie looked from one to the other, the shock on their faces like a comedy duo.

Archie stuttered, 'No way. No way did we attack the Queen. We attacked my dad . . . shit. Shit!' He ran his hands roughly through his hair, leaving it standing at odd angles to his head. 'Oh, my God. It wasn't like that.' Beads of sweat stood proud on his forehead. He swiped them with the back of his hand. 'My father is an Archer. We, I just wanted to humiliate him. He's done it to me often enough. I thought it would pay him back.'

'So Roderick pushed him over?

'No. It went wrong. I told Rod that my dad would be in the right hand flank third from the front as they were coming out of the High Kirk. They all have their positions, but for some reason on that day Major General Cornwallis had swapped positions with my dad. Roderick wasn't to know – he'd only ever seen a photograph and it wasn't a recent one.'

'I don't need to point out how this looks, given the other stuff.'

'What other stuff?'

Viv shook her head. Was he really this naive or was he taking the piss?

'The stuff I found on your computer, not to mention that you're harbouring a criminal.'

He looked genuinely confused. 'I've no idea what you're on about.' Ignoring the bit about the criminal. 'There's nothing on my computer that shouldn't be there.'

She raised her eyebrows then glanced at Roderick, who looked away.

Archie noticed the exchange. 'Rod, what's on my computer that shouldn't be there?'

Both Viv and Archie stared at him in expectation. He didn't speak. He stared at his foot as he scuffed it over the carpet. 'Would you believe me if I said I didn't know?'

Archie replied, 'If you didn't know then you didn't know. But someone does. So if not you . . .? It would have to be someone with access to the cyber hub.'

He turned to Viv who said, 'I agree. Who among your work buddies would want to set you up?'

Archie rubbed his hands over his face. 'None of them. I mean why would they? I haven't hurt any of them . . .' A questioning look flitted across his face.

'What? What did you just think of then?'

Archie shook his head. 'Nothing. It was nothing.'

'No, it wasn't nothing, otherwise you wouldn't have looked the way you did. Now what crossed your mind?'

'I'm embarrassed to say.'

Viv let go of a sigh. 'Come on, Archie. Don't be shy.'

'Well, Frances asked me to go out with her.' He laughed. 'There's no way that she'd do anything nasty just because I wouldn't go on a date with her. Anyway it was ages ago.'

Viv thought she wouldn't be too sure about that and instinctively rubbed her neck where the spike of the toothpick had pricked her carotid artery. 'How long ago?'

'A couple of months back.'

Viv's mind slipped into overdrive. If Frances had had a thing for Archie, it hadn't surfaced on the weekend away. She'd ignored him, even been rude to him. Was there malice in their lack of communication? Frances had been off her game after Viv rescued her from the sea. Why hadn't Archie gone in to help her? Or Gordon for that matter?

'D'you think she's ever asked Gordon out?'

'How would I know? She's desperate but not that desperate.' He snorted. 'I really don't believe she'd put my career at risk.'

Viv raised her eyebrows. 'No, you've done that all by yourself. Have you any idea how much . . . oh never mind. If you don't know then you shouldn't be in the job. You're supposed to be hyper aware of "National Security". She made the sign of parenthesis. 'Why would you do such a stupid thing?'

He looked sheepish. 'It was a bet.'

Suddenly the grubby carpet was the most interesting thing in the room to both Archie and Roderick.

Archie continued. 'It was only a way for me to get back at him, my dad. I'm so sick of being maligned. Everything, and I mean everything, I do is wrong. I just thought it wouldn't do him any harm to be humiliated for a change. He thinks he's so perfect. Every one around him has to live up to his expectations. I'm sick of it. I know it sounds juvenile but . . .'

He sounded convincing. Viv had known families who had driven their children to suicide because of their draconian attitudes to sexuality, using humiliation as a way of trying to control them. But Archie had more that he wanted to hide than his sexuality: his gambling wasn't anything to be proud of.

Archie stood up to his full height and ostentatiously cracked his knuckles. 'I'm sure you don't have to tell Marconi any of this.'

'I'm not working for Marconi.'

At first he seemed to relax, but realising that if she wasn't working for Marconi it must be someone higher up the ladder, he tensed.

She inclined her head in confirmation.

'I'm sure you could find a way . . . It was all a big ruse to get back at my family . . . nothing to do with the Queen.'

'Even if I believed that, I've got to report . . .'

Archie and Roderick flashed a look between them.

'Don't even think about making this any worse for yourselves that you already have. I mean at the moment you're probably looking at getting your knuckles rapped.' She looked from one to the other again, sensing that they were weighing up their next move. She took a step towards the door. Roderick moved forward.

She smiled, 'You already know that I'm capable of taking you down.' She was bluffing because although she could manage them one at a time, two at once would be a test. Archie sighed. But she saw Roderick tense and his weight shift onto the balls of his feet. He sprang at her but she raised her knee and caught him full in the groin. He crumpled as he hit the carpet. Archie got down to his knees and glared up at Viv as if it was her fault.

She shook her head. 'What? You think I'd let him take me down without protecting myself? Spare me. He'll not die.'

Roderick rolled over onto his side, gasping for air.

Archie said, 'You didn't need to hurt him so badly.'

She shook her head again. 'You're mad. You think I'm doing this for kicks? The pair of you should think seriously about handing yourself in. Explain exactly what you've told me and I genuinely think you'll get off with a warning.'

'Hah! You think?'

She paused. 'I suppose springing a prisoner from the cells will have to come with more than a slap on the wrists. You'll probably lose your job . . . and who knows what.'

Archie lifted Roderick's head and cradled it in his arms. It was so touching that Viv had to turn her back. The picture she had built up of Archie now seemed way off the mark. His reaction to Roderick writhing in pain was the reaction of a man in love. No wonder he was making such stupid decisions. Love was as close to madness as most people got, but could Archie be so naive?

***

She jogged from London Road to Fettes, then sprinted the last couple of hundred metres to the front steps where she caught her breath, bowed over with her hands on her knees. The car park was pretty quiet but she spotted Mac's immaculate Audi and smiled at how much care he took over his cars. Her Rav went through a carwash once a month if it was lucky, but the interior was like an office without the benefit of domestic staff. She headed straight to reception. The person behind the desk wasn't familiar so she gave her name and asked for DCI Marconi. She'd barely sidled over to the window to shake out her limbs a bit more when Mac tapped her arm and gestured with his head to follow him.

'Are you sure you need to do this?'

'No. I've just got something tickling at the back of my mind. You know a bit like an earworm only without the benefit of music.'

Mac shook his head. 'I guess. Right over here.' He pulled another chair over to his side of the desk and pointed to his own oversized leather seat. 'You take that since you seem to know where you want to navigate. Talk me through it as you go.'

She glared at him. 'You sure? I thought the whole point in having me snoop around was because you guys want to keep your noses squeaky clean.'

'How much stuff have you found that we would have to have a warrant for?'

She smiled and raised her eyebrows. 'Really?'

'Oh, just get on with it.'

She tapped on the keys, scrolling through CCTV footage that was definitely clearer than any she'd managed to retrieve. 'Wow. What a relief to see images that I can actually make out.'

He raised his hand. 'You can definitely keep that stuff to yourself.'

Mac's hands looked as if they belonged to a concert pianist and not the large super-fit cop sitting beside her. When she reached the section of film with Martin Martin standing behind her on the Royal Mile she was convinced she could see something inside his jacket which, if Mac would have the film enhanced, could turn out to be a weapon.

'Look here.' She pointed to Martin. 'There's no way he isn't carrying. And he's as nervous as . . .'

Mac leaned over and she caught a hint of his lemony smell. She sat back so that he could get closer to the screen. 'I can see that he has something. But it's a leap from . . . he might have sandwiches wrapped in tinfoil.'

She shook her head. 'Aye! Sure thing, Detective. You going to get that checked?'

He nodded. 'Sure thing, sarky.' He nudged her elbow. 'Right. What else do you need to see?' He wandered across his office to a coffee machine and gestured with a cup.

'No, thanks. I could kill a glass of water, though.'

Viv knew there was a water cooler at the end of his corridor, but more importantly, how long it would take him to get there and back. He glanced round the room as if checking that whatever was lying about was okay to leave where it was. He stepped out of the door and as soon as he did she took out her phone and photographed the first page of a file lying on his desk. She took a shot of the second page, and decided she was pushing her luck so tucked her phone back into her sock. She was scrolling through more footage when Mac returned with two plastic cups brimming with chilled water. She gulped the first one down then took her time with the next.

'I wonder . . . are you tracking Roderick's phone?'

He hesitated.

'Well, if you're not may I suggest . . .'

'Different laws apply. He's not . . .' Mac stopped and tapped his fingers on his lips. 'Hang on. I think I can make that happen.'

Viv shook her head. 'For fuck sake. Shouldn't that have been the first thing to do?'

'Watch it. We're not as incompetent as you think. We do, however, have to work within the law. Until we have a clear, unequivocal version of what happened outside St Giles' we couldn't make a charge of terrorism stick. But now and since his escape I think . . . well never mind what I think.'

She had no such concerns and could find her own way to track him now that she had photographs of his file, containing his phone number and address. She pushed the seat back from the desk and stretched her arms above her head. 'That yoga just about killed me.'

'And that would be exactly why you need it. I take it lover boy . . .'

'Don't even go there. He's not my lover boy and . . . never mind. I'm going home to a hot shower and a good night's sleep.'

He yawned. 'Me too. Want a lift?'

'Oh, that would be so good. I'm totally bushed.'

Chapter Twenty Six

Before hitting the hay for the night she slumped at her desk and groaned as she read an automated email reminder that she was meeting Josie, a friend from Paris, at the Book Festival the next morning. That had completely dropped off her radar. Should she reply? She didn't and went to bed.

By morning she was rested and emailed Josie back. 'See you at the signing tent at 11 am.'

This left her plenty of time for research. First up she posted a message on one of her hacking groups – she'd read a stream not so long ago discussing the ins and outs of tracking. While waiting for replies she made toast and coffee and listened to the news on the radio. The sun was streaming in through her sitting-room window. She licked the hot butter running down her chin and her fingers and mused at how tourists might be lulled into a false sense that Edinburgh was a sunshine capital. And, if the headlines were to be believed, the city was crimeless so long as the Festival was on. With her laptop and a cup of coffee she settled on the couch and revisited the Facebook pages she'd been to before. The police had not been diligent enough in removing all the information about the illicit party at Bute House. What she was accessing on social media sites was evidence that they hadn't followed the video trail to its conclusion and consequently she found a ton of stuff on Roderick and those he hung out with in cyberspace, including more video footage of the actual party.

She didn't recognise many of the faces but it wouldn't take long to pair them up with Face Book accounts if they'd been tagged. There was a theme emerging in the some of the posts that got her attention. One in particular, a group calling themselves 'The Neo-Jacobites', appeared to be extreme right-wing nationalists.

Their beliefs were further to the right of Genghis Khan's. Then she spotted it. The motif of a triangle with a thistle inside it and two swords crossed – she'd seen this before and didn't like the implication. The severed limbs in the photographs that Ruddy had given her both had this motif tattooed on them. And had Martin Martin's jacket not also had it on? She couldn't be absolutely sure. She shuddered. This was ugly. She checked the clock. Now this stuff would have to wait until later in the day.

By the time she'd dodged her way through the Grassmarket and along King's Stables Road she only had a couple of minutes to spare when she reached the pedestrian crossing that fed into Charlotte Square gardens. It was like walking through the door of the wardrobe into book Narnia. Viv felt immediately at home, knowing that everyone inside the perimeter fence was there for the same reason – to celebrate books and reading. Josie wasn't difficult to spot. Tall, broad, with her hair cut to a centimetre from her scalp and tinted cyclamen, she was a beacon. Viv tiptoed up behind her and tapped her shoulder. They hugged and hugged with Josie lifting Viv off the ground. Then, as if just remembering her, Josie introduced Viv to Suzanna, her new friend, who apart from the cyclamen tint, was a dead ringer for Josie.

Suzanna stuck out her hand. 'Good to meet you, Viv. I hear lots about you.'

'Oh dear. Never a good thing. Good to meet you as well. We should get going? Have you spotted which queue is ours?'

Josie pointed to a small group milling around outside a tent at the back. 'We're going in there. It's a workshop.'

'Okay. What does that mean?'

'It means that you're going to be confined with us for an hour and a half, Viv. There'll be a max of thirty people and we'll be discussing Samuel Beckett.' She grinned. 'You'll love it.'

Viv didn't know squat about Beckett and imagined that Josie was keen to go because since she'd moved to Paris all things from her home in Ireland had become exotic. It turned out to be a fabulous session, with one inevitable Edinburgh worthy who believed she knew more about the subject than the guy tutoring. Josie was less keen on hearing her views and Viv could see her becoming wound up by it. It was all part of the deal in Viv's view, although she did wonder what possessed someone to buy a ticket and come along with no intention of learning. After the session the three had lunch at Jamie's on George Street, where Josie spent the whole time shredding the poor interloper from the Book Fest. They parted trying to fit in another gig before Josie returned to Paris, but it wasn't likely given Viv's commitments.

On her way back to the West Bow Viv wandered through the National Gallery. Not in search of a Velasquez or Ramsay, but the first free loo. There were so many people with their necks cricked staring up at the walls she imagined everyone with a migraine by the end of the day. Eventually she found what she was looking for but had to join a snake of women with the same purpose. As with counting sheep on a sleepless night she'd learned a couple of visualisations to take her mind off peeing. But it was the same business as how not to think of an elephant. You had to think of one before you could discard the image. That's why when parents say things like, 'Don't put your finger in that socket', their toddler's finger reaches for the socket before the parent screams the next order. The image of lying on a beach in the Seychelles helped for a short time until a light wave broke on the shore, then she was in real trouble.

She rubbed her hands beneath the drier, cursing its design. Were they always fixed to the wall by men who never washed their hands after going to the loo? If they did they'd understand why the height of the drier matters. Too high and the water rushes down your wrists and forearms onto your cuffs, too low and water drips onto your new Louboutins. Not that Viv was a fan of anyone who'd made shoes that continued the tradition of foot binding. So with damp sleeves she returned to the gallery and sloped through to the back. As a child she'd visited here with the school. She recalled the sense of reverie, the silence. Her teacher's forefinger glued to her lips in a constant reminder of hush. It felt smaller now, but no less awesome. The notion of quietly contemplating art was a thing of the past. The galleries buzzed with conversation and guards loudly clearing their throats to prevent transgressive selfies. For Viv this was a local haunt, but today it was a tourist fest. She exited into a different kind of fest, where entertainers jostled for space to perform samples of their shows. Keeping audiences rapt was no easy job. Competition was cut-throat and the temptation to move from one act to another was overwhelming. Viv squeezed along the flagstone path leading to the Playfair Steps. Traders selling felt hats to silver jewellery beneath covered stalls took up more than half of the pavement. Once at the top of the steps she dodged over the road in front of a bus, the driver giving her a blast on his horn before she reached the other side. She waved, imagining how pissed off he must be, then continued to make her way towards the West Bow on the quickest route she could.

When she reached the Lawnmarket, the upper section of the Royal Mile, she took a right and stood in the exact position where Frances' beau had stood on the day of the attack. She glanced at the doorway to the Woollen Mill then up at the roofs. There was no way that the security guys who'd been up there wouldn't have been aware of Martin. She'd have to find a way of speaking to them, but how? She guessed they'd be wherever the Queen was. Where might they hang out when off duty? She knew a woman who'd know. She took out her phone and scrolled.

So much for a quiet night in. George IV Bridge was packed with posh coaches parked for the evening while their passengers sat, chilled to the bone, on the Castle esplanade watching the Military Tattoo. It was tricky to get from one end of the bridge to the other but she made it to Forrest Road without killing anyone. Sandy Bell's, a famous folksie pub that sold excellent beer, was within spitting distance of an MOD training hall. She now pushed vainly at the door. Then she tried again and it opened a few inches.

A man holding up his pint said, 'What's the password?'

She replied, 'John Brown's b . . .' but before she had finished the door swung open and half a dozen men whose body language wasn't without menace surrounded her. Using both palms she tried to push the one closest, close enough to smell his beery breath, but he was solid and didn't budge.

He said, 'Was that meant to be a joke?'

Two of the others jostled closer and she felt heat rising up her neck. Claustrophobia. 'Back off, guys. We're probably on the same team.'

One of them said. 'I doubt that.'

The others laughed. But not because it was funny. They stood in this formation for too long for comfort, with Viv sensing it was a test that she'd have to pass before she'd get to the next level. She locked eyes with the beery-breathed man and held the stare until his mouth showed a hint of a smile.

He stood back and said, 'What can we do for you?'

Viv said, 'I need help?'

They laughed in unison. Then one of them said, 'I'm sure we'd be up for that.'

Raucous laughter again.

Viv sighed. 'For fuck sake, this could be a matter of national security.' The words stuck in her throat. She almost gagged at the irony of using them for her own gain. No matter. It got their attention.

Beery breath said, 'How might that be of interest to you?'

'I work for the NTF.'

He raised his eyebrows and made a gesture to the others, and without further question they backed off and continued drinking. Three of them were on pints of orange juice. The other three looked as if they had the real thing, but given the seriousness of their duties she guessed it was probably non-alcoholic beer.

Viv glanced round the room and seeing no one that looked civilian guessed it had been taken over for military personnel.

He pointed to a seat at the back. They made their way through bulky bodies in tee shirts with graphics that strained to make sense over taut pecs and thick necks.

He said, 'This had better not be some kind of joke.' He nodded to the collection of guys they'd left behind. 'They're not keen on jokers.'

She launched in. 'The other day when Her Majesty was at the High Kirk there was a man standing in a doorway on the Royal Mile. I think he had something in mind. I could be wrong but from the footage . . .'

He held up his hand. 'You got any ID? Why would I speak to you about my job? If indeed . . .'

She didn't let him finish, but raked around in her pocket and showed him her NTF card. The photograph was poor but he nodded his acceptance. 'From the way he stood I think he was carrying.'

The guy snorted. 'We're not in some kind of US crime drama where the Marshal is a broad.' He faked an American accent.

Viv sighed a fuck-off sigh and shook her head, but continued. 'I think he didn't take action because he was beaten to it by the young guy running at the Archers' line-up.'

'You had a ringside seat by the sounds of it. Why?'

She didn't answer. 'I didn't see him on the day but have checked out the CCTV footage and I'm almost sure . . . '

He interrupted her. 'Well, that's where I become uninterested. See that "I'm almost sure"? That means no info from our side until you're absolutely sure.' He took a draw of his pint and Viv sensed she'd lost him. Still, at least she'd made contact.

She got up to leave.

He said, 'You got any contact details?'

She dug back into a pocket and retrieved a card with her email address on it and handed it to him. 'We're on the same side, for God's sake. Spare me the histrionics.'

Once back onto Forrest Road she ran her hands down the sides of her trousers. Then rolled her shoulders to avert the headache creeping up her neck. Must be testosterone overload. As she reached the end of the street she turned and looked back just in time to see someone step back into the doorway of Sandy Bell's. She rubbed her eyes. Tired. Was she imagining things? She continued down Candlemaker Row but stopped halfway and spun round. She wasn't imagining it, one of the heavies from the pub was following her. She should have expected nothing less.

He came straight up to her and stopped. One of the guys who'd been on orange juice.

'Been sent to watch over me?' Bravado, being the lesser part of valour.

To his credit he nodded. 'Only seeing you home. Hope it's not far.'

She gestured to the back of her building. 'Barely a stone's throw.' She pointed. 'See that top floor window.' They both stopped in the middle of the pavement.

He nodded.

'That's where I live. West Bow, top floor. Fraser on the buzzer. There, now does that save you the trouble?'

'Not really. I still have to see you home.'

She shrugged. No skin off her back.

Less than five minutes later they reached her door. She said, as she put her key in the lock, 'This is me then. Thanks for your company.' She closed the door behind her but stood for a few seconds and thought about what he would do. If she'd been told to follow someone home and had completed the task she'd retrace her steps. She opened the outside door again and looked right and left. He was propped against the wall to her left with one finger in his ear and the other hand holding his mobile phone. She closed the door and waited.

She texted Mac and asked him to send her more CCTV footage. If she could trace Frances' friend's journey to the Royal Mile it could help. But in the meantime she rooted around in the junk mail in her pigeon-hole. She had an idea and stuck her head back out of the door. No sign of her companion. She jogged back up to George IV Bridge, turned right towards Chambers Street. At the end of Chambers Street she made a right onto South Bridge. Up on the left she found that increasingly rare breed, an internet café.

Under a pseudonym she created an account for the dating agency that Frances used. Logged in and found Martin Martin's page. With a few more details she Googled him and eventually found a photograph of him with a group from the Royal Botanical Gardens, but not before being sidetracked by an earlier Martin Martin. An eighteenth-century tacksman whose tour of the Western Isles preceded Boswell and Johnston's. Fascinating, but it would have to wait. She printed off the photograph, then as an afterthought sent him a message. Enjoying how easy it was to adopt a disguise. Her next step, a trip to the Botanics, would have to wait 'til morning.

At home she checked to see if Mac had sent the CCTV footage. He had, along with a snippy message. 'I can guess what you're up to but I'd prefer you let me in on it.'

She replied, 'So far only following a hunch. Will get back to you when I've been through the lovely new footage you've lovingly sent me!' She could almost hear him shout obscenities at his screen on the other side of town.

The latest footage was jumpy and grainy. She swore in frustration at having to go back and forth, back and forth. 'Is this the best the digi age can come up with?' Eventually, through piecing one set of footage together with another, she managed to trace his route all the way back down the Royal Mile to where the road divided. He entered the screen from the Abbeymount side of the Palace. There was no way that she could ask Mac for even more footage so she'd have to find an alternative way.

By the time she headed to bed her eyes were so strained she could hardly see. It took a while to find sleep but when it came she was dead. From this unconsciousness she was sure she heard a doorbell ringing. Was it part of a dream? Her psyche having a laugh? It turned out to be reality and she almost exploded out of bed. Hearing Mac's voice through the entry system did nothing to smooth her ruffled state. She was tempted to tell him where to go, her finger paused over the release button.

'C'mon, Viv, you know you're going to in the end so you might as well press it now.'

He wasn't helping his cause. She shouted, 'Fuck off. It's the middle of the night.'

'Ah well, that depends on which continent you're on.'

'Did you hear me?'

'I heard you. Now let me in. I've got news.'

She pressed the button and strode back to her bedroom for an over-sized pullover.

He entered tentatively as if expecting her to throw something at him. If only she'd thought of it she would have.

'Coffee?' he asked.

She raised her eyebrows. 'Don't push your luck.'

They went into the sitting room, where Viv realised she had stuff on her desk that she didn't want him to see.

'We had a call from the Holyrood household. They've had an intruder. Only as far as the garden but still, game enough to get himself over the boundary wall, which is no mean feat.'

'Is that all? Surely that could have waited until morning. I need my beauty sleep.'

'Been burning the midnight oil?'

'No, I haven't. Just staring at a screen for too damn long. Did anyone see who it was? I mean did they get close enough to identify that it was male?'

'Yes. There are cameras all over the palace grounds. We'll find him. But what have you got? I know you well. There's no way you'd have given up a cyber chase halfway through. Spill.' He glanced at her desk.

She stepped proprietorially in front of it. 'Not a chance, buddy.'

'C'mon, what have you got to hide?'

She weighed up the pros and cons of telling him now rather than later. She pulled out the photograph of Frances' beau and handed it to him.

He screwed up his eyes. 'Is this the guy from the footage?'

She nodded. 'Sure is. His name's Martin Martin. He's Frances' new boyfriend. You know – the one she wouldn't tell us about.'

'How did you . . .?' He waved the question away. 'Was this on her computer?'

'No. I found it on . . . well, less said about that the better. I think he's used Frances as a way of getting details on the Queen's movements. If you think about it, her engagements for these couple of days were relatively last minute, only known by a few privileged souls and her inside team . . . You think the guy who broke into the garden at Holyrood knew HM was in residence? Does she sleep with the light on?' She sniggered at his disdainful expression. 'Just sayin', some people can't sleep without. And talking of sleep, are we done?'

'Not yet. Tell me exactly what you found in the cyber hub. You haven't given me any detail.' He tried to make eye contact with her.

She looked at her feet. 'I told you there wasn't much to find.' She glanced up. He wasn't stupid and ultimately she'd be safer if he knew what her plans were.

Her procrastination was obvious and he said, 'Well, what did you find that might be interesting? There's something you're not saying. Spit it out.'

'Apart from the fact that I'm sure Martin is the guy standing behind Archie on the CCTV footage. He has his hand . . . actually it'll be easier if I show you.' She took her laptop over to the ottoman and found the footage she wanted. 'There.' She pointed to the screen. Mac stepped closer then perched on the edge of the couch. She knelt beside him.

He zoomed in, which made the image even more grainy. 'I'll get someone to enhance this.'

'I think he's holding something inside his jacket. Look at his right hand.'

'We need to see more clearly. It's too poor to tell. He could be scratching an itch.'

'Sure.' She shook her head. 'I think I know what he does.' She edged in and found the dating website, and brought up his details. 'Seems to have trained in horticulture at the Botanics. I wonder if he was the guy in the Palace gardens?' Thinking out loud.

'We'll soon find out . . . Surely Frances knows the score?' He sighed, rubbed his elegant fingers over his face. 'Christ sake. She knows she . . .'

'What? That she shouldn't have a life? I found this.' She pointed to the photograph of the man with a group of colleagues from the Royal Botanical Garden. 'I thought I'd go and check them out. See if they know where he is now.'

'And when were you going to let me in on this little nugget?'

She shrugged. 'It might be a red herring. I'd have let you know when I found him.'

'This is serious, Viv.'

'Who's laughing?'

'What else have you been up to? And don't give me that look.'

'I've been and spoken to the marksmen who were on the roof.'

'For fuck sake! How did you find them?'

'I have my ways.' She grinned, but he wasn't buying it. 'Okay. You know that you're not the only person who asks me to do the odd job.'

He conceded but still looked peeved. 'You might keep me in the loop.'

'If you're meant to be in the loop then you'll be in the loop. It's not worth my telling you. Ditto if you give me work you wouldn't want me blabbing to anyone one else, especially not another branch of SIS.'

'Thank you, that's all I needed to know.'

She gave a little bow. 'Now can I get some sleep?'

He moved towards the door. 'You all right otherwise?'

'Never better.'

He batted her response into oblivion.

Chapter Twenty Seven

The following morning Viv had clients to visit, but had her sights set on checking out the Botanics later in the day. The sky was overcast, but so long as the rain stayed away the streets would still be heaving with tourists. With her usual slice of hot buttered toast and a cup of coffee she scanned her emails.

Angus had sent a reminder about his having friends round for drinks and the fireworks to mark the end of the Festival. She didn't really have an excuse not to go and was keen to see him again, although she wasn't sure about meeting his chums. She sent a brief reply, saying she'd do her best to get there. Good to keep her options open.

Edinburgh was a small place when it came to who knew whom. Rosie Hacket, Viv's first client, was a known gossip, a freelance graphic designer, with lots of work from the National Galleries' book department. However, her main occupation was networking and she never missed a single private view in town. Viv would be exhausted by the time she'd heard about her social exploits. Rosie had an Oxbridge radar. Everyone she'd met had 'double firsts' from Oxford or Cambridge or was sleeping with Prince Andrew. Access to such information made Viv nervous, since in the past she'd been blamed for passing on private information, which she hadn't, but it took a bit of convincing as to who the real source had been. Rosie lived in a lovely colony house off Pilrig. It was one of Edinburgh's hidden gems. Easy parking in a quiet street a stone's throw from the main artery of Leith Walk.

Rosie answered the door with a handset pinned to her ear. She gestured for Viv to come in as she continued her conversation. Viv was used to this. Rosie's inferiority complex made it easy for her to invent superiors. She said 'absolutely' so many times it made Viv giggle. Rosie might design beautiful book jackets but she didn't edit her speech.

Eventually she tucked the phone back onto its charger and held up two fingers. 'Two minutes. Promise it'll take me two minutes.' Off she bounded upstairs to have a shower, leaving Viv in the tiny kitchen to set up.

She was more than two minutes, but it gave Viv time to read the *Scotsman* lying on the worktop.

Rosie returned, rubbing her blonde hair to within an inch of its life.

Viv gestured to Rosie. 'You'd better leave me some.'

'Oh God, sorry. Habit.'

'What are we doing today?'

'Not much. It's going through a good phase. And I'm wearing it up more . . . out tonight though, so got to look glam.'

Viv raised her eyebrows. Rosie never looked anything else. Even now first thing in the morning she had on clothes that Viv might choose for a wedding. 'Anywhere nice?'

Rosie had already moved somewhere else in her head and looked quizzically at Viv as she sat down, and was wrapped in a cutting gown. 'Oh! Yes, there's a drinks party at the Parliament. Everyone's going. Since Her Maj is in town I think folks will attend, thinking she'll be there. But there's no way.' She tapped the side of her nose. 'Even if she is their closest neighbour.' She snorted. Then in a rare flourish of interest she said, 'You out tonight, Viv?'

Astonished ,Viv hesitated and her chance was lost.

Rosie continued, 'You know I've bought the most divine top from . . . oh, never mind. I'll show it to you when we're done. The First Minister will be there. I've not met her yet.' She said this as if at some time the whole population would get to meet Scotland's leader.

Viv said, 'I hear she's . . .'

Rosie interrupted, 'A pain in the arse.'

Viv sighed. 'Well, no actually . . . How's the book design world?' Better not to be drawn into that particular conversation. Alas, no luck.

'Actually, I've been approached to do the jacket of her biography. Not that I imagine she wrote it.'

Another subject Viv had to keep her lips firmly zipped about.

'If you could just bend your head forward slightly.' Scissors to the rescue.

'Apparently the Duke of Atholl will be there, though. Damn nerve. South African shop keeper.'

Rosie was vague about her own background, although it wasn't grand – she'd gone to Napier University, still regarded by the literati as a 'poly', and hated to talk about it. She never asked Viv anything about her time at Edinburgh University. Viv had heard that Rosie's dad was in insurance, but they'd never had that conversation either. As long as the ball was in Rosie's court the chat went swimmingly.

'You know the director is getting a divorce?'

Worried that she might unwittingly know who the 'director' was, Viv changed the subject. 'Any chance that you'll get to see the fireworks?'

'If the party goes on long enough we'll be able to see it from the roof. Doubtful, though. The forecast is for cloud.'

Viv took out her hairdryer and was about to plug it in.

'Oh, actually I think I'll put it up. So you won't have to use that.' She pointed at the dryer as if it was a weapon.

'Fair enough.' Viv twisted the damp hair up into a chignon and pulled out a few strands round the front. Rosie was pretty. Pale skin, pale blue eyes and a heart-shaped face, but there was something unattractive about her. Job done, Viv wandered back to the Rav, knowing it wasn't just the gossip that put people off Rosie.

What would life be without variety? Her next client, a pharmacist and musician, was as shy as Rosie was not. Viv parked in Thirlestane Lane at the rear of his Marchmont shop and banged on the staff entrance. Brian stuck his head out as if checking for the enemy and looked right and left before inviting her in. She smiled. It was what he did. He self-consciously stroked the top and sides of his head, his thin dark hair as precious to him as the golden locks of a princess. He was so convinced of their imminent extinction. Yet, if Brian had been about to lose the lot she'd have recognised the change in his follicles, and it would have gone by now – but there was no persuading him. He was a minimum-conversation, no-nonsense client, and it took less time to cut his hair than it ever took to find a parking spot. She noticed that he was shy but vain, since his appointments coincided with his orchestral events. He played the clarinet and once had invited Viv to a charity concert. Each member of the orchestra had been told to bring ten guests while Brian only brought Viv. The others were amazed that he had found anyone at all.

Today he was flustered and began by blurting out, 'Member of staff off sick. Not good for business. Meant to have all the answers at our fingertips.'

This she thought was code for 'As quick as you can'. And so she set to. 'Concert tonight?'

'Yes, five-night run for the Festival. Too many unnecessary rehearsals.'

'Shall I just do what . . .'

'Absolutely. No change.'

She felt a giggle rising and coughed to head it off. 'How are your audiences? The Mound is . . .'

'Good enough. We'll cover the hall rental.'

She knew she was pushing her luck but she said, 'What's the programme?'

'Crowd pleasers. Mozart, Albinoni's *Pachelbel*. You know, nothing too testing.'

'The clarinet concerto?' He shuddered and she almost sliced the top off his ear. 'Everything all right?'

'Someone walking over my grave.'

This was out of character – the scientist in him wouldn't normally think in those terms. She wondered what else was going on but didn't ask. He wouldn't allow her to use the hairdryer, in case the staff next door heard it, so she was through within fifteen minutes. She brushed him down, disposed of the hair in a bin outside the back door, accepted the cheque, which, as always, he'd written in advance, and with his next appointment in the diary, she was on her way. As she swung her kit bag into the car she remembered how generous he'd been when she'd needed info about drug cocktails and their effect on different body types. He'd sent her a link to a forum he was on which debated that very subject. She liked him, he was a 'ladder down' kind of guy.

Next stop the Botanics. The new entrance and shop had seriously boosted the number of visitors to the gardens and today was no exception. She dumped the car on Inverleith Place and jogged back to the front gates. What felt like a million yummy mummies with four-wheel drive push chairs were blocking the entrance. She couldn't work out whether they were going in or coming out, but eventually she managed to squeeze by them and find the information desk. A young woman, whom Viv guessed was probably a student working the summer break, smiled and said, 'Can I help you, madam?'

Viv drew out the photograph and passed it over the desk. 'Just wondering if you recognise any of the guys in this photograph.'

The woman stared at the photograph for a few seconds. Then pointed. 'This man works in the glasshouses. Not sure what his name is, but . . .'

Viv watched the woman's eyes dance away to the left over her shoulder. Viv turned and saw the man that the woman had identified. He walked straight towards them. Viv nodded her thanks to the woman and went to meet him. 'Hi there. I wonder if you can help me? Does this man work here?'

The man took the photograph and nodded. 'Yes, he did two summers.' He gestured to the woman behind the desk. 'Same sort of thing as she's doing. Filling in when permanent staff are on holiday. Could be trimming edges or working the till.'

'D'you remember his name? And where he moved on to?'

'I'm sure his name was Mark or Michael . . . no, wait, Marty. Yes, Marty. He was planning on going back up north. Trying to get full-time work at Inverewe Gardens. Lucky man if he managed.'

Viv nodded and said, 'Thanks, that's really helpful.'

'What's he done?'

Viv shrugged. 'Not sure yet. Got any idea what he might have done?'

'He was a live wire when he had a drink in him. During working hours you hardly knew he was here, he was so quiet. Always wandering about with headphones on. Big Corries fan.' He patted his chest. 'I'm a big Corries fan myself, but that was as much as we had in common.'

Something in his eyes made Viv think they'd had more in common than he was letting on, but she let it go. 'Thanks again.'

Chapter Twenty Eight

Viv laid her hand against the outside door of Angus's building and to her surprise it opened. She closed it behind her and ran up the stairs. The door to his flat was ajar. She knocked but received no answer so stepped inside.

Angus was standing with a bottle in one hand and a glass in the other. He grinned the most exceptional grin. If she needed persuading about his enthusiasm, that was it right there in that smile. He put his arm around her shoulder, careful not to get wine on her. He whispered in her ear, 'You've no idea how happy I am to see you.'

She kissed him, catching the side of his mouth. A voice she recognised called her name. She turned. 'Hello. I didn't expect to see you here?'

The First Minister replied, 'I could say the same thing. Good to see you, though. I'm glad I made an effort with my hair.'

Angus stared from one woman to the other. 'Well, I take it you two know each other.'

'Viv knows more about me than any other single human being. Whatever you do don't ask her for any quotes for the book.' She looked over her shoulder and lowered her voice. 'Actually if you did she wouldn't tell you anything. Viv is the soul of discretion.'

'She sure is.' Angus stared at Viv as she glanced around the room avoiding his eyes.

'I'm going up to the terrace. See you up there with a drink in your hand instead of your scissors.' The First Minister disappeared up to the roof.

Angus stood with his mouth wide open.

'Catching flies?'

'You never said.'

'As she said, "soul of discretion".' She play-punched his arm then kissed him on the mouth, since he didn't have a free hand to punch her back. 'What does a woman have to do to get a drink around here?'

He handed her his glass and filled it. 'I guess there are going to be many more surprises.'

She nodded. 'I hope so, don't you?'

He grinned. 'So, you going to give me the scoop on our FM?'

'Not a chance. But if you play your cards right I might scrub your back again.'

'I'll settle for that. Come on, let's go up, there are nibbles and lots more people I'd like to introduce you to. You'll probably know them better than I do.'

It was good to see the FM in jeans and a jersey. Viv couldn't imagine why she wore hideous immobilising heels and the tight dresses that she did. It surely wasn't in the rule book. The FM beckoned her and Angus over. Viv thought of Rosie, desperate to meet her, yet willing to badmouth her despite not having done so.

The FM said, 'This is Gordon.'

In unison Viv and Angus spoke then laughed. Angus said, 'You first.'

So Viv said, 'Glad to meet you.'

And Angus said, 'Delighted you could come.'

After acknowledging admiration of the roof terrace Angus excused himself to make sure the loudspeakers were working and that they'd hear the music for the fireworks. It was getting close to time and it would be a shame not to hear the concert broadcast on the radio.

He gestured with his head for Viv to follow him.

'I thought you wanted to introduce me to your friends?'

He laughed, 'A ruse, my dear, a ruse. I'm sure you saw it for what it was?' He dumped the bottle and pulled her hand to squeeze next to him in a position where they'd get the best view. Rosie had been right – it was cloudy and an east wind had got up, but at least it was dry. He engulfed her to stop her from shivering. Felt good. For the next forty minutes there was nothing to do but stare skyward and listen to the booms and bangs, oohs and ahs from everyone on the roof. She wasn't keen on huge displays of fireworks since the amount of money that was spent could keep an animal shelter going for a few years. Still, the up side of these was that after the last bang there would be a mass exodus of tourists, signalling Edinburgh's return to business as usual. She had felt Angus tense when the first bang went off, but he held her tight and relaxed into it. He wasn't being a very good host and as soon as the concert music finished his chums began to thin out. He didn't seem to mind.

'There's someone inside I'd love you to meet. Follow me.'

They descended the stairs and went into his study, where there were stuffed bookcases, a huge oak desk, with a large iMac and all surfaces shambolic with papers. There were two shabby wing-backed chairs. One occupied by an elderly man with a book open on his lap and spectacles low on his nose. 'Dad, this is Viv. The woman I told you about.'

He started to get up but Angus said, 'She'll not be worried if you stay put.'

Viv stepped forward and offered him her hand. He took it in both of his and looked straight at her, as if examining every blemish on her face.

'How do you do, young lady? It is very nice to meet you. I hope Angus will bring you to the house so that we can become better acquainted.' Very posh and very formal.

Not at all what she'd imagined. Not that she'd given his parents much thought. A man in tweeds and an army tie shouldn't be completely out of left field, even if a tad over-dressed for the occasion. She guessed this was a uniform for him. Then it occurred to her that he'd probably spent his life in uniform. That would account for the accent. Marbles abounded.

Viv glanced up at Angus, then over to the desk. His untidiness reassuring. Among the papers her eye caught a familiar face. She edged closer. Her shoulders tensed. It was Sal. She couldn't see the whole thing, but the photograph was definitely an image of Sal. She swallowed. What was going on?

'She's a busy woman, Dad. But I'll try and persuade her.'

The old man nodded and pushed ill-fitting specs back up his nose.

Angus guided her through to the kitchen. 'Thank you. I said I'd introduce you. He's been on his own for too long. Too much time to worry about his children. You might like the house though. It's less than an hour's drive away. It's thoroughly eccentric. Freezing cold and damp but eccentric.'

She considered her reply. 'I'm not much of a country girl. Too green. Makes me queasy.'

He looked disappointed. 'I see you as an outdoorsy type.'

'Don't be fooled. I'm not really a type at all. But pavements suit me.'

He removed his arm from round her shoulder and shrugged. 'Let's introduce you to some of the stragglers.'

'Actually I need to get going. Work.'

He nodded. Uncertain. 'Oookay. Does that mean that we might catch up later? Or will you be washing your hair?'

She laughed. 'I'm always washing my hair. But no, since we're sticking with the hairdressing analogies, it wasn't a total brush-off. I do have work to do.'

He rubbed her back. She tingled on her short trip home, but not in a good way.

Chapter Twenty Nine

Viv sat at her desk and wrote a list of things to do, prioritising the tracking guys she'd messaged earlier. Lists were a good way of allowing the knotted chaos inside her head to untangle. Martin Martin emerged as the next priority. She Googled him again and with every new snippet of his life, was struck by how odd his profile was. He'd make a good subject for Myers Briggs. He had a Facebook page but didn't post anything. The few photographs that were on it were only there because he'd been tagged in someone else's post. Still her search kicked up some detail from his past that she hadn't expected. Another photograph posted a year ago, taken outside the glasshouses at Edinburgh's Botanic Garden, reassured her that he was indeed employed in the horticultural world. She stared at his image. He didn't seem to be engaged with the group, standing slightly apart and looking away from the camera. Camera shy? What would she do without social media? Time to call it a night.

After an early coffee the following morning she returned to her desk, dissatisfied at seeing Martin only in photographs, and decided that serious measures had to be taken to locate him. She smirked at the screen as she discovered details of his latest home address. Nowhere near Inverewe. Within an hour she sat in the Rav outside Martin's flat in Iona Street hoping to catch a glimpse of him. It was early and she anticipated him heading out to work, but had no way of knowing whether he'd already left and she was edgy. Could she be sure of finding the right guy from such poor visuals? Yet surely if she saw him in the flesh she'd be able to confirm it was definitely the same person.

Conan Doyle had triggered an interest in footprints, but now forensics were much more sophisticated and the recent discovery of a person's 'gait cycle', their unique walk, had become as reliable as DNA. It exposed things about a person that the uninitiated wouldn't notice. She hoped she had his walk imprinted on her memory from tracking him on the CCTV footage.

The radio was on but she kept switching between channels. Eventually someone came out of the stair door. She sat bolt upright and put her mini-binoculars up to check if it was Martin. It wasn't. She sighed. Patience wasn't her friend. She picked and worried at a thread on her jeans before realising she'd made a hole. Again the stair door opened, but this time a woman with a buggy and a toddler by her side backed out and took off towards the main road. Finally, a few minutes after the eight o'clock news, Martin appeared, wheeling a bicycle. That scuppered her intentions to analyse his walk. He looked right and left as if deciding which route to take, then threw his leg over the bar, clipped on his helmet and cycled towards Leith Walk. She started up and followed him, almost losing him at the junction where he dodged into the middle of the road. She waited an age before filing out into the traffic. He took a right by Pilrig church, which made following him easier. There was nowhere for him to go until he reached the junction with Bonnington Road, where he turned left onto Broughton Road and continued toward Stockbridge. At the end of Hamilton Place he finally stopped, dismounted and parked the bike against a streetlight, and crossed the road to a café. Minutes later he appeared with a cup of something, and she wondered how he would negotiate the drink with getting back onto the bike to continue his journey. But he didn't get back onto the bike. He walked over to a bench in the square in front of Saunders Street and sat sipping his drink. She was parked on a yellow line facing west with her fingers crossed, hoping that wherever he was going next would be in the same direction. A traffic warden, edging ever closer to where she sat, forced her to make a decision. But just at that moment Martin was joined on the bench. Frances. Now this was interesting. She had to move or get a ticket. She drove up the first left on Leslie Place, round into Dean Terrace and dumped the car. She ran back to the bridge over the Water of Leith.

Martin and Frances sat side-by-side chatting, he with his drink and she playing footsy with the gravel. Their body language flirtatious; playful but not overly so. They chatted for ten minutes before Frances stood up and they kissed – pretty chaste. Viv crouched behind a four-wheel drive until Frances passed. Martin didn't make a move for another five minutes. He tossed his cup into a bin and went back for his bike. But instead of mounting, he walked the bike up the steep hill of Gloucester Mews onto Wemyss Place, then right on to Queen Street. She kept well back until, to her astonishment, he entered through the back gate of Bute House. What was he doing in there? She had been in to cut the FM's hair so many times and never once encountered him. What were the chances of that? That didn't mean he wasn't employed there. She thought through the possibilities. There was a small space, not big enough to be called a terrace, with pots and a bit of box hedging but surely not enough to warrant a gardener. What to do next? Should she return and rescue her car before it got towed? Or brazen it out and go into Bute House? She crossed the road and sidled in through the parking area. She could feign a change of appointment with the FM. She knew the security staff, so that wouldn't be a problem. From the garden there was an entrance through the basement. One long corridor with many rooms off it led to a door at the end. On the south side of that was a stairway leading to the home of the most powerful woman in Scotland. A lead-lined door required a certain kind of pass card. She stood at the wall watching Martin secure his bike and clip his helmet to the handlebars. He rubbed his hair and ran his hands through it a few times, moulding it into style. The act of a vain man and not what she'd expected. He opened a pannier on the back of the bike and took out a card on a ribbon. He swiped the door and pushed it open while placing the card over his head to hang round his neck. Once he was out of sight she leaned against the wall and imagined what jobs he might do within Bute House. Just because he'd trained in horticulture didn't mean that's what he did now. In fact, it was a complete shot in the dark that she'd caught him leaving home to go to any job at all. Good work so far and the day had just begun. She jogged back to the car, which had a ticket stuck to the windscreen.

Chapter Thirty

She drove back to the Grassmarket, and feeling peckish, nipped into Bella's. She flicked through *The Guardian* as she waited for her espresso and an almond croissant, then rocked back on her chair. Connections were beginning to stack up. Archie knew Roderick, Roderick was familiar with Bute House, Martin knew Bute House and was dating Frances who worked with Archie. So far the only crime that had been committed was the pushing over of an ancient Archer, a Queen's bodyguard. Intent to harm the monarch would result in more than a slap on the wrist but would be difficult to prove with what they had at the moment. Treason carried a life sentence. The up side was he could no longer be hanged, drawn and quartered.

Bella appeared with her coffee. 'You're looking distracted. Everything okay?'

'Sure. Looking forward to this, though.' She sipped the espresso and ripped off a piece of the croissant.

The door to Bella's opened and Gus walked in. She wiped her mouth with her napkin and smiled as he approached. She gestured to him to take a seat. 'You in for breakfast?'

'Well, now that I'm here I could join you. I saw you from the road and wondered if you'd mind company.' He was tentative.

'I'm glad to see you.'

He frowned. 'Probably not as glad as I am to see you.'

She sensed a question in there. 'Don't you believe it!' She leaned over and kissed him on the cheek. 'I am delighted that we are finally having breakfast together – although this isn't how I'd imagined it.'

Now he smiled. 'The fact that you've imagined it is very heartening.'

Bella came to the table with a flat white and laid it in front of him. He looked up. 'That's service for you. Thanks. Can I have one of those as well?' He pointed to the croissant.

'No can do. That's the last one. I've got . . .'

Viv interrupted. 'We'll share this.'

He started to object.

'It's huge. I can't eat the whole thing.' Which was a lie. She regularly scoffed one of these in the middle of her morning. She regarded it as a healthy carbs fix.

Bella disappeared and returned with an ordinary croissant and a jar of almond paste. 'This might work as a substitute.'

He grinned. 'Women! So resourceful.'

Viv's mobile rang and on spotting Mac's number she excused herself from the table. Outside on the pavement she listened as he brought her up to speed on recent developments.

'Ruddy's filled me in on Roderick. We've to go cautiously to avoid a media circus. Same old same old. As if we don't know what we're doing. I expect I'm getting the heads up so's to keep you in check.'

'What a nerve. The only reason he brings me in is to do the unorthodox stuff that you guys aren't supposed to touch. So I don't need looking after, I need more slack.'

'No need to get snippy – we're on the same team.'

'I don't give a shit that Roderick's father is an MSP.'

'Exactly! I rest my case. Keep calm and keep me posted on your every move.'

'Yeah, yeah. Like that's ever going to happen. Cheerio.' She smiled through the window at the concern on Gus's face.

Four girls teetering on platforms more suitable for the North Sea, wearing pelmets exposing ample thighs, staggered towards her. They giggled as they passed and she grimaced at their toxic wake, ducking so as not to inhale spray from armour-like hair-dos and a cocktail of cheap scents. She couldn't work out if they were returning from, or starting early for, a night out. She shook her head and grinned as she wandered back into Bella's.

'Everything all right?'

'Yes. Completely normal. Don't you love living at the centre of the universe?' She waved to Bella who came to the table with a fresh cappuccino without Viv having to order it. Too much espresso and she'd be jangling. 'Mind-reader. Thanks, Bella.' She blew over the top of the cup, separating the froth from the coffee. 'Mmmm. I'm so looking forward to this.'

'Thanks for being so tolerant with my dad. As I'm sure you could tell he's old school. Keen to see me settle.'

'And you?'

'Not so much. I'm not a great catch.' He tapped his temple. 'Too messed up.'

'There's no such thing as sanity – only versions of madness that have become socially acceptable.'

He smiled. 'No, really. No one could sleep in the same bed as me and get out alive.'

'Wow. Are you boasting?'

He laughed. 'I wish. No, I get night terrors. Kick out probably; even punch out. Who'd want to be on the receiving end of that?'

She thought of Frances, who had no recollection of her behaviour in the night. 'Do you know it's happening? I mean when it's happening or afterwards if you fall back to sleep would you remember what you'd done?'

'I have so far. Crikey, it would be terrible if I didn't. I hope there isn't some poor . . . Well best not to go there. This is pushing my luck, but I wondered if you would come and visit the old house. You'd have to wear your thermals even though it's August.'

Her belly clenched. What was he really asking her to do? He already knew she was a body and soul townie. 'When did you have in mind? I've got a job on that means I can't go anywhere at the moment but . . .'

He shook his head. 'No. No, it's fine. It's not right of me to ask.'

'No, it's fine to ask. But I've got to finish what I've started.'

He nodded. 'I suppose. There's not much that I can't do so long as there's wifi.'

'Let me see how I get on. It might be that I get it wrapped up within a couple of days, then it'd be no problem.' She sounded unconvincing even to her own ears.

'How long have you known the FM?'

'Since way before she had titles.'

'She sounded so familiar with you. It made me think of all the things in a woman's life that it wouldn't occur to me to ask about.'

Viv raised her eyebrows in a question.

'Well it hadn't occurred to me ask her who cut her hair or who she goes to for beauty treatments. But those are the people in a person's life who get to know them intimately.'

She nodded. 'Can't deny that. But we also have an unwritten contract that we wouldn't share that info. I mean how long would my clients keep using me if I gossiped? Not long I'll tell you. Edinburgh is a village. I'd soon be unemployed. Ditto when I write for . . . oh never mind.'

'No, go on, I'd love to hear this. I thought you said you were a hairdresser.'

'I am, but as I said before I do . . .'

'Yes, I'm getting it. But . . .whatever that other stuff is that you're doing I'd love to hear about it.'

'There's not much to tell. I occasionally write things for a newspaper under a pseudonym. And I do a bit of, let's call it research, for the police.' She laughed at the look on his face. 'Don't look so surprised. There's no such thing as a stereotype. You should know that. There's always more to people than you think, and the more people try to put others into boxes the more they'll find them squealing to get out. Tidy people are a myth. People can look tidy, but their lives, their psyches, rarely are, and if they appear that way it's by design and you've got to ask what they're covering up. You know – swans and all that.'

His eyebrows knitted.

'Swans look beautiful on the surface but are paddling like fury beneath.'

He nodded. 'So how come you know so much about people? Can't just be hairdressing.'

'It could be hairdressing, but I did a degree in anthropology, and you might as well know that I also have a PhD.'

His face was a picture of doubt. He sat back in his chair. 'So that's why Mac called you doc?'

She grinned. 'That's what he calls me when he's pissed off with me, but yes if he did call me "doc" that would be why.'

He rubbed his hands across his face then broke into a smile. 'This is a learning curve. You're too brainy for me. I'm a simple soldier cum biographer. I mean I'm not much of a thinker.'

'Now I know you're lying.'

'No, I'm not.'

'But that's what I mean. You are presenting a stereotype that isn't true. It's what people have come to expect, but it simply isn't true. Convenient maybe, but true not so much!'

Bella slipped a saucer with the bill on it across the table. They both grabbed at it. She won.

They walked back up the Grassmarket and she reached up and kissed him on the cheek. 'I'll let you know when this job is done.'

'Or let me know if there's anything I can do to help.'

She nodded and continued on up the West Bow.

Chapter Thirty One

She returned to the flat and immediately booted up her laptop. YouTube had come up with the video of the MSP's son drinking vodka in the kitchen at Bute House. Someone took that video, so there were others there on that night up to similar high jinks. If she found them she'd probably find Roderick again. First she scoured his social media pages and followed leads to friends from the same school he'd been to. The original video was filmed during a school leaving party so they might now be spread a bit wider geographically. The FM's son had been coerced into hosting it since his was the only house big enough to accommodate so many.

Eventually she found one young man who hadn't deleted his photographs. The inside of Bute House was too grand not to be recognised. They'd even taken a group photograph sitting on the staircase in the public entrance, with each boy holding a bottle of beer up and cheering for the camera. No video of this, though. She wondered if they had all just been mucking about or had the video been taken intentionally to embarrass the FM? If they'd wanted to really embarrass her they'd surely have caught her own son doing something naughty. But they hadn't; they'd filmed the son of an MSP.

She sat back in her chair and tried to think herself into what the mood on a night out with a crowd of young guys might be like. Perhaps exultation at being released from school uniform? Or at the prospect of leaving home? What about girls? Fear of girls? After all, they'd spent their school days exclusively in the company of boys. It was an interesting choice to have a party, marking a rite of passage, without girls. Didn't they want a night with girls, and if not, why not? Best not to jump to conclusions. What else could this mean? She continued scanning the photographs. From what she could see they weren't particularly bad. No one was snorting coke off the FM's desk with a fifty-pound note. If the worst thing they'd done was swigging vodka in the kitchen, the FM had gotten off lightly. Not much of a story and yet it had been splashed over the front pages of national newspapers. A slack weekend for the press? Or more to the story than she'd picked up? The slightest slur with a politician was game on. The FM had gone away for a night and hadn't expected or given her permission for the party but, if the stories had any foundation, her son had been bullied into letting his mates in with their booze. What had started as a few beers had grown legs when the media got hold of the video. No smoke without fire. Was the video given to them by the photographer? Or had it gone viral on YouTube? Something else to check.

Where did Martin Martin fit in with any of this? He knew Bute House, he'd dated Frances, he was on the CCTV footage with his hand tucked into his jacket. It wasn't much to go on unless they found something which proved he intended to shoot the Queen. Archie had taken responsibility for the attack on the old Archer, with a reluctant Roderick. Roderick and Archie were more than friends. Did Roderick and Martin know each other? She rubbed her hands over her face, too many connections swirling round her head. She settled down to a session with Facebook. First she relocated the page with the photographs and wrote down all the other places in Edinburgh he'd 'liked' and matched those with others who'd been at the party. She checked those 'liked' pages with the ones on Martin Martin's page. A laborious task, which took an age, but paid off. It couldn't be coincidence that the Turkish café on the shore at Leith Docks came up again and again. She sat back and stretched, then jumped up. Time for another outing.

The phone rang. She stared at the number on the display. It was Jules, the editor of a newspaper she wrote the occasional column for. It had been a while since she'd heard from her. 'Hi, Jules. Long time no hear.'

'You know the form, Viv. Internet's a bogie. No one needs a pen and paper any more.'

Viv chuckled. She hadn't heard that saying in ages. 'It's okay, I'm not fishing for work.'

'No, I hear you're busy doing a job for Marconi.'

'Well, you heard wrong. I'm busy cutting hair as usual.'

'You'd give me a heads up if you got wind of anything?'

'You wish. Besides since when did you need actual facts? From what I've read recently information comes more embellished than it used to.'

'You've no idea how difficult it is to get folks to pick up a newspaper, even if it has an outrageous headline or tits on the front page . . .'

Viv smiled. Jules was never one to mince her words. 'Don't even go there.'

'Oh, it's fine for anyone selling a car to go there, but not for me trying to sell local news.'

'Spare me your histrionics. Life's a bitch and all that. Now surely that isn't the only thing you rang for?'

'No, we're needing help on features and you're my first call.'

Viv was pretty far down Jules' list of freelancers. She laughed again. 'Sure. When were you thinking about?'

'Staff problems. A maternity cover coming up. Could become permanent if she goes gooey on me.'

'I'm not interested in anything permanent, so no need to dangle that myth in front of me. I might be able to do a couple of features though, but not straightaway.'

'You can't be that busy with hair.'

Viv could almost hear Jules grin. She must have got hold of some snippet that was worrying at her, and she'd not let it go until she got what she'd called for. But there was no way that Viv could give her anything new about the Queen's attack. Was there another mole or was it the same person giving details from the NTF?

'Look, Jules, when you've got specific dates send me an email and I'll see what I can do.'

'Sure you don't have anything to share with me?'

With the sound of an intake of breath Viv visualised Jules at her desk drawing in a lungful of nicotine, not a care for the non-smoking law.

'You know me. Not the sharing type.'

'It's not what I've heard. You and Buchanan the biographer . . .'

Viv shook her head. So it was the FM Jules was interested in and not the Queen after all. 'Bye, Jules. I'll let you know.' Too late, she was speaking to the dead tone.

Viv glared at the handset. Nothing in this town was sacred. She sighed. Then a message pinged into her inbox. One of the guys from the 'Hacker Cracker' site had come up with a code to track Roderick's phone. It took her a few minutes to install but once completed she was ready to follow him wherever he was heading.

She packed her rucksack then made for the loo. She locked up and took the stairs two at a time. The screen on her phone had a map showing a flashing red dot following what she prayed was Roderick on the move with his phone. The dot was moving too quickly for him to be walking or running so she assumed he must be on a bicycle or in a car. When the red dot began to speed along a straight trajectory she realised he was on the old railway track and the only way he'd be going that speed was on a bike. It wouldn't take him long to reach the Turkish café, if that's where he was going. Fingers crossed.

Heavy traffic meant much drumming on the steering wheel, but once she made it onto Inverleith Row and turned right onto Ferry Road it was a clear run. She kept an eye on the flashing red dot until it came to rest. She reversed into a parking space and got out. With her phone in her palm it was easy to trace the actual building where the flashing dot had ceased to move at speed. It was the Turkish café. He would recognise her if he caught sight of her so she made her way back to the car, which at fifty metres from the café gave her an excellent view of the door and a row of bikes chained to the railing on the opposite side of the road. All she had to do was wait and see who else turned up or came out.

Leith had had a makeover in the last decades. Old bonded warehouses had been transformed into chic flats, and corner shops had become delis. Pubs and restaurants occupied sites which had previously harboured sailors and prostitutes. Not so long ago a woman wouldn't have dared walk the streets here unless she was for sale, and those women were always at risk. She wondered where they were now. Her phone vibrated. 'Hi.' It was Mac.

'Where are you?'

She hesitated. 'Em, I'm in Leith.'

'And what would you be doing there? You sound cagey.'

So far she hadn't let on to Mac that Roderick had been in Archie's flat or that there was a connection between Roderick and Martin. 'I'm near the Turkish café on the docks. I've traced Roderick's phone. I haven't laid my eyes on him yet so maybe someone else has his phone, but I'm hoping he's there. I just want to see who he's meeting.'

'You and me both. I'm on my way.'

'No, wait! There's no need to come here. I've got this covered. It's not as if I have to do anything other than watch . . . I'll report to you what I see.'

'Sure, Viv. We've enhanced that section of film with Martin Martin that you pointed out and although we can't be absolutely sure we believe there's a high risk that he was carrying something metal.'

'But even if he was I've only made the connection between Roderick and this Neo-Jacobite group . . .'

'We wondered if you would get there.'

'What do you mean you wondered if . . .?'

'Hang onto your hat. Nobody is keeping anything from you – we just couldn't be sure and there are some things that it's best we don't get caught snooping around in.'

She interrupted him. 'No, but it's fine if I get caught and hung out to dry for it.'

He didn't rise.

She continued. 'Oh, never mind – you don't need to come . . . hang on.' The door to the café opened and a group began walking towards her car. She swung round in her seat and kept her head down, pretending to search in her rucksack as Roderick, Martin and another man walked right past the car in animated conversation.

'Shit. He's on the move with Martin and another guy.' Her brain went into overdrive. 'I know it's a leap but the third guy has an arm missing.' She took the risk and said, 'Ruddy showed me photographs of severed limbs with tats on them that look a lot like a motif that I came across again on these guys' Facebook pages. I'll need to move and follow them on foot. They've just turned into a one-way street.' She grabbed her rucksack and with the phone pinned to her ear, set off at a safe distance behind the three men.

Mac said, 'Are you sure?'

'About what?'

'The tattoo?'

'Well, I'd need to see those photographs again, but it seems too much of a coincidence that both of the limbs had the same tat that turned up on the Facebook page of . . .'

'Spit it out. What else?'

She was conscious of not getting too close to the threesome, but had to make sure she wouldn't lose them.

'I may have spotted the motif on a jacket that Martin was wearing. It was from a newspaper cutting. A grainy photograph of him with colleagues from the Botanics. I'm almost sure he had the shield with the thistle and the swords but he had like a name badge over it so I could only make out the edges of it.'

She heard him heave a huge sigh. 'And you were going to tell me this when?'

'I'm still not sure how they all connect but it seems more than bizarre that Roderick and Martin are meeting with some geezer who is missing his arm, wouldn't you say?'

'Does the guy with the arm missing have a beard?'

'No. He's tall, reddish brown hair over his collar, reddish complexion – probably a boozer. He's wearing a khaki shirt with one sleeve tucked in on its self, jeans and trainers. Apart from the missing arm he looks innocuous. I mean he wouldn't stand out in a crowd if it wasn't for the arm. Martin is carrying a cycling helmet and wearing a pale blue Lycra top and skinny jeans. Roderick is wearing . . .why am I telling you this?'

'Because you know that whatever they are up to Roderick has to be brought in. I've got a car on its way.'

'But if he's part of something bigger isn't he more useful out and about? If you have him in for questions . . .?'

He interrupted her. 'It's the law, Viv. He absconded and he's at large – not out on a jolly.'

'I get that. But he could still be more useful out here, even for the day? Hang on.' A set of car sidelights blinked and all three men stopped and got into a vintage Nissan Bluebird. She stepped into a doorway and took a photograph on her phone of the registration number. Once they moved off she reported the number to Mac and raced back to the Rav.

'Be careful, Viv.'

'I'm in my car, Mac. I'm not about to jump out in front of them.'

'I know you. The guy with his arm missing is no gentle giant, not the kind of man who cares about gender.'

She heard the clunk of Mac's car door and the engine start up. It wasn't difficult for her to catch up with the Bluebird, since it was queuing in the lane to turn right off Constitution Street towards Leith Walk. 'I've got them in my sights. They look as if they're heading up the Walk towards town. I'll keep following until you join me. The traffic's dense, so I'd have to try hard to lose them.' It suddenly occurred to her that they might be on their way to Martin Martin's flat. Sure enough. They took a left onto his street, parked and got out. She doubleparked behind a delivery van. 'They've stopped on Iona Street. This is where Martin has a flat.'

'Stay on the line.' A serious warning tone, unlike his usual self.

She flicked the mobile onto speaker. 'They're not going to his flat, they've gone into a pub. I wonder . . .'

'No wondering. Stay put. I'll be ten minutes, tops. There should be a patrol car there any second now. Bye.'

The van driver in front of her closed his back doors, jumped into his cab and indicated to pull into the traffic. She was so busy watching the van that she almost missed the armless man come out of the pub and walk in her direction. She lifted her phone again and put it to her ear keeping her head tilted down until he passed. He passed by but went round the back of her Rav, stepped up to the driver's door and yanked it open.

He glared at her. 'Out!'

She hesitated.

'Get the fuck out!' He grabbed her arm and began to haul her from the car.

She glanced around to seek help but there wasn't anyone on foot. She kicked out at his groin but he jumped back. Before she knew what was happening he had her by the hair and pulled her head clear of the car.

'What the fuck are you up to? You've been tailing us from the docks. Now, who are you working for and what do you want?'

'Let go of my hair, fuckwit,' she fired back, in no doubt that her words would be inflammatory.

He gripped her hair tighter. She squealed. Only having one hand didn't inhibit him. Now that she was up close to him she could see how worn his face was. His nose was a map of thread veins, and his eyes showed that his liver had worked overtime. Still, however hard his body had been taxed his grip was plenty strong enough and he was determined to hold on.

'I repeat. What the fuck do you want?'

She swallowed. Disgusted by his sour breath. Through gritted teeth she said, 'Not you, so let go of my hair, you shit!'

He screwed the hair tighter. She squealed again and punched out at his gut. It was hopeless. There wasn't enough space for her to pull her arm back and land a decent blow. He had trapped her between the car seat and the door. She kicked out at his shin and connected. He swore and twisted her hair so tight that she thought she felt the roots snap.

'Bastard. I couldn't give a toss about you.'

'So who are you giving a toss about? You're not following my wheels for nowt.'

'Wheels? More like a pram you've got there with two . . .'

He pushed his body against her, then brought his knee up in a ferocious blow to her groin. It might not have done the damage that it would have to a man, but she doubled over. She remained bent for a few seconds then whipped her head up and connected with his chin. She heard something crack.

'Bitch! You'll regret that.' He bundled her back inside the car, pushing her over the handbrake and gear stick, clambering in clumsily. Then he pulled the door closed and released her hair. He clicked the locks. She rubbed her scalp and fingered a handful of hair that fell onto her shoulder, no longer attached. Incensed, she punched out at the side of his head, but he now had an open flick knife pointed at her thigh.

'Who the hell are you?' she said.

He brandished the knife close to her face. His gums were bleeding. 'Never mind who I am. What are you doing tailing me?'

'I told you I couldn't care less about you.'

'So if it's not me it must be Martin.'

She didn't answer.

He drew the knife up to her neck. 'Don't think this is for decoration.' He suddenly jerked around to check out the back seat, as if expecting someone or something to be there.

A patrol car drove past on the other side of the road. Sweat trickled down her sides. The knife reminded her of a barber's cutthroat razor. Its edges paper thin and sharp. One silly move could slice an artery. She took a deep breath.

But as if he sensed she was building up to move, he sneered, 'I wouldn't if I were you.' He brought the knife up to her cheek. The sun caught it and it glinted dramatically.

She took another long breath, glanced in the rear view mirror and saw two police officers walking along the pavement towards the Rav. They were chatting then suddenly stopped and one of them spoke into a little microphone on the edge of his uniform. He began looking around. To her dismay they about turned and walked back the way they'd come. She bit her lip.

'Aye. You can bite your lip all you want. But you're no going anywhere until you tell me who you are and why you've been tailing me.'

'Christ! Listen to yourself. You're like a broken record.'

He shook his head. 'You've got balls.' He raised the knife and with a tiny flick nicked her cheek. Blood trickled down her face. 'Your face could be destroyed in a second with this.' He turned the knife from side to side, staring at it with admiration.

She wiped the warm blood with the back of her hand, catching it before it dripped onto her shirt. Where the hell had the cops gone? She glanced again in the rear view mirror. No sign of their returning. She persisted. 'What's your name?'

He snorted. 'What, we becoming fucking mates now?'

She shook her head. 'My name's Julia. I work as a PI. One of Martin's exes has paid me to . . . '

'Don't make me laugh. You think I zip up the back?'

'No. But if you don't believe me you should ask him.' She nodded towards the door of the pub where Martin Martin had appeared with helmet in hand and was looking right and left.

Martin shifted from foot to foot. He hadn't spotted them inside the car. Both Viv and her captor watched as he ran his hands through his hair. He was definitely edgy, his head moving from side to side. He glanced back into the pub, then turned left and marched off in the direction of his flat at the other end of the street.

Her captor screwed up his eyes and held them on Martin's back until he disappeared into his building. Then he twisted round to face her. 'No way of checking that now,' still brandishing the knife.

Viv was in no doubt that having one arm didn't make him less of an opponent. His upper body was toned and his grip had been vice-like, but she had to get out of the car before he really lost patience and used the knife to greater effect. She stretched her arm down to the floor as if about to pick something up.

'Don't fucking try . . .'

Too late, she balled her fist, flicked her wrist backward into his face, and with all her strength and agility pushed the release button on the door and stumbled out. He dropped the knife but grabbed at her shirt. The sound of linen tearing gave her the impetus to give one almighty yank and she was free. He scrambled over the passenger seat but she was already too far away for him to catch her. She ran and ran until she reached Leith Walk. Mac had said ten minutes tops. Where the hell was he? Glancing back there was no sign of anyone following – if he'd any sense he'd have taken himself in the opposite direction. She was about to continue up the Walk when a patrol car raced round the corner. She ran onto the road as if she was going to jump in front of it. It screeched to a halt.

'Were you sent by DCI Marconi?'

The female driver nodded. 'What happened to you?'

'Never mind, I'm fine, but I think Roderick Howarth is in that pub.' She gestured along the street. As she pointed she saw Roderick and the one-armed guy getting into the Bluebird. 'Quick. They're getting into that car.'

The patrol car shot off and managed to cut in front of the Bluebird. Both men jumped out and ran in different directions. Roderick towards her. He spotted her and dodged round a car and into the middle of the road. She followed, causing a four by four to do an emergency stop. The man inside shouted at her as she waved an apology and bolted after Roderick. He made the mistake of glancing back and bumped into a large delivery man carrying a box which he let fall. The van man stumbled and took Roderick down with him.

As she caught up he lay on the ground in submission and smiled at her. 'We've got to stop meeting like this.'

She couldn't help but smile back. She grabbed his hand, noticing that her own hands were covered in blood. She pulled him to his feet. He squeezed her hand then released the tension as if he might take off. She pushed one arm up behind his back. 'Now don't make me hurt you.'

He relaxed. 'I don't think you . . .'

Another police car turned and parked across the middle of road, blocking traffic from entering.

Roderick whispered. 'Shit.'

She said. 'You didn't think I'd come alone?'

He shook his head. At the far end of the road she saw another couple of police cars block the way and the officers got out and ran towards Martin Martin's building.

Roderick laughed. 'They've got the wrong address.'

She knew if it was Martin they were after then they had the right address. Another police car arrived. Buses, they were just like buses. More officers joined the others outside Martin's flat. They had earpieces and were obviously listening to orders. The four of them left the door to the flat and walked toward the pub. But before they reached it the door burst open and a group of men, she counted seven, ran at the officers screaming a chant that she couldn't make out.

'You know what they're saying?'

Roderick shrugged. 'It's "freedom", in Gaelic.'

'For God's sake, do they think they're in a Mel Gibson movie?'

He bristled. 'You've . . .' He didn't get the chance to finish.

Mac appeared with another officer who smartly snapped a set of handcuffs onto Roderick's wrists.

Viv grinned.

Mac started at the sight of her. 'What happened to you?'

She'd forgotten that she had a bloody face and put her equally bloody hand up to wipe it again. It was dry. She left it alone. Viv turned to Roderick as he was ushered to a patrol car. 'What's your friend's name?'

He grinned. 'Which one?'

The bravado of youth. She pointed to the man who'd nicked her face with the knife. 'Him.'

Mac shouted back as he jogged away toward the dispersing men. 'Don't worry. We know who he is.'

Roderick was bundled into the back of the car. Viv stared at the men that the officers had rounded up and recognised one from a photograph on Facebook. What the heck were they all up to? She wandered back to the Rav and grabbed her phone and her rucksack.

She read a text message from Ruddy. 'You can stand down. Mac and his cavalry will sort out the rest.'

There were a lot of officers around now, as if they'd been expecting more trouble than they'd got. A van arrived and the men who'd been rounded up were put into the back and driven off.

Mac came back to speak to her. 'Don't know how much we'll get from this lot but it'll take some playing.'

'What do you mean? I'm still in the dark.'

'The Neo-Jacobites that you discovered on Roderick's pal's Facebook page, well most of these guys are recruits. They've set up a network of "extreme nationalists", pretty underground until now. Not worried about who they hurt, be it the Queen or the FM.'

'Really? They don't see any difference between them?'

'Nope. Neither the Queen nor the FM sees the world their way and neither panders to their extreme right-wing views about Scots' superiority. Oh, and the fact both targets are women adds some serious tension to the mix.'

'Have you actually got a real threat?'

'Yes. There'd be no point in picking them up if we hadn't.' He grinned. 'If you hadn't spotted Martin Martin on that CCTV footage we might have missed him. But you did and when we started looking into who he was the Marine Force got touchy. He's been under their surveillance since he sent map coordinates of remote bays around the coast to an email account they've been worried about. Oh and his pal, the guy missing part of his arm, is the brain behind it. He's a pal of Becky from the outdoor centre. Too many nice coincidences, don't you think?' He wasn't expecting an answer and continued. 'We don't yet know what part she plays but we're hoping she's an innocent who was in the wrong place at the wrong time. You didn't get your trip in the helicopter for nothing, Viv. The boats you saw were dealing. Only now we know what they were bringing in.'

She rolled her bloody hand. She held it with her other hand to stem the flow.

Mac looked around then shook his head.

'No way! You can't just leave it like that . . . I bet it's guns. Was it? Were they bringing in guns? And those fancy fags from the cave?'

He shook his head again. 'You're totally wasted on cutting hair.'

'Why don't I feel flattered by that? . . . Surely the Queen and the FM are safe now, though?'

He shook his head. 'No one can ever be completely safe. Those nutcases,' he nodded to where the police van had been, 'are the tip of the iceberg. An attack on either the Queen or the First Minister is what they have planned. To get rid of either would be a coup.'

'So, wait a minute, let me get this straight. They're actually willing to kill the Queen or the FM in the name of nationalism?'

He nodded. 'Sure. It's not any kind of nationalism that you or I would recognise. It's fascism with a blue and white face.'

'You mean a shield emboldened by a thistle and a couple of swords . . . What about the boats on the coast?'

'They're not in our jurisdiction, but I think we helped discover not only what they were bringing in but where they were coming from.'

She raised her eyebrows in a question. 'The fag ends?'

'Baltic.'

She blew out a long breath, frustrated but understanding that he wouldn't give any more away. 'So the weekend away was worth it?'

'In so far as it helped you make the connection between Frances and Martin. We've known for a while that someone was leaking titbits about the First Minister's itinerary. Wherever she's been on duty or off she's had a few of these unsavouries pitching up and heckling. Then she had a meeting with the Queen this week, which was rescheduled at the last minute and still they turned up at Waverley station. Their presence has become consistent with more of them in the last few weeks. It just felt as if they had gained confidence and momentum. Something had changed. Thank God you recognised Martin on the CCTV.'

'What'll happen to Frances?'

'Not sure yet. But she'll be charged. Never work for us again.'

She glanced up at the sky. 'You see that's my problem. Because there is no "us" any more, is there? You're all tied together like a knotted ball of wool. Is that deliberate?'

He sighed. 'Too many questions for now. I have to get back. I'll catch you later.'

She touched her cheek.

He hesitated. 'You okay?'

She nodded. 'Sure. Just need to get cleaned up.'

Mac still didn't move. 'You want to go over what happened?'

Whenever he used that voice she welled up. She swallowed and shook her head. Another car pulled up. Simon got out, and as routine demanded, pulled at his shirt cuffs as he approached. She smiled. We all have nervous tics. He headed for Mac. They shook hands. A flicker of alarm passed over Simon as he noticed her face.

She wiped her cheek, smearing the dried blood and opening the wound. She gave them both a brief nod and slipped into her Rav, pulling the door shut. She caught a whiff of her assailant's odour and instinctively put the window down. She switched on the engine and gripped the steering wheel. Her legs began to shake, so she took a few long, slow breaths. That didn't improve them. What she needed most was to run. But the Rav would be no good to her double parked in Leith. She switched the radio on, turned up the volume and drove back to the West Bow on adrenaline.

Chapter Thirty Two

Her legs didn't stop trembling until after she ran full pelt from the parking space and up the stairs to her flat. Adrenaline must have somewhere to go. Inside she stripped off, dumping each item in a pile at the bathroom door, and stepped into a warm shower. As water powered from the showerhead she flinched and cursed as it reopened the gashes on her cheek and hand. She stared at the pool of pale pink water gathering in the shower base. Getting dried was tricky. Who'd have imagined that such small cuts could produce so much blood? She stared at her face in the mirror. He had caught her twice, once on the cheekbone the other, just below, was not so deep.

It took ages to fiddle around patching herself up with butterfly plasters but eventually she stemmed the blood flow. Defo not looking her best. Time for tea. With the kettle on she stood with her back to the worktop, soothed by the familiarity of its gentle bubbling. What intelligence did Mac have that he wasn't telling? Would those guys really have had a pop at the Queen or the FM? Surely their best chance of getting what they wanted was a First Minister whose sympathy and energy went into making Scotland independent? Clasping a mug of hot tea she made her way into the sitting room and plonked herself on the couch. She flicked on the TV. BBC News 24 had nothing running on the skirmish in Leith; no surprises there. She searched for the Scottish news – not the right time. She switched off, unsure why she was still in the habit of flicking on the TV when the internet was the place to find anything and everything. But she found nothing there either. Too early or too sensitive?

With her mug on the floor and feet tucked beneath her on the couch, she pulled the throw over her shoulders. Maybe if she closed her eyes for a few minutes she'd feel better.

She was woken by loud bangs. Gunshots? She sat bolt upright on the edge of the couch, and rubbed her eyes remembering that fireworks mark the start of the Tattoo. It was getting dark and she was peckish. She groped for the remote again and flicked the TV on but still didn't find any coverage. Her muscles objected to every movement and the only thing she could muster the energy to do was crawl to bed and sleep, but her mobile vibrated in her jacket pocket still on the heap outside the bathroom. She was in no mood to chat but the vibration persisted. She couldn't stand it. She staggered up the hall and checked the screen. She tensed, thought about ignoring it, but didn't, 'Hi Angus, how are you?' She hadn't given him her mobile number.

He said, 'Fancy meeting up for that dinner?'

'Frankly, no. I've had a day and a half.' She gently prodded her raw face, proud of her assertiveness.

He was hesitant but persisted, 'I could cook for you.'

She raised her eyes to the ceiling and heaved a sigh, 'Thanks, but no-can-do.' She was about to say, 'some other time' but realised there wouldn't be another time. She wasn't only tired. She didn't trust him. The photograph of Sal on his desk stuck in her mind like a grain of gravel in her shoe. She said, 'I have to go.'

'Is that a substitute for "I'm washing my hair"?'

Her hesitation was all he needed.

'Ah. Okay. Probably see you around.'

'Look, there's someone else trying to get through. Bye . . .'

Astonished and wary Viv said, 'Sal, good to hear you. Has Mac been in touch?'

'No Viv, he hasn't. What happened this morning is all over Fettes. Are you all right?'

'I'm looking like shit, but I'll heal. How about you, you okay?'

A long silence, then, 'I miss you. Is there anything I can do to help?'

Viv stalled, 'Well I'm sure some of your famous macaroni and cheese wouldn't go amiss.'

Sal didn't answer immediately.

Viv said, 'No don't worry, I was only . . .'

'No, no, I'd love to. It's just I'm amazed, glad you'd let me help.'

'A woman will go a long way for a decent mac and cheese.' She almost heard Sal smile.

'Don't move. I'm on my way.'

Less than an hour later the buzzer sounded. Her belly contracted, she rubbed the roots of her hair as she answered.

It was Mac's voice. 'Hey, Viv it's me. I won't stay long but I thought . . .'

She released the catch and leaned on the doorframe until he appeared. Like her, Mac always ran up the stairs. He arrived breathing hard but nowhere near collapse.

'Sal's on her way. I think I nicked her parking space.' He grinned. 'Nothing like a gooseberry to spoil a wee cosy tete-a-tete.'

She shook her head again, 'You're nuts. She's only going to make me dinner. Nothing sophisticated enough for you mind.'

He winked and leapt back before her fist connected with his upper arm. 'I'm just surprised that she's . . .'

'You and me both. I'm dying to hear what's happened to Sam.'

The buzzer sounded again and Viv released the door downstairs. They waited as Sal's footsteps clip-clopped up to meet them. She dropped two bags of groceries and leaned against the bannister. 'Wine, we all need wine,' she panted.

Mac lifted the bags and took them into Viv's kitchen. Sal stretched her hand up to touch Viv's cheek. 'Does it hurt?'

'Stings.' She held Sal's hand and kissed her fingers.

Mac clattered around opening cupboards, 'Where are the glasses?'

They smiled and went down the hall to help. When they were all comfortable in the sitting room, with wine and nibbles, Mac said, 'I know you think you didn't gather much intel on the west coast Viv, but you did. These thugs have been running rings round the Marine Police. And Frances, our mole, I'm amazed at how naïve she's been, how naïve I've been. Gullible isn't the word. I must have been blind.'

Viv opened her mouth to speak but Mac raised his hand. 'No let me finish, I have to take some of the responsibility for this . . . So, Frances goes on a dating site, not wise in her position, but not illegal. Starts seeing some guy whom she allegedly had no idea was angling to meet her for the sole purpose of info gathering. She doesn't believe she was giving anything away that wasn't in the public domain. But she's wrong. The guys in the cyber hub were the only ones who knew that the Queen's meeting with the FM was changed at the last minute. Not even sure it had filtered through to their aides. That wasn't reported so she's either unbelievably stupid or she thinks we are. I'm inclined to think it's the latter. And don't get me started on Archie . . . it's curtains for him.'

Sal went to speak, but Mac shot her a look so she lifted a few crisps and sat back on the couch and let him continue.

'Finding and following Martin Martin was the stroke of genius. We'd have taken a while to connect him to Roderick, and joining the dots between him and this bunch of thugs on the coast was a long shot but . . . look what happened when you took the punt. Who'd have thought that a tat on a severed arm would lead us, well you, to the downfall of such a powerful ring? I'm talking about guys from Eastern Europe and South America who, we knew were connected but . . . Viv it's a really big deal what you've done.'

'Okay, okay I get it . . . Is there a way out for Archie?'

'Not a chance. Pain in the arse though, losing two listeners in one week . . . Impressive string of events Doc.'

'Glad to be of service, but can we ease up with the praise? Right now I'm starving.'

Sal stood and wandered out to the kitchen. 'I can take a hint.'

Viv said, 'No stay.'

But Sal called back, 'I've already heard it.'

Mac shook his head. 'You'll be offered promotion. You want my job? I've seriously slipped up on this.'

Viv laughed, 'Don't be an arse. If you hadn't given me the footage I'd never have . . . '

He interrupted her, 'You have to learn to take credit. I know you're not interested in money. But prestige, the next challenge?'

Sal shouted from the kitchen, 'No! No more challenges.'

Viv and Mac stared at each other, and shrugged surprised by Sal's vehemence.

Sal stuck her head round the door and pointed a cheese grater at Viv, 'You've had quite enough adventure for now. Please, promise you'll stay safe for a while?'

'I never knowingly put myself in danger. I've had a . . . scuffle today but I was never really in . . .'

Mac snorted, 'That is total bull and you know it. That cutthroat could have severed an artery or anything. Don't tell porkies. You were in danger. Your attacker, is a total sociopath, no badges from the Mother Theresa Foundation for him any time soon. If you knew what he's been doing with young women.'

Viv held up her hand, 'Okay. I get it. But I can't take any more details. Let's eat.'

Mac stood, stretched then laid his hands on his hips, 'Good job Viv, really good job. I have to get back to Fettes to process things, so I'll leave you two to it.' He raised his eyebrows then grinned. Both Viv and Sal shook their heads in disbelief as he nipped out into the stairwell. They stood on the landing and listened to him chortling all the way to the bottom.

'He's right Viv, it is a big deal to have bust up that ring. It's been a huge thorn in the side of Strathclyde and Lothian. I know. I know we're not supposed to call them that any more, but both forces have been plagued by illegal drug running, guns appearing on the streets, and women, well girls . . . Just think, maybe you could have a holiday?'

'Is that an invitation?'

Sal flushed, 'Could be.'

'And Sam?'

'Let's eat then we can talk.'

Sal opened a delicious bottle of Barolo.

After they'd eaten they lounged with legs stretched out on the ottoman.

Sal swirled wine in the base of her glass, 'We were duped.' She laughed, 'Deception is the new black.'

Viv screwed up her eyes and shifted to face Sal. 'Deception is the old black.'

Sal nodded. 'You're right. Sam wasn't interested in me any more than Angus was in you.'

This made Viv sit up. 'What d'you mean? What does Angus have to do with . . .' She refilled their glasses then tucked her feet beneath her on the couch. 'So there's a connection between Angus and Sam?'

Sal nodded, 'Yes. Let's say they've worked together and . . .'

'Were they together together?'

Sal nodded again. 'You could say that, although she said he was doing all the running. I wouldn't trust her as far as I could spit. They've played us . . . I saw her emails.'

Viv raised her eyebrows, 'What, you just happened to see them?'

'Well, not exactly. But she became weird when you were around. Overtly physical, always asking questions about you. I'm not a forensic psychologist for nothing. Best way to get to know someone is to check their communications and since I was never invited to her flat I checked her phone . . . I should have known.' She held up her hands in defeat, 'but at least I found out what they were up to.'

'So let me get this straight, Angus was coming on to me as a way of making Sam jealous? And she was doing the same with you to make him jealous? How absurd is that?'

'Takes all sorts. But I'm telling you we've been played like fiddles. So, I say you and I call the next tune.'

Viv snorted, 'I'm not looking for a new band . . .'

Sal edged over to her on the couch and dropped a light kiss onto her lips. 'Me neither.'

THE END

Vicki Clifford is the author of three previous novels featuring Viv Fraser. Beyond Cutting and Digging up the Dead each received an honourable mention by the Rainbow Awards USA. The Viv Fraser Mysteries were shortlisted for the Diva Literary awards 2017.

She lives at the centre of Scotland with her husband, two dogs and thousands of ailing vegetables.

You can find out more at:
www.vclifford.com
Or
Amazon UK: http://amzn.to/2thMEnb
Amazon USA: http://amzn.to/2sy6KMU
Facebook: http://bit.ly/2sE5umB
Twitter: @VicClifford

Printed in Poland
by Amazon Fulfillment
Poland Sp. z o.o., Wrocław